THE SPIDER STRAIN

AND OTHER TALES FROM THE PULPS

THE SPIDER STRAIN

AND OTHER TALES FROM THE PULPS

JOHNSTON McCULLEY

WILDSIDE PRESS

THE SPIDER STRAIN

*Part of the Wildside Pulp Classics Series,
selected and edited by John Gregory Betancourt*

Published by:
Wildside Press
P.O. Box 301
Holicong, PA 18928-0301
www.wildsidepress.com

CONTENTS

THE SPIDER STRAIN

I.

Love, and Mystery.

IT WAS not the first time that John Warwick had felt very thankful that his training as a member of society, and in the world at large, had been such that it enabled him successfully to talk about one thing and think of something else entirely different at the same time.

He managed to maintain the conversation with the charming young woman at his side, and while he did so, he considered that there was something taking place in which he was greatly interested, and sensed that there would be something in the nature of a climax soon.

John Warwick guided his powerful roadster along the pretty highways on the bank of the river, beneath overhanging boughs of trees dressed in their autumn foliage.

Now he allowed the great engine to drive the car at a rate of speed that almost took one's breath away — and now he throttled it down until the car crept, purring, along the highway, seeming to rest before another burst of speed.

He was driving in that fashion for a purpose. Silvia Rodney, the young woman who sat at his side, believed that it was because Warwick was nervous, and she smiled happily, for Warwick's manner led her to believe that he was about to address her on a subject a young woman always likes to hear discussed by a man she more than admires.

Warwick's real purpose, however, was to discover just why he was being followed, and by whom. He had known for the past two hours that he was being followed by somebody. He was aware that he was being watched closely as he ate luncheon with Silvia Rodney at a little inn far up the river, but he had been unable to locate the person who had him under surveillance. And John Warwick had a perfect right to feel a bit nervous about it.

Known to the world at large as the one remaining member of an old and respected family of culture and wealth, the truth of the matter was that John Warwick was a criminal of a sort, a clever member of the band controlled and commanded by The Spider, a supercrimimal who had been the despair of the police of Europe in days gone by, and who still was active, though not to such a great extent.

Ruined by men who had called themselves his friends, John Warwick had joined The Spider's band at the supercriminal's suggestion, and had become a valuable man to the master crook. He maintained his position in society, for there he was of the greatest value to The Spider. He would be of value only as long as he remained free from suspicion. His successful work had antagonized criminals who were fighting The Spider, and Warwick knew that they would expose him if they ever got the opportunity.

Knowing that he was being followed and watched, John Warwick speculated as to the identity of the person or persons doing it. Were they officers of the law who had grown suspicious of him? Had he made some fatal slip that had put them on the right track? Or were they criminals antagonistic to The Spider and his band?

Warwick did not betray his nervousness and anxiety to the girl at his side, and nobody could have told from his manner that he was thinking of annoyance or trouble. He indulged in his usual brand of small talk, spoke of things to be seen along the road, chatted of the beauties of the scenery, gave the impression that he was a bit bored by it all — and, in reality, was very much alert.

"Great old season, autumn — what?" Warwick said now, glancing at Silvia.

"It is, indeed, John," the girl replied.

"True to all the forms of life — and all that sort of thing," he went on. "I always did admire a man or woman in the autumn of their existence — mellow with age, rich in experience, wise to the ways of the wicked world, and all that sort of silly rot! Live and learn — what? Quite so! A man gets really fit to live about the time he has to die. My word!"

"John Warwick, you are speaking like an old man, and you certainly are not one!"

"Thirty-four, dear lady!"

"I am twenty-six myself."

"Refuse to believe it!" Warwick declared. "Must be spoofing me, what? Don't look a day more than eighteen!"

"John Warwick, you are trying to flatter me!"

"My word! Couldn't be done, dear young lady! Not the proper sort of words in the old dictionary — none nearly strong enough. Webster chap should have met a girl like you — would have invented a lot more good adjectives!"

"John Warwick! I'll be angry in a moment!"

"Angry? My word!" Warwick gasped. "I always had a suspicion that girls liked to hear men say that sort of thing."

"But I am not a silly girl!" Silvia Rodney declared, pouting a bit — and she turned half away from him and looked at the river sparkling in the bright sunshine.

John Warwick managed to glance at her from the corners of his eyes — and sighed.

Silvia Rodney was the niece of The Spider. When Warwick first joined the supercriminal's band, he had made a pretense of paying a great deal of attention to her — it gave him an excuse for visiting so much at the mansion on American Boulevard where The Spider had his home and headquarters. This acquaintance had developed into love with a speed that was truly amazing. John Warwick, a man of society, hunter of big game, world roamer in days gone by, the man many women had sought for husband and could not capture, had fallen in love with the sweet, unassuming girl — and had been forced through circumstances to hold his tongue.

For from Silvia Rodney had been kept the knowledge of her uncle's true character. She had been taught to believe that he was the representative of a certain European power, and that he was working in the interests of humanity.

John Warwick was too honest to speak to her of love without telling her that he was a criminal of a sort — and The Spider had forbidden him doing that. He knew that Silvia Rodney returned his love, and was wondering why he did not ask her to become his wife.

Warwick had been a ruined man when he had joined The Spider's band. But, because of his excellent work, he had gathered a small fortune again; and The Spider, by way of reward, also had engineered a campaign on the Stock Exchange that had netted Warwick almost a quarter of a million dollars.

Warwick was all right financially now, yet he remained true to The Spider, not through fear of what might happen to him if he left the supercriminal's band, but out of gratitude to The Spider for his help.

There were times when John Warwick wished that he might marry Silvia Rodney and cease his nefarious work. It had not been so very nefarious at that. The Spider and his followers committed thefts, but generally on the side of right. Ill-gotten gains were what they generally took from their victims; and now and then The Spider contracted to obtain and return something that had been procured by improper means from its rightful owner. There were worse criminals than The Spider and his people, but nevertheless, what they did was outside the law.

Warwick stopped the roadster in a grove beside the highway and helped Silvia Rodney out.

"Dear young lady," he said, "we will walk about one hundred feet through these woods and come to a high place overlooking a bend in the river. It is the most beautiful spot in the entire state, especially at this time of the year."

Warwick led the way through the brush, and finally they emerged on the top of a giant rock at the river's edge. Silvia gave a little cry of delight at the scene that unfolded before them.

A great river was at their feet, curving into the distance, and the woods on both shores were dressed in red and brown and gold. In the far distance, they could see the city.

They sat down on a fallen log to watch the scene — and John Warwick sighed again.

"Why — why not say it, John?" Silvia Rodney whispered to him, after a time.

"Pardon?"

"Must I say it?" she asked.

"My word! Whatever can you mean?"

"John Warwick, there seems to be some deep and dark mystery about you," the girl said. "Perhaps it is forward of me to speak in this way, but I flatter myself that I am a modern young woman, not bound by every silly and narrow-minded convention — and I always like to have mysteries solved. John Warwick, you have been in — in love with me for a year!"

"Certainly, my dear little lady!" Warwick replied. "What man would not be?"

"John Warwick, I want you to know that I am speaking seriously. A woman always can tell when a man really is in love with her. And — and I should think — that a big, wise man — could tell when a girl — was really in love with him."

"My word!"

"And you know that I — well, that I am!" she gasped. "And yet you — you never speak of it. I suppose that it must be because I am not good enough for you."

"Oh, my word! You're a great girl — and I'm a regular rotter, really."

"I know better than that — you are nothing of the sort!" she declared. "And I'll not have you defaming yourself in that way! Perhaps it isn't at all nice for me to speak in this way, but I must have an explanation, John. I — I cannot go on in this way! Is it that you don't — want me?"

"Oh, my dear girl!"

John Warwick turned away from her and looked up the broad river. He had faced charging elephants and infuriated tigers, he had been in many a close corner during his work for The Spider, but never in his life before had he faced an ordeal such as this. The charming girl who sat at his side was more formidable, in her way, than a jungle filled with wild beasts.

"What is it, John?" she asked now. "Is it something that you cannot tell me?"

"I — I am not good enough!" he replied.

"John Warwick, I have been investigating you a bit. Alice Norton has spoken to me about you a hundred times, and she has known you from boyhood. You have been a good, clean man, John. You were a bit wild in college, and just after you graduated, but your wildness consisted mostly of globe-trotting and hunting lions, and things like that."

"I suppose so," Warwick sighed.

"There is nothing in your past life that would keep a nice girl from becoming your wife."

"My word! Regular paragon — what? Example to be held up to erring youth, and all that sort of thing!"

"Now you are trying to make me laugh and change the subject. And I refuse to do anything of the sort, John Warwick! We are going to have an explanation here this afternoon — or I never shall go riding with you again, or talk to you when you visit my uncle."

"Oh, I say! Condemn a chap, and all that?"

"I mean it, John!"

Warwick looked up the river again — and saw nothing. He was feeling very uncomfortable, to say the least. He was remembering his promise to The Spider, and he did not want to lose the sweet companionship of the girl at his side.

Silvia Rodney touched him on the arm. "Silly man!" she said.

"Beg pardon?"

"I think that I understand, John. You have wanted to speak to me for some time — I could tell. And you have not, because — well, because of my uncle, I suppose."

"But what could your jolly old uncle have to do with it?" John Warwick asked. "You mean that I am afraid he wouldn't give you to me, if I were to ask him?"

"I suppose you think that I am a silly girl who is blind and deaf and dumb," she said. "My uncle seems to think so, too. Why, John, I have known the truth for two years, at least, but never have let my uncle find out. I felt a bit badly about it at first — and then I discovered that my uncle isn't so very bad after all. He was bad in his youth, but now he and his men and women are working more in the interests of right than anything else. I know that my uncle is The Spider, the supercriminal!"

"My word!"

"It is the blood that flows through his veins," she went on. "His father was a famous criminal. My own father was associated with my uncle for some time before his death. I am resigned to those facts now, John."

"My word!"

"And you are not so very bad, you see. What have you done recently? You recovered an idol that had been taken from India. Uncle received money for that, of course, and so did you, yet it was honest in a way to have the idol returned. Then you recovered a famous painting that had been stolen, and so it found its way back to its original owner. You committed burglary to get it, and yet it was honest, in a way. So, you see, things are not so very bad."

"My word!" Warwick gasped again.

"And so, John, if that was the reason why you did not

speak —"

"But I am a crook!" he protested. "Can I ask a sweet girl to become my wife when I am a criminal, when I am liable to arrest and incarceration at any moment?"

"John, if the girl loved you, she would be willing to run that risk."

"My dear lady! Since I have been working for your uncle, he has aided me in building up my shattered fortunes. I could maintain my place in society now and have a wife at my side. And I do want you, dear girl! But I cannot have you — unless The Spider releases me. If he would do that —"

"I feel sure that he will, John. He loves me, you know, and will do anything for my happiness."

"We shall ask him," Warwick said.

"You let me ask him, John. Let me tell him everything. I feel sure that it will be all right."

"You'll marry me, if The Spider releases me?"

"Of course!" she said. "So we — we are engaged, now?"

"I suppose so — provisionally."

"Well —"

John Warwick faced her again, and saw her smile and her trembling lips. He took her into his arms quickly, and kissed her.

"Let us hope and pray that The Spider will be merciful!" he said.

They got up and started walking back through the woods toward the roadster. Suddenly, Warwick remembered! During his conversation with Silvia, he had forgotten about his belief that he was being followed and watched.

Now he was doubly alert as they walked back through the brush. He glanced around the grove as he helped the radiant Silvia into the roadster, but he saw nothing suspicious. He started the car, turned it into the road beside the river, and drove it toward the distant city.

Once more he maintained a conversation, a more animated one this time, but he was busy thinking and planning. He was driving at a good rate of speed when they went around a sharp curve in the road; then he stopped the car suddenly, backed it up, and waited.

Presently another car shot around the curve — a roadster as big and powerful as Warwick's. Only one man was in it. His face flushed as he caught sight of Warwick and realized that he had been caught. He bent his head and drove on furiously.

"What is it?" Silvia had asked.

"Had an idea that chap was following us," Warwick explained, "I've been feeling it for a couple of hours. Thought I'd catch him by stopping quickly and letting him drive past."

"Who was it, John?"

"I have not the slightest idea, my dear," Warwick replied. "But I'll jolly well find out, you may be sure! Can't be having unknown fellows following me around, what? My word, no!"

II.

Under Orders.

ONE hour later, John Warwick was pacing the floor of the big living room in the residence of The Spider on American Boulevard.

Silvia Rodney was closeted with her uncle in his den on the upper floor of the house. Warwick was nervous. He dreaded his coming interview with the supercriminal, which he knew he would be forced to hold as soon as Silvia came down the stairs.

"Feel like an ass, what?" Warwick told himself. "Might be a silly college youth, and all that sort of thing! Peculiar how some things work out in this old world! Never seem to know what is going to happen next. My word!"

He paced the floor for nearly another half an hour, consuming cigarette after cigarette; and then a radiant Silvia came down the stairs and rushed into his arms.

"Everything is all right, John," she said. "And you are to go up immediately and see him."

"Think I'd better take a gun along?" Warwick asked.

"Nonsense!"

"Your jolly old uncle might turn violent, you know — me capturing his pet and only niece, and all that sort of thing. Might decide to have revenge, or something like that."

"I don't think you need fear him, John."

"Well, I'll toddle up the stairs and have the dreaded ordeal over with, at any rate. No particular use in postponing it, what?"

Warwick hurried up the stairs and knocked at the door of The Spider's den. A gruff voice bade him enter. Warwick did so and closed and bolted the door behind him, as was customary when holding a conference with the supercriminal in his office.

The Spider sat in the usual place behind his big mahogany desk, in his invalid's chair, his fat hands spread out before him, his flabby cheeks shaking, and his little, piglike eyes glittering in a peculiar fashion.

"Sit down!" the supercriminal commanded; and once more he spoke in a gruff voice.

John Warwick sat down, and the Spider looked at him until Warwick began to feel uncomfortable.

"Say it, jolly old sir, and get it out of your system!" Warwick suggested finally.

"There doesn't seem to be much for me to say, Warwick. I want to secure the happiness of my niece, of course. It was a great shock to me to learn that she was aware of the nature of my business. I had believed that she was ignorant of it."

"Deuce of a shock to me, too, sir," John Warwick admitted. "I had no idea that she had guessed the truth."

"Perhaps it is for the best that things have worked out in this manner," The Spider went on. "She tells me that you will not marry while you are continuing your career of crime."

"Certainly not, sir — never think of it!" Warwick declared. "It wouldn't be fair to her."

"I'm glad you look at it in that way. You have your fortune back now, of course, and can give her a good home. You need play criminal no longer — for you are playing at it! You are not a criminal at heart. I suppose that I shall have to release you as a member of my band, Warwick. All that you know, you will have to keep secret, of course, but I feel that I can trust you to do that. So I am going to give you your release, Warwick."

"Thank you, jolly old sir!"

"After you have attended to a couple more matters for me," The Spider added.

"Oh, I see! Something already planned — what?"

"Yes — two things. As soon as they are accomplished, you are to be a free man, and then you can marry Silvia and settle down as a respectable citizen."

"The old world isn't such a bad place after all — what?"

Warwick said. "Man gets his reward in time, and all that sort of silly rot! Feel like a new man already! My word!"

"Don't be hasty, Warwick! These two things that I have mentioned are far from being trivial."

"Oh, I gathered that much!"

"You may begin work on the first just as soon as you please and do it in your own way."

"Orders, old sir and employer?"

"Exactly. I presume that you are acquainted with Mrs. Burton Barker?"

"I am," Warwick replied grimly. "Her husband was one of the group of men that robbed me of my fortune."

"Then this work should be a pleasure for you," said The Spider. "You may have observed that Mrs. Burton Barker wears a peculiar locket on a long gold chain."

"I have noticed it often, old sir and employer. No matter how she may be dressed, she always wears the silly thing. She's always twining the chain around her fingers and playing with it. I've wondered many times why she persists in wearing it when Barker could buy her all sorts of jewels, if she wished them."

"That locket happens to be an important bit of merchandise," the supercriminal said.

"I am to get the locket?"

"You are."

"As soon as possible?"

"Yes," The Spider replied. "And the sooner you can get it, so much the better!"

"It seems like a silly thing to steal!" Warwick declared. "You could buy all you wanted for about fifty dollars each."

"You couldn't purchase that particular locket at any price, and there is not another in all the world exactly like it!" declared the supercriminal.

"Some sort of history connected with the foolish thing?" Warwick wanted to know.

"Something like that, Warwick. You just get that locket as soon as you can and leave the rest to me. There will be ten thousand dollars in it for you — if you succeed."

"If I succeed!" Warwick gasped. "My word! Always succeed, don't I? Couldn't afford to fail — simply couldn't — when I am so nearly done working for you, could I? Fall down at the last moment, and all that sort of thing? Certainly not! My word, no!"

"Getting possession of that locket might not be as easy as it sounds," The Spider warned him.

"How is that, old sir?"

"It happens that there are some other persons very anxious to get their hands on it."

"Ah, I see!"

"And they are so anxious that they will go to about any length to get it, Warwick. You will have strong competition, in other words. This will amount to more than merely snipping a locket from a chain worn by a woman."

"What is the silly old locket, anyway?" Warwick wanted to know.

"I may tell you about that later," The Spider returned. "You'll have enough on your mind in planning to get it and outwit the others at the same time."

"And the others —"

"I can tell you absolutely nothing about them, Warwick. Another man is after that locket of Mrs. Burton Barker's, but he will not make an attempt to get it himself. He has assistants, however, and I do not know them. You'll have to be alert, on guard, and find out things for yourself."

"My word! Deep and dark mystery — what? And all over a silly bit of a locket that —"

"Allow me to tell you that it is not a silly locket, Warwick! It is a very important locket, and we must have it. Do you under-stand? We must get it!"

"Very well, old sir. I'll get the thing. I'm going to some sort of an affair at Burton Barker's place this very evening — going to take Silvia with me."

"Be careful, Warwick!"

"Invitations are already accepted, old sir and employer — and it'd look rather peculiar if she did not go. I always do my work best when everything appears natural — understand? Somebody might get suspicious if everything did not."

"But, Silvia —"

"She'll be in the way — bother me, you mean? Bless you — no! She probably will dance with a lot of chaps and give me time to do my work. I'll be more careful, too, if she is there — be afraid of making some silly mistake and wrecking our happiness. By the way, do these — er — other chaps of whom you spoke know that I am going after that locket?"

"They know that I am after it, and that you are one of my trusted men," The Spider replied. "And so, naturally, they will think that you are on the job when they see you at the Barker place."

"Suppose they will be there, too? Are they the sort that could go to a place like that?" Warwick asked.

"I haven't the slightest idea, Warwick."

"I'd better lose no time then, what? I'll get to work as soon as possible — nab the silly thing before anybody else can!"

"That would be best, I think. Do you want any help?"

"I fancy not," Warwick replied. "I'd probably work much better alone in such a case. I may use Togo, if it proves necessary. He is worth a dozen ordinary men."

"Very well; have it your own way and use your own methods," the supercriminal told him. "All I'm interested in is the proper result. I want that locket, Warwick. I must have it — and I don't want you to fail!"

"My word! You speak as though I always had failed!" Warwick complained. "Never failed yet, have I?"

"There is a first time for everything, Warwick," said the supercriminal, "and I am not eager for this to be your first failure. Keep your eyes open for the others. I am sorry that I can give you no definite information concerning them."

"Then I suppose I'll have to be suspicious of everybody — what?" Warwick said. "I'd better toddle along now, old and respected sir! I have to see Silvia again, hurry home, dress — all that sort of silly rot. 'Bye!"

"Good luck, Warwick!"

"Thanks, old sir and employer! I fancy that this will not be a very difficult job. Getting a silly locket that hangs on the end of a chain — my word!"

"Ten thousand in it for you, Warwick. That will pay for a honeymoon."

"Not for the sort that Silvia and I intend having, but it will help some," Warwick replied "'Bye!"

Warwick left the den of The Spider, and hurried down the stairs to where Silvia was waiting for him.

"Everything is jolly well all right, dear girl," he reported "I have a couple more tasks to perform for your uncle and then I am to be — er — free. Understand? And then —!"

"You'll be careful, John?"

"Of course! My word! Be jolly well careful when a mistake would mean my losing you! We are going to Mrs. Burton Barker's place tonight, remember!"

"Will you have work to do there, John?"

"Now, now! Little girls should not ask too many questions, you know!"

"But I am interested!" Silvia declared. "And perhaps I might be able to help you!"

"Heaven forbid!" Warwick exclaimed fervently. "Allow you to run into danger — what? My word!"

"Oh, perhaps you think that I am not clever enough to help you," she accused. "Please remember, sir, that The Spider is my uncle, and some of the same strain of blood that is in his veins flows through mine!"

"Why, my dear girl!"

"And I'd like to help you," she coaxed.

"But I don't fancy that you can in this — er — particular case," Warwick told her. "Perhaps you may in the other — the last one — we'll see about it later. We can't afford to take any unnecessary risks, you know. I'll tell you a bit more about it tonight. Have to toddle along now — dinner, dress, all that sort of thing. 'Bye!"

Warwick kissed her again, and then he hurried out to the curb. But he shivered as he sprang into his roadster.

"Just fancy a girl as sweet as Silvia running the danger of arrest to help me steal a silly locket," he mused as he drove rapidly up the boulevard. "My word! It isn't being done! Not the proper sort of thing at all — what?"

III.
Togo Shows Emotion.

TOGO was the peer of all Japanese valets, as John Warwick often had said — and yet he was more than that. Though the world in general did not suspect, Togo himself was a valued member of The Spider's band, and had been for years before

John Warwick was induced to join it.

Togo had worked for the supercriminal in the old days in Paris, and he knew many things about the band that even John Warwick did not know. The deeds of The Spider and his men and women were mild now to what they had been in those days before an accident made a cripple of the supercriminal and prevented his active physical participation in the band's doings. Though he could not get about except in an invalid's chair, yet The Spider remained the brains of the band.

Warwick and some of the others knew that in the den of the house on American Boulevard there were great filing cases that held many interesting documents. Some of these related to criminals, some were of such a nature that they could have been used against prominent men, and others were documents regarding police officers and detectives.

Whereas any well-regulated police department kept a rogues' gallery of crooks, The Spider maintained his rogues' gallery of peace officers, knew their peculiarities, their weak spots, and their strong points. But only Togo and few of the old-timers knew of other things that were in those secret archives — things that related to days gone by, little accounts that the supercriminal sought to settle from time to time, in some as the creditor and in some as a debtor.

Togo was also sincerely attached to John Warwick. Several times, he had given Warwick valuable aid, and on one occasion had saved him from exposure and arrest. When Warwick returned to his rooms this day, Togo opened the door for him, stepped back, and bowed, flashing his teeth in a smile.

"Honorable Jap, I am a bit late," Warwick said. "Kindly have dinner sent up from the restaurant downstairs just as soon as possible. There is a little social affair this evening at the home of Mrs. Burton Barker, and I am obliged to attend. Beastly bore, I suppose, and all that — but it happens to be necessary."

"Yes, sar!" Togo said.

"Togo, I was driving with Miss Silvia Rodney this afternoon, and a chap betrayed particular interest in me."

"Sar?"

"He appeared rather anxious and eager to know all about my comings and goings, and all that sort of thing. I maneuvered to get a glimpse of him, finally. My word! Very common-looking chap at that — very common indeed!"

"Policeman, sar?"

"If he is, he is a new one on me, Togo, old top. I fancy that he is no policeman, or anything of that sort. I have a faint idea that the chap is one of those criminal fellows. The sort that always are poking their noses into the business of other folk — you know!"

"Yes, sar!"

"It might be well, old boy, if you kept your eyes and ears open a bit around here, what? We've been bothered before now by fellows who were inclined to cause us a bit of annoyance, haven't we? Getting rather sick of it!"

"I understand, sar."

"If anybody should come prowling about —"

"I shall attend to him, sar!" Togo promised.

"There you are — always bloodthirsty! My word! Assassinate the whole world if you could, what?"

"Only if the world was against you, sar!"

"Um! Thanks!" Warwick said. "Faithful chap, and all that! Well, keep eyes and ears open, old boy. And toddle right along now and order that dinner!"

*   *   *

Half an hour later, Warwick was eating dinner in the living room of his suite, Togo serving it. When he came to coffee, Warwick leaned back in his chair, puffed at a cigarette, and regarded Togo carefully.

"I've a bit of news for you, old top — astonishing news," he said, presently. "You are as much a comrade in arms as a valet, and so you should know."

"Thank you, sar!"

"You know our flabby-cheeked friend with whom we are associated now and then in a little enterprise? Quite so! Well, I have to tell you, honorable Japanese, that before very long I shall be leaving his band."

"Sar?" Togo cried.

A swift change came over Togo's face. For a moment the Japanese, who seldom showed emotion, revealed his feelings, and in no uncertain manner.

"Oh, everything will be quite regular, honorable Togo!" Warwick assured him. "I am not turning traitor, or bolting, or anything like that. My word, no! I'm thinking of getting married, old boy — understand?"

Togo grinned.

"I see that you do understand," John Warwick continued. "And a married man should not be doing things that might get him into trouble with the police, should he? So there you are! Our friend, whose name need not be mentioned here at this moment, has agreed to — er — release me after I accomplish two certain things. You gather that all in, honorable Togo?"

"Yes, sar!"

"Excellent! Your own future is provided for, of course. I'll need you with me as much as before, and all that. It's up to you to say whether you remain with me or go back to where you can — er — be more active in the service of our flabby-cheeked friend."

"I shall be glad to remain, sar," Togo replied.

"Good! I have to accomplish the first task of the two tonight, if I can, at the residence of Mrs. Burton Barker."

"I am to help, sar?" Togo asked eagerly.

"Um! I fail to see at this moment just how you can help, old top. Sorry! Like to have you in those last two little games if I could, and all that. But this is a strictly society affair, you know — dress-suit stuff."

"I understand, sar."

"I've got to get a little locket —"

"A locket, sar?" Togo cried.

"My word! Whatever is the matter with you? Why shriek at me in that fashion?" Warwick demanded, putting down the coffee cup. "Are you beside yourself — what?"

"Your pardon, sar!"

"But I fail to understand, confound it! Never knew you to act so in the world! Have you been drinking?"

"No, sar!"

"Explain, then!"

"I — I was startled, sar."

"I should think you were! And you certainly startled me! Almost made me choke, confound it!" Warwick exclaimed. "What do you mean by such a thing?"

"You mentioned a locket, sar. I — I was wondering if it could be *the* locket."

"Honorable Japanese, it is merely a silly locket that a foolish woman wears on the end of a long, ridiculous chain. Why our flabby-cheeked friend wants it is more than I know — and I suppose that it is none of my business. He didn't happen to take me into his full confidence this time, confound it!"

"Then it must be the locket," Togo said.

"What locket?" Warwick demanded. "Am I always to be surrounded by riddles? My word! It's enough to make a man take to drink, and all that sort of thing!"

"I — I cannot tell you, sar, if The Spider will not," Togo said. "I am sure you will pardon me, sar."

"My word! What mystery is this? I had thought that it was just a silly locket that somebody wanted badly enough to pay for. Other chaps are after the thing, too, it appears. Jolly old Spider told me to watch out for them!"

"Then it must be the locket I mean," Togo said. "You must be very careful, sar."

"Do I happen to have a reputation for being reckless?" Warwick demanded. "My word! A man would think that I was about to abduct the sultan of Turkey, or some little thing like that."

"It seems to be only a very simple thing, sar, but, believe me, it is not!" Togo told him.

"How on Earth does it happen that a woman like Mrs. Burton Barker is wearing a locket there could be so much fuss about? Why, the woman has had the thing for years! It seems to be a sort of pet of hers. Everybody wonders why she wears the thing. Impression is abroad that she is superstitious, and all that, and thinks the fool locket brings her good luck. Can't fathom this thing at all!"

"I — I certainly wish that I could tell you, sar, but I dare not without the permission of the master," Togo declared. "But I beg of you to be most careful, sar, and to watch out for those others you have mentioned."

"It seems to me that I have accomplished tasks far more difficult than this," Warwick said. "Is the greatest diamond in the world concealed in the thing, or some silly rot like that?"

"I believe that the locket is not of very great value in itself, sar," Togo replied.

"I fancy not, since I am to receive only ten thousand if I succeed in getting the thing. Sure you can't tell me more about it?"

"I dare not, sar!"

"My word! How very disgusting! Never did like such mysteries — get on a man's nerves, what?"

"If I only could help you, sar!" Togo exclaimed. "At least, sar, please allow me to be in the neighborhood of the Barker residence this evening. You may have need of me, sar. And, if you expect to be married soon, you will want nothing bad to happen."

"I should think not!" Warwick said. "But, this is amazing! Thought it was just a silly locket!"

"It is called the Locket of Tragedy, sar!"

"My word!" Warwick exclaimed, staring at the valet. "What a perfectly silly name to give a locket — and a cheap one at that! Nothing very tragic about Mrs. Burton Barker, I'm sure. She is just a silly butterfly of a woman!"

"It is true that she may have that appearance, sar," said Togo. "But, if you will pardon me, she is nothing of the sort. She is a dangerous woman, sar!"

"You know her?"

"I know of her, sar," said Togo. "Be on your guard, sar, when you attempt this thing. She may be expecting somebody to make an attempt to get the locket. And if you are suspected —"

"I understand, honorable Togo. Thanks, too, for this surprising warning. I always considered the woman rather shallow myself. Sort of a little girl masquerading in a grownup's costume, what? I've known her for a score of years, since she was a girl —"

"Pardon, sar!" Togo interrupted. "But, during all those years, were there no times, when you were traveling, when you did not see her and heard nothing of her for years?"

"Of course! She was in school — and then she came out and spent the usual time abroad —"

"Ah!" Togo said significantly.

"So that is it, eh? She got mixed up with The Spider while abroad — what? Why, it can't be possible! The girl had a mother who watched her like a hawk!"

"Nevertheless, sar, something happened at that time that influenced this woman's whole life."

"She never looked like a woman of tragedy to me!" Warwick

declared. "Can't imagine old Barker marrying a woman of that sort — his fancy always ran to the other kind."

"Perhaps her husband knows nothing of it."

"Of what?" Warwick asked.

"Of the locket and what it means," Togo replied.

John Warwick got up and began pacing the room. Togo piled the dishes on the tray, carried them into the hall, and rang for the waiter in the restaurant below.

"Never heard of such a thing!" Warwick grumbled. "All this row about a locket and a foolish woman! I'll bet there's nothing to it after all! I'll get the thing as quickly as I can and take it to The Spider. If I can't get a locket from a woman like Mrs. Burton Barker, I must be getting old, slowing up — what? My word, yes!"

Warwick walked to a dark corner of the room, stepped to a window there, and looked down at the street. The lights were just being turned on. A stream of automobiles was passing, men of affairs going to their homes from their offices.

Warwick glanced across the street, where there was a drug store with windows brilliantly lighted. He stepped closer to the window — and looked again. Standing before one of the store windows and looking at the apartment house was the man who had followed Warwick in the roadster.

"He's watching me rather closely — what?" Warwick told himself. "I'll have to look into this matter, I'm afraid. Always did detest a mystery!"

He stepped to his desk, got an automatic pistol from one of the drawers, and slipped it into the pocket of his overcoat. He put into his coat pocket a tiny pair of pincers so sharp that they would cut through strands of any ordinary metal — say, a gold chain. He called to Togo to order the chauffeur to have the limousine in front immediately and then put on his hat and coat — but not his gloves.

"You'll be careful, sar?" Togo asked.

"Naturally!" Warwick replied. "Can't understand this sudden idea that I may get reckless! Never knew me to be reckless before, did you? My word!"

"And I cannot help you, sar?" Togo implored.

"Oh, you may happen to be in the neighborhood, if that will appease you in the least," Warwick answered. "Fail to see how you can be of help to me, though."

"Thanks, sar!" Togo cried. "Perhaps I may be of service to you, sar! It will be a difficult task, I fear. It is not the easy one you seem to think, sar."

"Nonsense!" Warwick exclaimed. "Upon my word, I never heard such utter rot before! I'll have the silly old locket before midnight — make you a good wager on it! I never saw you quite like this before, honorable Japanese! Makes me wonder what the old world is coming to, you know. Nonsense! A man would think, from your actions and words, that I was going into a battle, or something like that!"

Togo's answer rather startled him. "You are, sar!" Togo said.

IV.

One Known Foe.

JOHN WARWICK left the apartment house, stepped out into the street, and then walked briskly across it. He entered the drug store and purchased a package of cigarettes. There was no particular sense in that, since he had an ample supply in his rooms, and even some in his pocket, but it gave him a chance to pass within six feet of the man who had been watching him.

Warwick did not give him as much as a glance as he entered the store. The man moved down the street a dozen feet or so, and stood by the curb. Warwick walked from the drug store, stopped to light one of the cigarettes he had purchased, tossed away the burned match, and then whirled around and stepped up to the man at the curb.

"See here!" he exclaimed, in a low, tense voice. "I'd like very much to be informed just as to why you show such a remarkable and unusual interest in my affairs!"

"What's that?" the other snarled.

"I fancy that you both heard and understood me," Warwick said. "You followed me this afternoon, while I was out motoring, and now I find you loitering around the place where I live."

"Well, what about it?"

"Why, I don't fancy it at all!" Warwick told him. "I ought to have an explanation, and all that sort of thing. My word! A fellow hates to have somebody prowling around and watching him. It isn't quite the thing, you know!"

"I've no doubt that you do object to being watched," the other man said.

"Just what do you mean by that?" Warwick demanded.

"None of your business!"

"See here! I am in the habit of being addressed in a respectful manner, confound it!"

"Well, what are you going to do about it?" the other asked, sneering once more.

"Why, confound it, sir, I can break you in two with my bare hands!" Warwick declared. "Do you imagine that I am a weakling just because I happen to be wearing evening clothes? Keep a civil tongue in your head when you are speaking to me!"

"I didn't say that I wanted to speak to you, did I? You began this conversation, didn't you?"

"I did — and probably shall end it!" said Warwick. "Why have you been following me, and all that?"

"I didn't say that I had been."

"Ah! Trying to evade the question, are you? What? My word! Do you fancy that you can indulge in repartee with me? Answer me straight now!"

"Attend to your own business! I'm getting sick of your talk!" the other told him.

"I have half a notion to hand you over immediately to the police chaps!"

"You try it, and we'll mix. I think you're crazy, if anybody wants to know!"

Warwick suddenly stepped closer to the man and grinned at him. Warwick understood now. He could handle this man physically, and with ease and he knew that the other knew it. Why, then, did this man taunt him to combat?

To cause a row, probably, and make it necessary for Warwick to go to police headquarters and settle it, or make charges — to delay John Warwick, in fact, and prevent him getting to the residence of Mrs. Burton Barker on time. The fellow might even hope to mar Warwick's face early in combat, in such a manner that Warwick would not be presentable and could not go to Mrs. Burton Barker's at all.

So Warwick grinned, and stepped closer and spoke in a tone somewhat lower.

"Your work, sir, is as coarse as your manners," he said. "You will observe that there is a patrolman just across the street. He is an old friend of mine. I give him a box of cigars now and then, and always speak to him when we pass in the street. If you start anything with me, sir, I shall knock you down, order him to take you to the station, simply announce that I shall appear in court in the morning — and go on my merry way. Your little plot would not work then, what? You'd fail and look jolly well silly, and all that sort of thing. Make a regular ass of yourself! My word!"

"You think you're smart, don't you?"

"Certainly not! Smart? Oh, I am a regular stupid ass!" Warwick said. "I don't know much of anything — but I can see through your little game!"

"I guess there are a few things that you don't know, all right!"

"Perhaps — and perhaps not!" Warwick told him. "But I do know this much — if I catch you prowling around me any more, I am going to handle you, and not in a delicate manner, either. And if you happen to have a couple of friends, I'll handle them, too."

"Quite a boy, ain't you?" the other sneered.

"Enough of one to do that," Warwick answered. "Going to tell me why you have been following me and prowling about?"

"Do you think that you can bluff me just because use happen to belong to The Spider's gang?"

"Spider's gang? My word! What on Earth are you talking about?" Warwick asked blankly.

"I suppose you've heard of The Spider!"

"Are you once of those nutty fellows, off your feed, bats in the belfry — all that sort of thing?" Warwick demanded. "I never heard such nonsense! Ought to be incarcerated and held for investigation! Liable to run amuck and slay women and children!"

"Oh, I guess we understand each other!" the other said. "That line of talk doesn't get any too far with me, you want to understand. I'm wise!"

"That is fortunate," Warwick observed. "There are but few wise men remaining on Earth, and we have desperate need of them all. I am under the impression that I have been wasting valuable time talking to a silly ass. Spider's gang! My word!

Whatever can that mean? However, cease following me around. I can't have a lunatic trailing me all the time — frighten my friends to death!"

"It probably will frighten some of them, all right!"

"Now you are talking in riddles again!" Warwick declared. "I see that my limousine is waiting, and so I cannot waste any more time on you. Just a friendly tip, my man — if I find you annoying me again, I shall feel compelled to deal with you personally!"

John Warwick's voice lost its light tone and became menacing as he spoke, and his eyes narrowed and glittered for an instant. The other man recoiled, but regained his composure again almost instantly and stepped nearer Warwick.

"Maybe you'd like to try to do that little thing right now!" he said.

"Ah! You'd like very much to have me, wouldn't you?" Warwick exclaimed. "But it happens that I have an engagement — a rather important engagement —"

"Yes, I know all about that!"

"You do, eh? It appears to me that you are a bit too much interested in my personal affairs. My word! You seem to know as much as my private secretary would — if I had one. I'd advise you to remember that little tip of mine!"

John Warwick glared at the man, and then hurried across the street to where his limousine was waiting. He told the chauffeur to drive him to the residence on American Boulevard, and there he picked up Silvia, who cuddled up beside him in the big car and seemed to be very happy in so doing.

"Are you going to tell me what you are going to do tonight?" she asked.

"Little girls should not ask too many questions," Warwick told her. "It isn't much of a task, really."

"I think you are mean if you don't tell me!"

"Promise to keep it a dark secret?"

"Of course!"

"And you must forget it as soon as I have told you, and keep your mind off it. You don't want me to fail, do you?"

"Certainly not, John!"

"Very well. Mrs. Burton Barker always wears a little locket on the end of a long, gold chain. I am to get that locket. Don't ask me why, for I do not know. Your jolly old uncle wants it for some purpose, and that is enough for me. Now, you forget it!"

"Very well, I'll try, only I'm not so sure that I can," Silvia said. "But I'll not bother you, John."

Warwick glanced through the window as the big car speeded toward that section of the city where pretentious residences predominated. The Burton Barkers had an imposing mansion surrounded by lawns that were fringed with big trees.

It was one of the show places of the city. Warwick knew it well, had been in almost every room of it. He often had inspected it while Burton Barker was having it constructed, and afterward he had been a guest there scores of times. That was when he had believed that Barker was his friend.

Barker still thought that he believed it. Barker was not aware that John Warwick knew he had conspired with other men to rob him in business deals. Warwick would not have known it, had not The Spider proved it to him. Warwick had no repugnance, therefore, in committing a crime in Burton Barker's residence while he was a guest there. He remembered that Barker had robbed him in his own house, while pretending deep friendship.

The limousine turned into the driveway and came to a stop before the house. Warwick helped Silvia out, and they entered. Many guests already had arrived, the orchestra was playing, and the scene was one of wealth and splendor.

They greeted their host and hostess, and for an instant Warwick's eyes rested on the locket he was to get. It still hung on the end of the long heavy gold chain, and Mrs. Burton Barker was twisting the chain around the fingers of her left hand, as she seemed always to be doing.

John Warwick danced once with Silvia Rodney, and then handed her over to another partner, and walked slowly through the rooms, nodding to his friends and acquaintances, acting as though he were searching for somebody, but, in reality, spotting any strangers who might happen to be present.

If it was to be his lot to face foes, he wanted to know their identities, if possible. From what had been told him, he did not know whether his antagonists would be strangers or persons with whom he was well acquainted.

One thought dominated his mind — that The Spider expected success and would not countenance failure. John Warwick had been ordered to get the locket worn by Mrs. Burton Barker, and the supercriminal expected him to get it.

Warwick passed on through the rooms, went to the veranda, strolled there and smoked a cigarette, and retraced his steps to the house again. Some belated guests were arriving. Warwick wandered toward the foot of the stairs to inspect these late-comers.

And then he almost lost his composure for a moment and stepped quickly aside, where he would not be observed. Greeting the hostess was the man who had followed him in the roadster in the afternoon, and with whom he had talked in the street before the apartment house just before starting for the Barker residence.

The man was in proper evening dress, and he greeted Mrs. Burton Barker in the approved manner.

John Warwick was puzzled to a certain extent. Mrs. Burton Barker was talking to the man as if she had been acquainted with him for some time. Was he in her employ, trying to protect the locket, and did he suspect John Warwick of planning to purloin it? The thought almost made Warwick shudder, especially when he remembered how the man had spoken regarding The Spider, for Warwick lived in continual fear of the day when suspicion would be cast upon him.

Or, was the man talking to Mrs. Burton Barker merely one of those others who were making an attempt to get possession of the locket before The Spider's people could?

While fussing around and pretending to be bored, Warwick watched the pair closely. To all appearances, the man was merely exchanging polite greetings with his hostess, but John Warwick knew that they might be speaking of important things that had to do with him. Mrs. Burton Barker was a clever woman in a way — she was able to smile and laugh, and at the same time speak of serious affairs and let those near think she was indulging in small talk, and Warwick knew it well. He had been trained in the same social school.

"Have to make sure of my ground — what?" Warwick told himself. "Must use strategy, and all that sort of thing! Can't be making some silly mistake and getting into trouble at this stage of the game. It wouldn't do at all! My word, no!"

He wandered down the corridor and approached them from another direction. He watched the man's face, made an ineffectual attempt to read his lips and ascertain what he was saying, regarded Mrs. Burton Barker carefully, and tried to imagine what she was replying.

Warwick noted that this man spent more time with his hostess than any of the other guests, and that increased his suspicions.

"No use working in the dark — what?" he told himself. "Have to ascertain a few things, I fancy!"

Warwick straightened his shoulders, managed to get a smile on his face, and then started walking directly toward Mrs. Burton Barker and the man with whom she was talking.

V.

Into a Trap.

MRS. BURTON BARKER smiled a welcome as John Warwick approached, for she always had admired him, but Warwick was not certain at the present time whether the welcome was sincere. The man standing beside her glared at Warwick for an instant, and then quickly regained his composure and got a blank expression into his countenance. Mrs. Burton Barker introduced him to Warwick as Mr. Marlowe, and the two men bowed coldly.

"This world is a queer old place — what?" Warwick said. "For instance, Mr. Marlowe is almost the exact image of a chap with whom I had a peculiar controversy today."

"Why, how was that, John?" Mrs. Barker asked.

"I was out motoring with Miss Rodney," Warwick explained. "A chap seemed to be following us. I managed to get a good look at him. And this evening, just before I started here, I caught the same chap watching the place where I live. Made me a bit angry, don't you know — went across the street and protested to him about it. Chap talked to me like a silly ass!"

"But why on Earth should he have been watching you, of all persons?" Mrs. Barker asked.

"Don't know, I'm sure."

"And you say that I resemble him?" Marlowe queried, a

smile twitching his lips.

"Enough to be a twin of his," John Warwick replied. "I refer to looks, of course — face and form and all that. Voice somewhat similar, too."

"Of course it wasn't Mr. Marlowe?" Mrs. Barker said.

"My word! Never said that it was!" John Warwick protested. "I meant that it is peculiar how you'll meet a chap and think how much he looks like somebody else you have met. Only a certain number of types in the world, I fancy! Deuced peculiar, isn't it? Always seeing somebody who looks like somebody else!"

John Warwick grinned, and for an instant his eyes met those of Marlowe squarely.

Mrs. Burton Barker turned away then, to greet some of her other guests, and Warwick and Marlowe stepped to one side, and started walking toward the den that had been set aside as a lounging and smoking room for the male guests. There happened to be nobody in the den when they reached it.

"So you followed me here!" Warwick said, in a low voice, as soon as they were alone. "I'll have to ask you for some sort of an explanation, I fancy!"

"It happens that I am here as an invited guest," Marlowe told him. "Are you the social censor hereabouts?"

"My word, no!" Warwick exclaimed. "It is nothing in my life what sort of person Mrs. Barker wishes to invite to her residence. But you followed me — that's the point!"

"And why should I follow you?"

"That is precisely what I am eager to know," Warwick told him. "There's no confounded sense in it! It annoys me, really! I can't be having it, you know."

"And just how are you going to stop it?" Marlowe asked.

"Why, confound it, I'll simply handle you, if this thing continues! Don't you think you'd better give me some sort of an explanation?" Warwick said.

"Explanations are not necessary," replied Marlowe. "They'd be a waste of time and breath. I guess we understand each other, all right. Yes, I guess we do!"

"You are a very poor guesser," Warwick told him. "My word! Follow a chap around all day, and then refuse to tell him the reason for it! It isn't done, you know! It isn't right at all!"

"Stop trying to throw a bluff, Warwick! I happen to be wise, you know."

"I know nothing of the sort! You may be old man Wisdom himself, for all I know — or merely a silly ass! Come, now — give me an explanation. I think that I am entitled to it."

"Why not ask The Spider what you want to know?"

"There is some more of that Spider stuff!" said Warwick. "What on Earth does that mean? Are you dippy, and all that sort of thing? Bats in the belfry — what? My word!"

Marlowe stepped nearer to him and spoke in a lower voice. "Suppose, Mr. Warwick, that we walk out on the veranda, or around the lawn, where it will be possible for us to talk without running a chance of being overheard," he said. "We may be able to arrive at an understanding of some sort."

"Very well," Warwick replied. "I certainly must have some sort of an explanation!"

They made their way through the corridor and to the veranda, where there were several couples sitting around in the semi-gloom between dances, and Marlowe went slowly down the steps to the lawn and started following a walk that curved around the house toward the flower gardens at the back.

Warwick, smiling faintly, followed at his heels. Streaks of light came through the branches of the trees here and there, and yet there were plenty of dark and shadowy places where an assault could be staged without much trouble. John Warwick was alert and cautious. He did not intend to have this fellow, Marlowe, catch him off guard and eliminate him for the time being.

"Well, talk!" he said, after a time. "I fancy that we'll not be overheard around here — what?"

"Warwick, as I said, I am wise to you," Marlowe began. "I happen to know that you are The Spider's trusted right-hand man. Don't take the trouble to deny it — for I know! And I know, also, that you are under orders right now."

"Orders? My word!"

"Orders to get possession of a certain something that is at present in the residence of Mrs. Burton Barker."

"Oh, I say!"

"That is attached to the person of Mrs. Burton Barker. I'll go as far as to specify. So you see, I understand the affair perfectly, Warwick. I happen to be connected with certain persons who do not care to have you succeed in your little undertaking. In fact, it is my particular business to see that you do not succeed. Now you understand fully why I have been following and watching you."

"My word!" Warwick gasped. "I never heard such utter piffle in all my life before. Cannot understand it at all! Quite beyond me, and all that sort of thing!"

"Yeah? Well, that kind of talk doesn't fool me a bit, Warwick!" Marlowe told him. "You might as well save your breath. And you might as well give up all intention of trying to do as you have been ordered. For you are not going to succeed this time, Warwick, though you have done some clever things before."

John Warwick threw back his head and laughed.

"Most remarkable conversation!" he said. "It's all utter rot, of course; but allow me to tell you that, any time I set out to do a thing, that thing is done! I always succeed, old chap! Understand? There's no such word as failure in my personal vocabulary. My word, no! However, I am glad that you have told me this interesting little tale."

"Are you going to keep on trying to throw that bluff?" Marlowe demanded. "Maybe you think that I don't know a thing or two. The best thing for you to do is to forget your orders. You'll run into trouble if you try to carry them out!"

John Warwick laughed again, softly, as if at an excellent jest, and then turned back toward the house.

"I fancy that this conversation has been quite a waste of time," he said. "I might have been dancing, and all that sort of thing. Silly ass to listen to you — what?"

"You'll be a silly ass if you don't take the advice I gave you," Marlowe said. "You may not think that you are up against a tough game, but you are!"

Now they were passing a clump of brush that grew close to the walk and threw a deep shadow over it. Warwick had noticed it as they passed it before, had watched it searchingly for a moment or so, but had seen nothing that looked suspicious. He glanced at Marlowe now, but Marlowe was walking half a pace ahead of him and seemed to be giving the brush no attention at all.

"Well, Warwick, are you going to give it up?" Marlowe asked. "Are you going to take my advice?"

"Advice is something I rarely accept from a chance acquaintance," Warwick replied.

He chuckled again. And suddenly two men sprang from the dark near the clump of brush, and launched themselves upon him. At the same instant, Marlowe whirled around and sprang.

Warwick darted backward, and his chuckle died in his throat. He had been half expecting such an attack at first, but had grown to think that it would not materialize. Now he found himself fighting against overwhelming odds. He had an automatic in his pocket, but he had no chance to draw it, and, furthermore, he did not care to fire. He wanted publicity no more than these other men.

One of the men was throttling him now, preventing an outcry; another was trying to trip him and hurl him to the ground; Marlowe was gripping one of his arms, and also watching the walk ahead. Two more men came from the darkness and joined in the fray.

Warwick, his back against the clump of brush, fought as well as he could. He tried to hold off his antagonists, to clear a space through which he could dart to the walk and run down it toward the veranda. But he found that they were too many for him.

"Quiet as possible, men!" he heard Marlowe command. "We don't want a row that will attract any of the guests! Do your work quickly! Clever, is he? He walked right into the trap!"

The pungent odor of chloroform assailed Warwick's nostrils. He tried to fight furiously, to hold off unconsciousness, to keep from being a prisoner in the hands of these men, but they held him in such manner that he scarcely could put up a struggle.

Their voices seemed to come to him from a great distance. He felt his senses going, tried to strike and kick. He called himself a fool for not guarding against surprise better while taking that walk with Marlowe, when he might have known there would be some sort of a trap.

And then the drug had its way, and Warwick ceased to call himself anything.

*　　　*　　　*

As the limp form dropped to the ground, Marlowe issued his orders quickly and in a low voice.

"Get him across the lawn and into the machine! Take him away as quickly as you can — and for Heaven's sake, don't make any mistakes! Watch him carefully! I'll let you know when to release him — when my work is done!"

One of the men grunted in reply, and then two of them picked up the unconscious Warwick and carried him across the Barker lawn, from shadow to shadow, dark spot to dark spot, careful not to be observed. Close to the curb, on the side street, a limousine was waiting, its curtains drawn, its engine purring, a chauffeur sitting behind the wheel.

John Warwick was tossed into the limousine, and it left the curb and ran down the street, gathering speed. Two of the men had entered it with Warwick; the two others hurried down the street in the opposite direction.

And Marlowe, grinning like a fiend, walked slowly through the grounds and approached the veranda from the opposite direction. He went along the railing, tossed away a half-smoked cigarette, and passed through the open front door. Ten minutes later he was being introduced to a certain young woman guest and was asking her to dance with him.

The young woman was Silvia Rodney.

VI.

Togo Takes a Hand.

THAT particular brand of nausea which follows a dose of chloroform had been experienced by John Warwick before; and when he regained consciousness now, and experienced it again, he kept his eyes closed, pretending to be under the influence of the drug and waiting for his brain to clear.

Warwick realized that he was stretched on a couch of some sort; and he heard the voices of two men in conversation. His wrists were lashed together in front of him, but his ankles were not bound and there was no gag in his mouth. After a time, he opened one eye and glanced around the room.

It was a medium-sized room furnished in quite an ordinary manner. There were half a dozen chairs, a table, and a buffet. Warwick could see a closed door and two windows at which the shades had been drawn. Two incandescent lights burned in a chandelier.

The men were still conversing. Warwick could not see them, for they were beyond his feet, and he did not want to turn his body yet and let them know that he was conscious.

"Ain't nothin' much to it," one of the men was saying. "We keep this bird here until Marlowe telephones that he's turned the trick, and then we give him another dose of chloroform, take him in the car out to the edge of the park, and drop him there. When he comes back to Earth, he can go home — and he won't know where we kept him. That's all."

"I thought he was one of these clever ones."

"He is — but he ain't as clever as Marlowe, I reckon. We haven't anything to worry about, anyway — we do as we're told and cash in on the coin."

"What's all this about a locket, anyway?" the other asked.

"You can search me! All I know is that Marlowe is crazy to get his hands on it — some secret, I suppose. None of our business! The big idea is to keep this man Warwick from getting it for The Spider — understand?"

"I don't believe there is any Spider!"

"Don't fool yourself! I guess Marlowe used to know all about him over in the old country. There's a Spider, all right, and he's a tough bird to go up against! I don't want him and his gang after me any — not any!"

Warwick groaned and turned his head, and then sat up weakly and held his lashed hands to his face. He heard the two men get out of their chairs and start toward him. So they were as much in the dark regarding the locket as he was, were they? They were merely engaged to detain him until Marlowe had obtained possession of the thing, and then were to release him.

"Alive again, are yuh?" one of the men asked.

"What — what is the meaning of this?" Warwick gasped. "Oh, yes — there was a fight —"

"It wasn't much of a fight, I guess — you didn't have a chance!" said the other, laughing.

"Where am I?"

"That's somethin' you ain't supposed to know, Mr. Warwick. Here you are, and here you stay for the time bein' — and if you try any funny tricks, you'll wish that you hadn't."

"But — what is the idea?" Warwick demanded.

"I guess you know all about that. Anyway, we ain't prepared to answer any questions," one of the men told him. "We're just here to see that you remain for a time."

"How long?"

"Until we get orders to let you go — and let that be an end of your questions," the other growled.

Warwick looked at them more carefully — and two precious thugs they were. He glanced rapidly around the room. He had been in corners as close as this before, and had escaped. He realized that these men meant him no real harm physically — but they were interfering with his work. The Spider had told him to get that locket from Mrs. Burton Barker, and had warned him to be on guard against foes — and the supercriminal expected nothing except success.

"Better just take it easy, Mr. Warwick," one of the men told him. "We don't want to muss up a gent like you, as has done some nervy things in his time, but we'll have to do it, if you try any tricks. We got our orders."

"I don't fancy this at all, my men," Warwick said. "Confound it, I escorted a young lady to an affair this evening, and I should be there dancing with her now. What'll she think of me if I desert her in this manner?"

"It's hard luck, but it can't be helped."

"If you men aid me to get back there, I'll make it worth your while — and forget all about this."

"Well, we need the money, but it wouldn't be healthy for us to let you you go," one of his captors replied. "We'd get ours, if we did! So we can't talk along them lines, Mr. Warwick."

"I'll pay your own figure," Warwick said.

"Nothin' doin', sir!"

Warwick knew that the decision was final. He got slowly to his feet and paced around the room. But when he tried to get near the door or one of the windows, one of his captors always got in front of him. He tried the cords that lashed his wrists, and realized that they had been tied well. There seemed to be no present way of escape.

"Might as well take it easy," one of the men assured him. "A little wait won't hurt you any — and maybe you can get back there in time to take your young lady home. You can make up some whale of a story and be a hero." The man laughed raucously, and the other joined in.

"I suppose you realize," said Warwick, "that you could be sent to prison for doing such a thing as this."

"Oh, we ain't worryin' any about that, sir. This scrap is strictly between ourselves, and neither side is goin' to call in the police. If we go to prison, a certain gent of The Spider's gang will go right along with us!"

"What do you mean by speaking of The Spider's gang?" Warwick asked.

"I suppose you don't know — oh, no! You never heard of The Spider and his gang, you didn't. You ain't been workin' for him for more than a year — oh, no!"

"My word! Never heard such nonsense in my life!" Warwick gasped. "Can it be that you have made a mistake, got the wrong man, and all that sort of thing?"

"Not any, we ain't — and you might as well cut out the bluff!" came the reply.

Warwick continued walking around the room, and after a while he sat down on the couch again.

"What time is it?" he asked.

"A few minutes to eleven," one of his captors told him. "I guess you'll be turned loose about midnight — so you ain't got long to wait. Better just take it easy!"

Warwick engaged in no further conversation. He felt his bonds whenever he had a chance, and convinced himself that they could not be removed easily. He thought of dashing to a window, but he knew that the two men would be upon him before he could accomplish his purpose And the window might be in the second or third floor — he could not tell. This might be a cottage, or a cheap lodging house. Warwick did not even know in what part of the city it was located.

To all appearances, he had resigned himself to his fate. He yawned once or twice, and asked for a drink of water. One of the men went out of the room, and returned with the drink within a short time.

While he was gone the other watched Warwick closely, a revolver held ready in his hand.

Though he did not show it in his countenance, John Warwick was beginning to get frantic. He would fail— and from The Spider there would be no forgiveness. The supercriminal had warned him that he did not want failure this time. Warwick could not imagine why he had not been more careful. Here he was, a prisoner, and Marlowe and the others having every opportunity to achieve their desire.

He thought of Silvia Rodney, too, and knew that she was worrying because of his absence. Was he to lose Silvia because of failure to get the locket from Mrs. Burton Barker? Would The Spider, angry at his failure, keep him as a member of the band instead of granting him his release?

But there seemed to be no way of escape. The two men watched him closely, and if he got up to walk around the room, they left their chairs and remained close to him. A wrong move, a shriek for help, would cause them to spring upon him. They might even render him unconscious again — and then he would, indeed, be helpless and unable to carry out the orders of The Spider.

He wondered whether Marlowe had the locket already. For the hundredth time, he asked himself what that locket could be, and what secret it held.

"Well, are you going to keep me here all night?" he growled.

"Until we get orders to turn you loose."

"My word! This is disgusting — what? Liable to make you chaps pay for it in the end!"

"We ain't scared much!"

"Fancy I'll square accounts with you before we're done!" Warwick said.

He began pacing the floor again, walking from one corner of the room to the other, while they drew nearer and watched him carefully. He glanced toward the door — and saw that the knob was turning slowly!

Warwick's heart almost stood still. He guessed that the man on the other side of the door was a friend instead of a new foe, else he would not be so furtive about his entrance. He glanced at the door now and then, maintaining a conversation with the two men, at the same time edging toward the window, and acting as if he were about to make a break for liberty, thus causing them to watch him closely. Their attention was attracted from the door.

Warwick glanced that way again — and saw that the door had been opened a crack. Suddenly it was hurled wide open, and a form darted into the room. The door slammed shut.

"Hands up!" a stern voice commanded.

Warwick's captors whirled around. They found themselves menaced by an automatic. And they beheld the malevolent, glittering eyes of one Togo, John Warwick's Japanese valet.

VII.

In the Conservatory.

WARWICK gave a glad cry and darted to the wall, following it until he reached Togo's side, keeping from getting between Togo and the other two.

"You are all right, sar?" Togo asked.

"Quite all right, thanks," Warwick replied. "Hand me that weapon, old boy, and I'll keep these two thugs covered while you take these confounded cords off my wrists. And, if they lower their hands or make a move —"

He left the sentence unfinished. There was no need to finish it. The two men before him knew what he meant, and they did not relish the look in John Warwick's face.

He held the automatic, and Togo unfastened his wrists. Warwick motioned toward one of the men.

"He has a revolver, Togo — get it!" he ordered. "And then you may search the other. We can't be letting them retain weapons — what? My word, no!"

Togo carried out the command with alacrity, and returned to Warwick's side with two revolvers and one knife. The two men had backed against one of the walls of the room, and still held their hands above their heads.

"Sar, may I attend to them?" Togo asked.

"My word! Always bloodthirsty, aren't you?" Warwick said. "What would you do with them, old top?"

"I shall teach them never to annoy a gentleman again, sar!"

"This gentleman would not have been annoyed, Togo, old boy, if he had been thoroughly awake," Warwick said. "Serves me right — what? Teach me to keep my eyes open, and all that sort of thing!"

"But, sar —"

"Besides, Togo, we haven't time to play with these two precious thugs. And they treated me decently, at that. Just where are we, Togo, by the way?"

"In a little cottage, sar, at the edge of the city."

"Um! And how do you happen to be here?"

"I was about the grounds at the Barker residence, sar," Togo explained, "and saw the attack on you. I could not interfere at that time because there were so many, and because — it would not have done to create too much of a disturbance, sar."

"Quite correct!" Warwick said.

"When they took you away in the limousine, sar, I engaged a taxicab that happened to be passing the corner, and followed. I have the cab waiting near here, sar."

"Excellent, Togo, old top! We'll use that cab in short order. And these men —"

"Please let me handle them, sar."

"You may use that peculiar method of which you are a master and put them to sleep," Warwick said. "Take the largest one first — he has the ugliest face. If the other makes a move, I'll indulge in a bit of target practice — what?"

Togo sprang to do Warwick's bidding. His hands found the man's throat, his thumbs pressed against certain spots in the back of the neck, there came a groan and a gasp — and one of their foes was unconscious on the floor.

The other had watched from the corners of his eyes. He gave a shriek of fear as Togo turned toward him — but the shriek died in his throat as Togo's thumbs pressed home. He, too, was allowed to sink to the floor.

"We must hurry, Togo!" Warwick exclaimed. "This delay may mean failure, you know."

Togo led the way through the front of the little cottage, and out into the open air. He ran down the walk to the street, Warwick at his heels, and came to the taxicab. Warwick commanded that they be driven to the Barker residence, and he promised rich reward if the journey was made in record time.

"Feel like an ass, Togo!" he said, as the taxicab lurched along the street. "Got caught napping — what?"

"I told you that this was a dangerous adventure, sar."

"So you did! Never imagined I'd run into such violence while trying to get a silly locket from a foolish woman!"

"But that locket is no common one, sar."

"Can't be! Other chaps seem determined to get it," Warwick said. "Mighty glad you were Johnnie-on-the-spot, old boy! Feel gratitude, and all that! Must reward you someday."

"I was glad to help, sar."

"Always glad to be of service when there is a promise of a row, eh?" Warwick said.

"Yes, sar," said Togo, grinning.

"Togo, old top, this night may be my Waterloo. Wouldn't be a bit surprised if I fail to carry out the orders of our flabby-cheeked old friend, what? Other chaps have had an hour or more to get away with that locket."

"It is possible, sar, that they will take ample time and work slowly, thinking you are being held a prisoner," Togo said.

"Hope you're a good prophet! Dislike very much to fail at this juncture — might cause me all sorts of troubles and disappointments, old top."

"Pardon me, sar, but you have not failed yet. Even if they have it by the time we reach the Barker place, sar, we may be able to recover it."

"How's that?"

"That man Marlowe — I know of him, sar."

"You do, eh? What about the chap?"

"He is an old foe of The Spider's, sar."

"Is, eh? Then the jolly old Spider will be more than angry if we do not succeed tonight. My word! Have to make every possible effort, and all that sort of thing!"

"If this Marlowe gets away with the locket, sar, we might follow him and get it ourselves."

"Might, certainly. Rather get it from Mrs. Barker, however. Like to outwit the chap instead of using violence. Silly ass of a thing — that locket! Can't imagine what The Spider wants with it. Buy all you want for fifty dollars each. Locket of Tragedy, eh? Rot! Utter rot, I say!"

The taxicab stopped on the corner nearest the residence of Burton Barker, and John Warwick and Togo got out, and the former rewarded the chauffeur handsomely. And then he led the way across the velvety lawn, keeping well in the shadows.

"I'll have to make it appear that I've been wandering around the grounds and smoking — what?" Warwick whispered. "I'm going inside immediately, old top. Can't endure the uncertainty, and all that sort of thing."

"I'll remain in the neighborhood, sar," Togo said. "You may have some need of me."

"Good enough!" Warwick replied. "Be somewhere along this walk, so I can locate you quickly, if it is necessary. Luckily, those chaps didn't muss me up much. 'Bye!"

Warwick went into the residence of Burton Barker through a side entrance, dodged the others, went to the room that had been set aside for the gentlemen guests, and there brushed his clothing. His linen had not been soiled, he was glad to observe. He was still fairly presentable.

And then he made his way slowly down the broad stairs and came to the hall below. The orchestra was playing, couples were in the mazes of a dance, others were chatting in the conservatory and in the refreshment rooms.

Warwick stood at the entrance of the ballroom as if bored by the scene, and watched the dancers. His eye caught Silvia's; he nodded, and she flushed with pleasure. Then his eyes moved on — and presently he had located Mrs. Burton Barker.

He was glad to find that she still wore the locket at the end of the long chain. So Marlowe had not had the opportunity to get it yet — else he was waiting for an appropriate moment. John Warwick felt hope bubbling in his breast again. There still was a chance of carrying out The Spider's orders.

Another dance began, and Warwick noticed that Marlowe was dancing it with Mrs. Burton Barker. He stood back a short distance from the door, so that he could watch them without being observed. Silvia also was dancing, so Warwick did not have to give her his present attention, and was free to attend to The Spider's business.

"Must get that silly locket!" Warwick told himself. "Never do to fail now — what? Marlowe chap had his chance and didn't make the most of it. Have a try at it myself now, I fancy. Have to keep my eye on him, though. Wonder if he has any more assistants about? Must be alert, and all that sort of thing!"

The dance came to an end, and Marlowe and Mrs. Burton Barker passed within a short distance of Warwick as they walked into the hall. Warwick watched closely as Marlowe took his hostess to the refreshment room. It was evident that the man was trying to flirt with her — and she was the sort of woman who always is ready for a flirtation with any presentable man.

They went toward the conservatory. John Warwick guessed that Marlowe might make an attempt to get the locket there. He could engage Mrs. Burton Barker's attention and snip the thing from the end of its chain easily. Perhaps he would be able to make her believe that she had dropped it while they were walking through the hall and thus escape suspicion.

Warwick followed them into the conservatory, where there were many couples walking about. He dodged those he knew, and made his way behind a bank of foliage and bloom. Marlowe and Mrs. Burton Barker were on the other side of it, just sitting down. From where he stood, Warwick could watch them closely without being seen by them. They were indulging in small talk that meant nothing, and Warwick sensed that Marlowe was merely waiting for an opportunity.

Suddenly Marlowe bent closer to Mrs. Burton Barker, and the tone of his voice changed.

"Do you know, you are the sort of woman that fascinates me," he said.

Mrs. Burton Barker laughed lightly and bent away from him, and once more Marlowe moved closer to her.

"I mean it!" he said. "You are a wonderful sort of woman — quite beyond the ordinary a man meets every day."

"You are good at flattery," Mrs. Barker observed, thus asking for more of it.

"It is not flattery, but the truth!" Marlowe declared. "Didn't you notice that I was interested more than usual? Trust a woman to know when a man is interested!"

Warwick saw him bend toward her again — and smiled. He knew what Marlowe was doing. In a moment, he would become too enthusiastic, Mrs. Barker would put up her hands to ward him off, and then Marlowe would —

"Don't be foolish, please!" Mrs. Barker was saying, but in a tone that said she liked to have him foolish.

"I'd rather spend five minutes with you than hours with a silly, flighty girl," Marlowe went on. "When a man finds a woman who combines beauty with intelligence, he has found a treasure. Your husband is a very lucky man."

"I fear that there are times when he does not believe that," Mrs. Burton Barker said.

Marlowe suddenly bent nearer to her — and she did exactly what John Warwick had known she would do, she put up her hands, and turned her face away, trying to act the timid, modest, half-frightened girl, making an attempt to avoid a caress.

Warwick watched more closely now. He saw Marlowe lean forward again, put his face close to hers and whisper some foolishness — and while he did it, his left hand went forward, a bit of metal flashed in the uncertain light of the conservatory as the gold chain was snipped, and the locket was in Marlowe's hand and being conveyed to his pocket.

VIII.

Another Attempt.

JOHN WARWICK stepped back silently, walked around the bank of foliage and bloom, and confronted them.

"Pardon," he said, "but I believe I have a dance with our charming hostess."

Marlowe already was upon his feet, his eyes bulging, regarding Warwick as he might have looked at a man from the grave. Warwick smiled at him peculiarly.

"Must not monopolize Mrs. Barker," he said "My word! Haven't danced with her for quite some time! Pleasure I cannot miss this evening — what? Must assert my rights, and all that sort of thing!"

"Of course I'll dance with you, John," Mrs. Barker said.

"My word! You've lost your precious locket!" Warwick exclaimed.

Mrs. Burton Barker gave a gasp of dismay and felt at the end of the chain. Instantly, she was in a panic.

"Oh! I must find it!" she cried. "See — the chain is broken!"

"Probably caught it against something and snapped it," Warwick said lightly.

But he gave Marlowe another look, and Marlowe realized that Warwick knew what had happened.

"Imagine you'll find it without much difficulty," Warwick went on to his hostess. "Saw you come in here — and you had the locket on the chain then."

"You're sure?"

"Absolutely!" Warwick replied. "Probably dropped it around here some place. Easy to find, what? Just close the conservatory door — and then we know the locket is somewhere inside."

Marlowe glared at him, and Warwick chuckled. Mrs. Burton Barker was looking around the floor, her hands clasped before her.

"I must find it — must find it!" she repeated.

"Good-luck locket — what?"

"Yes — a talisman," the woman replied. "Why don't you help me find it?"

"No doubt it'll be found almost instantly," John Warwick observed, meeting Marlowe's eyes again. "Locket can't run away — what? My word, no! Have to be right around here some place! Let's look!"

They pretended to search. Warwick watched Marlowe closely from the corners of his eyes. He saw Marlowe drop the locket against the bank of flowers and then pretend to stoop and recover it.

"Here it is, Mrs. Barker," he announced.

"Oh, thank you!"

"Chain probably worn through," Warwick observed. "Fine gold, you know — little jerk would break it. Better have it repaired, dear lady — what?"

"I shall have it repaired in the morning," she said.

A servant approached with the intelligence that some guest wished to see the hostess, and Mrs. Burton Barker, promising to dance with Warwick later, took her leave. The two men were left alone.

Warwick stood before Marlowe, his hands upon his hips, and chuckled at the other man, whose face depicted his rage.

"Coarse work, what?" Warwick said.

"Think you're smart, don't you?"

"Why didn't you bluff it out, old chap? Didn't have the nerve? My word! I was standing behind the plants, you know, and saw you snip the thing."

"This isn't the end, Warwick!"

"Trying to threaten me now? Oh, I say! Doesn't ruffle a single feather of mine, really! My word, no! Calm in the face of danger, and all that sort of thing. By the way, better engage a new crowd of thugs. Those you have at present aren't quite up to the standard. Managed to get away from them, you see."

"I see!" Marlowe exclaimed. "May I ask how you did it?"

"Quite simple. Friend of mine saw me being abducted, followed, got into the cottage, overpowered the chaps, and rescued me."

"That damned Jap, I suppose."

"Wouldn't curse him, if I were you!"

Warwick warned. "He's quite the man, you know — been no end of help to me on several occasions. Don't like to hear him spoken of in that tone."

"Suppose we just put aside this high-falutin' talk," Marlowe said. "We understand each other — it's war between us. We're both after that locket. And I'm going to get it!"

"You had it a moment since and didn't retain it," Warwick reminded him. "My turn now, what?"

"Not if I know it! If you get that locket, Warwick, you'll be a very clever man!"

"Oh, I say! Not that, surely! Well, can't stand here talking to you all evening. Have to toddle along!"

"And I'll toddle right along in your wake," Marlowe informed him, angrily.

"Still following and watching me — what?"

"You can bet that I am!"

"And a lot of good it will do you!" John Warwick said. "Making a regular ass of yourself — you are! Have to toddle! 'Bye!"

He whirled around, walked through the conservatory and entered the wide hall. He saw Mrs. Burton Barker at the foot of the stairs, talking to a couple of guests forced to take leave early, and went toward her.

"Sure you have your locket?" he asked, when the others had gone.

"I have it in my hand," she answered. "It gave me quite a start to find it missing. I'm glad that you noticed it, John."

"You make quite a fuss over that locket, what?"

"It — it is a good-luck thing, John. I'm a bit superstitious, you know — always was, in fact."

"Don't seem to remember anything of the sort," Warwick

told her. "Always regarded you as an ultramodern young woman who didn't believe in rot."

"It is just a fad of mine," she said.

"Let's see the locket a moment — maybe I can fix it."

"I'll have it repaired in the morning, John; you needn't bother now."

"You'll be dropping it somewhere, and then you surely will lose it," he told her. "Better let me tie it on the end of the chain."

He lifted the chain and looked at it closely. She handed the locket to him, and he started fastening it to the end of the chain. He knew that was the only way. If she took the locket upstairs, she probably would hide it some place where it could not be found easily. There was a chance of getting it while she was wearing it.

Silvia Rodney approached at that moment with a man with whom she had been dancing, and stopped to speak to Mrs. Burton Barker.

"Dear hostess almost lost a locket," Warwick said. "Found it again, however. Trying to fasten it to the chain again."

His eyes met Silvia's for an instant, and the girl smiled at him. Marlowe approached and joined the group.

Warwick finished attaching the locket to the chain, and stood back. Mrs. Barker was making an attempt to show that she was not agitated, that she had almost forgotten about the locket. But she was watching it closely, Warwick knew. Her fingers played with the chain continually, and now and then ran down it and touched the locket at the bottom.

"Shall we dance?" Warwick asked.

They entered the ballroom and danced. He had no chance to get the locket. He wished he might detach it in such a manner that he could kick it into a corner and pick it up afterward. But he knew that he would have to wait until Mrs. Burton Barker's mind was centered on something else. It might be disastrous to make an attempt to get the locket now.

They finished the dance, and walked into the wide hall again. Marlowe was talking to Silvia and the man who had been dancing with her, and Warwick led Mrs. Barker toward them.

"Why not the veranda and smokes?" Marlowe asked lightly.

Warwick flashed a look at him, but agreed. They all moved out to the veranda, walked toward one end of it where there were easy chairs. They seated themselves and lighted cigarettes, and indulged in some more small talk. Warwick and Marlowe were watching each other carefully, each fearing that the other would make an unexpected move.

Warwick began wondering how the thing was to be accomplished. It had seemed so simple compared to some things he had done — merely snipping a locket from a chain and getting away with it without arousing suspicion. He began to tell himself that he must be slowing up, to let such a man as Marlowe prevent him from carrying out the orders of The Spider. He would have to be doubly careful about it now. He wasn't quite sure that Mrs. Barker believed the locket had been lost accidentally in the conservatory. He couldn't afford to run any grave risk, when his future happiness and that of Silvia Rodney depended upon his success.

Mrs. Barker addressed a remark to him, and he bent forward to reply. At that instant, the lights in the house went out.

There came a chorus of exclamations from the ballroom. Chairs scraped on the veranda as guests got to their feet. Mrs. Burton Barker started to say something, and the sentence was broken off in the middle.

John Warwick sprang to his feet, for he suspected a trap of some sort. It would be like Marlowe to have a confederate snap off the lights so that he could work in the dark.

Then there came a sudden rush of men over the railing. Warwick felt himself hurled to one side. He heard an exclamation of fear, and Marlowe's whispered commands.

Warwick realized what was taking place, then. They were kidnaping Mrs. Burton Barker. They probably would carry her a short distance across the lawn, tear the locket from the chain and get away with it. Marlowe would remain behind, and probably take part in the search for the assailants, thus freeing himself of any suspicion.

It all occurred in a short space of time. Warwick sensed that Marlowe would have him attended to, also. And so he darted noiselessly to the railing and vaulted over it to the ground. He brushed against another man, who instantly grappled with him. Warwick started to fight. He felt his throat gripped, felt a peculiar pressure —

"Togo!" he whispered hoarsely.

"That you, sar? I thought it was one of the others," Togo gasped. "Did I hurt you, sar?"

"No! Silence, old top! Let's see what's going on here!"

Those inside the house were crying for lights. Servants were calling to one another, and Warwick heard something said about a fuse burning out.

He crouched at the end of the veranda with Togo. He realized that Mrs. Burton Barker was being lifted over the railing, and a whiff of chloroform came to his nostrils. Marlowe was talking loudly now, as if to cover the confusion. Warwick heard Silvia's voice, asking what had happened.

And then he gripped Togo by the arm and led the way around the end of the veranda. He knew that Marlowe's men were ahead of them. He watched and saw them cross a space between two dark spots — four of them carrying a woman.

He darted forward again, with Togo at his heels, whispering explanations and orders.

"Taxi still at corner, sar," Togo whispered in reply.

Across the lawn they followed the men, careful to avoid being seen. The odds were great, and Warwick did not care to attempt a combat and come from it vanquished. The men ahead were running now. They dropped the unconscious form of Mrs. Burton Barker beside a clump of brush.

Warwick stopped there just an instant. It was as he had expected — the locket was gone.

IX

A Lost Locket

AGAIN, John Warwick darted forward, Togo close behind. Warwick was in a rage now. He did not believe in using violence toward women. He always had prided himself on avoiding the use of it whenever the orders of The Spider compelled him to deal with those of the gentler sex. And he did not intend to let four thugs assault a woman in that manner, chloroform her, and steal something that he himself wished to get into his possession.

He stopped behind a tree. The four men were at the curb, mumbling among themselves. It was evident that they were

waiting for a motor car, and that the driver had missed his cal-
culations.

"Let us get at them, sar," Togo whispered.

Warwick was just angry enough to agree. He gave the signal
and, with Togo, rushed forward.

They hurled themselves upon the four like twin hurricanes.
John Warwick went into action like a battleship, showering
blows on all sides, but he worked silently, conserving his breath
and strength as well as he could.

Togo sprang for the throat of the nearest man, and had him
stretched unconscious on the ground in an instant. Then he
reached for the second. But the others were putting up a fight,
now that the first shock of surprise was over. Warwick and Togo
found that the three of them were a match, a little more than a
match. With his back against a tree, Warwick fought as well as
he could, and Togo tried in vain to clutch one of his antagonists
by the throat and put him out of the combat.

Warwick sent a second man lurching to the ground with a
well-directed blow. The odds were even now. Togo screeched
once and hurled himself at one of the thugs, and the man turned
and ran. Warwick made short work of the other.

It took Warwick only a few seconds to search the three men
on the ground — and he did not find the locket. Lights were
blazing up in the house again, and male guests were rushing toward him. They crowded about him, demanding to know what
had happened.

Warwick explained in a few words. Some men had attacked
Mrs. Burton Barker on the veranda as the lights went out. She
was beside the clump of brush now, unconscious from chloroform. He had taken after the men. Here were three of them —
and another had got away. Togo, the Japanese valet, was after
that fourth man.

The male guests made short work of the three on the
ground. They were picked up and taken to the house, to be held
there until the police could be called. Mrs. Burton Barker was
carried inside, too, where the frantic guests were huddling together and talking in whispers of what had occurred. They
supposed it was an attempt at robbery; they felt of their neck-
laces and rings, to be sure that they had not suffered loss.

Warwick remained on the lawn for a quarter of an hour, and

at the end of that time Togo returned.

"He got away from me, sar," Togo reported.

"Well, it can't be helped, old chap."

"They — they got it, sar?"

"I imagine that they did, Togo, honorable Jap. That was the scheme of course. The man who escaped evidently had it."

"And now, sar —"

"Now, old top, I shall be compelled, for the first time in my life, to report to The Spider that I have failed. And he was particular to tell me, too, that he didn't care to have me fail in this case. He will rave and roar, I doubt not — almost have a fit, and all that sort of thing."

"You are not going to give up, sar?"

"I am not, honorable Jap. Marlowe is the head of this gang, and you can wager that Marlowe remains in the house so that nobody will suspect him. Sooner or later, Marlowe will get that locket from the man who has it."

"Then we watch this Marlowe, sar?"

"We do," Warwick said. "I have to go into the house now, of course. You may remain outside, Togo, and use your own judgment."

"I understand, sar."

"Never heard of such a fuss — all this row over a silly locket! Wonder what the thing is, anyway!"

"I feared there would be trouble, sar."

"Spider told me as much, but I scarcely believed him," Warwick said. "Imagine I look a pretty specimen now. One of those beggars caught me a clip under the eye — be black in the morning. I'll go into the house now, old top!"

Warwick made his way to the veranda. He discovered that he was a hero. The male guests had told their fair companions that John Warwick had followed the four men who had assaulted and robbed Mrs. Button Barker and accounted for three of them.

Warwick pushed his way to the stairs and up them to the second floor. Servants rushed to his aid. In a bathroom he inspected himself. There was a cut beneath one eye. His collar was torn, his tie soiled, and there was dust on his clothes.

"Pretty sight!" he complained as he bathed his bruised knuckles. "My word, yes! A bit of a row, and all that, but one of the chaps got away!"

Burton Barker rushed into the room, bubbling his thanks and reporting that his wife was all right again — and would descend and order the dance continued.

Then Marlowe stepped into the room.

"Good boy, Warwick!" he said, grinning. "You certainly handled those fellows!"

"Where were you?" Warwick asked nastily.

"It happened so quickly, I didn't realize what was taking place," Marlowe lied. "One of the fellows hurled me back along the railing, and by the time I could get to my feet, they were gone with Mrs. Barker — and you were gone, too. Miss Rodney was nervous — I escorted her inside as soon as the lights came on again."

"Very kind of you — thanks," Warwick said.

"You certainly battered up those three prisoners. They are saying that half a dozen men jumped on them."

"Silly asses! Ought to go to jail!" Warwick said.

"They'll go to jail, all right!" Barker declared.

A servant pushed in and called him, and Barker hurried away. The others could hear a woman wailing in one of the other rooms — Mrs. Burton Barker had discovered that her locket was missing. They could hear her shriek that it must be recovered, could hear Barker giving orders to his servants.

Warwick dismissed the servants who had been helping him, and began putting on a fresh collar one of them had brought. The cut beneath his eye had been bathed and court-plaster applied, but Warwick knew that it would be a bad sight in the morning. He turned from the mirror and saw Marlowe watching him.

"Well?" Marlowe asked.

"Three of your men are going to jail," Warwick said in a low tone.

"That's their fault."

"They are liable to talk, aren't they?"

"I'm not a bit afraid of that," Marlowe said. "They'll take their medicine, and they'll be paid for doing it. They did their work well, you know."

"I suppose so."

"You didn't have a chance, Warwick! It was a good fight

while it lasted, but it didn't last long. It might have been different if you had been given plenty of help. I don't understand why The Spider didn't give you help."

"There goes that Spider stuff again!"

"Oh, stop the bluff, Warwick! I'm wise, and you know that I am wise! I say it is a wonder that he didn't give you help."

Warwick stepped close to him. "Very well — since you know so much!" he said. "If I am working for some chap you call The Spider, let it be known that I never need much help!"

"This was the time you needed it, Warwick!"

"Got three of your men, at any rate!"

"But one got away, eh? And so you didn't get the locket!" Marlowe laughed, sneered, and turned toward the door.

"Lots of time yet to get that," Warwick hurled after him.

"Not a chance, Warwick — not a chance in the world! You've had your last look at that little trinket. And what you'll get from that boss of yours will be plenty — don't forget that for a moment. He could not have taken you into his confidence, or you'd have made a better attempt to win out. This was a mighty important deal."

"Don't know what you're talking about, I'm sure!" Warwick said.

"Well, you've lost, Warwick!"

"Game isn't over yet!" John Warwick observed. "Seen lots of them won in the last half of the ninth inning, you know. Rally — all that sort of thing!"

He passed Marlowe and went down the stairs. He intended to keep his eyes on Marlowe, even if he had to send Silvia Rodney home in the limousine alone. Marlowe, he knew, would get possession of that locket sometime. He would find Togo out on the lawn and tell him to hold the taxicab in readiness.

But Togo had disappeared for the time being. Servants with electric torches were searching the lawn for Mrs. Burton Barker's locket. That lady was trying to force herself to believe that it had been torn from her while she was being carried across the lawn — when, in reality, she knew that the assault had been for the purpose of getting the locket.

Mrs. Barker was on the veranda herself, almost hysterical, directing the search, refusing to go to her room. Some of the guests were taking their departure. The orchestra was still playing, and some of the couples were dancing as if nothing had happened. It was a tribute to their hostess.

Warwick went down among the others and pretended to join in the search. For the first time since he had joined The Spider's band, he felt a dread of the supercriminal. He almost feared the interview that he knew he would be forced to hold with him. The Spider did not countenance failure. He had instructed Warwick to get that locket, and he expected success.

It would be like The Spider to refuse to release him from the band and allow him to marry Silvia, and Warwick told himself that he never would marry her unless he was released. He would get the locket yet, he told himself. He would follow Marlowe day and night, with only Togo to help him — he'd get that locket if he was forced to use violence against Marlowe and his men, if he had to turn burglar or highwayman! He never had failed The Spider before, and he did not intend to fail now!

The search came to an end — and the locket had not been found. Warwick went back into the house, and received thanks from a pale Mrs. Burton Barker. He saw that she was making a brave fight to retain her composure, and he wondered again what the locket meant to her, what it meant to others. Locket of Tragedy, Togo had called it, but John Warwick didn't see any sense in that.

He met Silvia in the hall, and they stepped to one side.

"You'll be a handsome man in the morning," she said, laughing a little.

"Do not rub it in, dear lady!" Warwick told her.

"Aren't you ashamed of yourself, getting into a brawl while acting as my escort?"

"It is a serious matter!" Warwick whispered. "Dear lady, I have failed for the time being — they got away with the locket."

"How did it happen, John?"

"Marlowe — that chap you danced with — is at the bottom of it. He got Mrs. Barker to the veranda purposely. Those chaps sprang over the railing when the lights went out, grasped her and chloroformed her, rushed across the lawn with her, took the locket and left her there. My luck, I suppose, that the man who had the locket in his possession escaped.

"Then there is no chance of getting it, John?"

"I haven't quite given up yet. Going to watch this Marlowe

chap. Old Togo's about, ready to help. Have to get the thing, or your jolly old uncle will be furious. Might force me to remain in — er — his employ, and all that."

"Perhaps it will all come out right, John."

"Let us hope so!" Warwick said.

Marlowe stepped up to them. "Pardon me, but I believe that I have this dance with Miss Rodney," he said pleasantly. "Our hostess wishes the ball to continue, despite the annoyance she has experienced. As a compliment to her —"

"Of course! Naturally!" Warwick said.

He surrendered Silvia and watched them as they started dancing. He felt a twinge of jealousy, but told himself it was because Marlowe was the man and because Marlowe had bested him for the time being.

He could not help admiring Marlowe's courage. The fellow was carrying it off well. He was an excellent foe, John Warwick thought. And he became more determined to get the locket, if it took him weeks!

X

A Surprise

SILVIA RODNEY danced the encore with Marlowe, while Warwick walked up and down the hall and now and then stopped to speak to some acquaintance and dodge hero worship.

Warwick was wondering just who Marlowe might be and how Mrs. Burton Barker had become acquainted with him. He intended to get a line on Marlowe and keep in touch with the man. He simply had to get the locket! Everything depended upon it — his future standing with The Spider, his own happiness, and that of Silvia.

He wondered why Silvia was dancing with Marlowe so much, since she knew now that Marlowe was a foe to them all. Her face was radiant when Marlowe returned with her and handed her over to Warwick.

"Now I'll dance with you, John, and then, I think, we'd better go," Silvia said.

Warwick could do nothing but go out upon the floor with

her, but he managed a whisper.

"Please make it short, Silvia. I want to watch Marlowe and follow him. A great deal depends on it, you know. Simply must get that locket, what? He'll lead me to it, and all that sort of thing. Have to triumph in the end, or your jolly old uncle will walk around my collar. My word, yes!"

"Aren't you going to take me home, John?"

"Will it make you very angry if I send you alone?" Warwick asked.

"Of course!"

"But, in such a case —"

"I'll be angry, nevertheless. And how will it look to the others, John? Will they not suspect something?"

"Have to cover it up in some manner," Warwick said. "Might get out at the first corner and return."

"Oh, let the old locket go!"

"Dear girl! Your jolly old uncle will be enraged."

"I'll smooth it over for you, John."

"Afraid it would be a difficult task in such a case. Uncle seemed very keen on getting the thing, remember. Some sort of a secret connected with it, and all that. Appears to be vastly important, though for the life of me I cannot understand why."

"Well, you let it go and take me home!"

"Just as you say, dear girl, but I fear that we are making a mistake," Warwick told her, sighing. "Take all the blame myself, of course, and all that. My word! Jolly old uncle probably will roar like a lion. May refuse to — well, you know, dear girl!"

"You leave it to me, John. You've never failed before, have you?"

"Never!"

"Well, uncle cannot raise so very much of a row, then."

"Can't he? I've seen him angry!" Warwick said. "Rather face a tiger unarmed. My word!"

They finished the dance and went toward the hall. Marlowe was just taking leave of Mrs. Burton Barker, and he grinned at John Warwick as he approached. Silvia went for her wraps, and Warwick stepped out on the veranda for an instant.

He walked along the railing, until there came to him from the darkness a peculiar hiss that he recognized.

"That you, Togo?" he asked.

"Yes, sar."

"Follow our man when he leaves — I cannot."

"Yes, sar."

Warwick walked back to the doorway, entered, and continued along the hall toward the stairs.

"Better luck next time," Marlowe whispered as he passed.

"Hope so!" Warwick growled.

"Should have had help, you know. You were up against a tough proposition."

"A proposition of toughs, you mean."

Marlowe's face flushed. "Bad loser, are you?" he sneered.

"Haven't lost yet, you know," Warwick retorted.

"You haven't? Don't fool yourself!"

"Lots of time yet — game's young."

"Not this particular game!" Marlowe said.

"May find out different," Warwick told him. "Rally, you know — all that sort of thing. Seen it lots of times. Advise you to keep your eyes and ears open."

"Oh, I'll be watching out for you!"

"That's an excellent idea," Warwick observed.

He went on up the stairs for his things. He met Silvia; they spoke to Mrs. Burton Barker, and went out to the limousine. Soon they were speeding down the avenue and across the city.

"Oh, cheer up, John!" the girl said.

"Don't feel like it, dear lady. Not used to failure — what? Rather gets me, you know, and all that. My word, yes!"

"It will be all right, John."

"Not so sure about that. Have to report to your jolly old uncle as soon as we reach the house, I suppose, and take what is coming to me."

"Why not put it off?" she asked.

"Never do in the world. Make a full report, and maybe he can get the silly locket by sending somebody else after it — somebody who is not a bungler."

"But you were fighting against odds!"

"Makes no difference," he declared, "Always fought against odds before and won. Makes no difference at all!"

They rode for a time in silence, Silvia snuggling close to his side.

"When we get home," she said presently, "you wait until I

talk to uncle."

"Afraid it'll do no good," Warwick replied.

"Nevertheless, John Warwick, you wait until I have talked to him, and then you can go up and — er — take what is coming to you."

"Very well. Put off the evil hour a few minutes, at any rate," he said. "Imagine I'll get an awful wigging! My word, yes! Probably be told I'm a worthless beggar, and all that sort of thing. First time I've failed, you know — not used to it!"

"Perhaps there'll be a chance yet."

"A slight one," Warwick admitted. "I gave Togo orders to follow that Marlowe chap. By the way, you seemed to like to dance with him."

"John Warwick, are you jealous?"

"My word — no! Just remarked it!" Warwick said.

"Well, you'd better not be jealous, sir! That is something I'll not endure! Here we are at home!"

Warwick told the chauffeur to wait and escorted Silvia inside the house. She left him in the big living room and went up the stairs to The Spider's den. She knew that he would not have retired, that he would wait to tell her good-night.

John Warwick spent a bad quarter of an hour. He paced back and forth across the room, fearful one moment, defiant the next, wondering what he could say to The Spider to justify himself. He decided that he could only explain and ask the supercriminal to be merciful.

And then Silvia came back down the stairs.

"How did he take it?" Warwick asked.

"Oh, I scarcely think he will have you shot, John."

"Angry, I suppose?"

"You'll find out soon enough — you are to go right up and see him," she replied.

"Hope the old chap isn't too hard on me," Warwick said. "Can't dare to think of losing you, little lady."

He held her in his arms for an instant, kissed her, and then started slowly up the stairs.

Outside the door of the supercriminal's den, he paused for a moment to gather his courage. Warwick was a man who did not like to confess failure. He knew that The Spider probably had spoken kindly to Silvia, but he would not let that affect the manner in which he received John Warwick.

Finally, he opened the door, entered, closed and bolted it behind him as was the custom, and then whirled around to find The Spider in his usual place behind the big mahogany desk.

"Sit down, Warwick!" The Spider said. "And give me your close attention while I explain something about that locket."

"I regret —"

"Silence — and listen! It is getting late, and I am a tired man. I just want to tell you, Warwick, of the importance of that locket. Several years ago, the woman you know as Mrs. Burton Barker was spending her first season abroad. Her mother was with her. In a peculiar manner, the girl saw a crime committed. She was young and romantic, and she took a fancy to the man who committed it — one of my men."

"I understand, sir."

"Without her mother's knowledge, she kept engagements with this man. He saw in her only a foolish and romantic girl, and he kept up the acquaintance to get information. Her mother was rich, as you know. This man of mine intended to get all the information he could and probably lift the mother's jewels."

"I understand."

"He let the girl know that he belonged to a famous band of criminals. He let her know too much. The Locket of Tragedy was the property of a famous Parisian, and this man of mine got it one night while looting an apartment. It was called that because it had been owned by persons who met violent ends. It had quite a history, and many a collector stood ready to pay a handsome price for it."

"I see," said Warwick.

"A queen who poisoned herself owned it once, and then a famous courtesan who was tried for murder and executed. Almost every owner of the locket met with violence. My man got it as I have said, and he showed some of the loot to the girl who now is Mrs. Barker. She wanted the locket, and he let her have it, thinking he could steal it from her later. He didn't dare refuse at the time, for he needed more information before attempting to rob her mother of a fortune in jewels.

"Before he could regain the locket her mother took a sudden notion to return to the States, bringing her daughter with her, of course. The night before they departed, this slip of a girl got possession of a bit of tissue paper. That paper is still in existence, and is enough to send me to prison for the rest of my life, and to send other men there. The authorities of Paris would pay a fortune for it.

"She returned to the States, and I sent my man after her with instructions to get the locket and the paper, which she kept in it. He failed, and returned, and I sent two other men. She did not wear the locket in those days — she had it hidden somewhere. I sent her word that, unless she returned the locket and the bit of tissue, I'd have her criminal sweetheart slain. She had spunk — replied that if I did she would hand the paper over to the police.

"She had us there — understand? She threatened to hand the things over the first month she did not receive a letter from this man she admired. We were safe as long as he wrote those letters — and I saw that he did write them.

"Then she got married, and began wearing the locket. It had grown to be a sort of duel between us by that time. She did not surrender the things even after being married. I tried a score of times to get the locket and what it contained, and I failed. I let the thing slide, as the saying is, let her hold the sword over my head.

"Last month, Warwick, she got no communication, for the simple reason that this man of mine had died. I ascertained that she was making investigation — she thought that I had made away with him, understand? She was ready to hand that locket to the police and tell her story."

"And the others —" Warwick asked.

"Members of a band antagonistic to me. They learned of the locket and its secret. They wanted to get it and send it to the authorities of Paris themselves — wanted to see me and some others sent to prison. Do you understand what that locket meant to me, Warwick? If those others got it, if Mrs. Barker retained it, I was doomed. That is how important that locket was to me!"

Warwick gave an exclamation of horror. So he, by his failure, had doomed The Spider — and perhaps himself. For, if an investigation were made, it might lead to Warwick and other new members of the band, too. And, as for Silvia — why, her life would be ruined! She would be pointed out as the niece of a supercriminal.

"It would be a case of chickens coming home to roost!" The Spider continued. "My crimes the last few years, since that accident that made me a cripple, have not been what the world would call extra bad. I have reformed to an extent, as you know. But in the old days, I did many things for which I still could be punished."

"Sir, I —" Warwick began.

The Spider silenced him with a gesture.

"So you can see the importance of that locket," the supercriminal went on, "And when you sent it to me just now, by Silvia —"

"Sir?" Warwick gasped.

"It was a great relief to me. It meant everything. It meant that I shall not have to spend my last days in some prison. And I am so thankful, Warwick, that I am going to quit. I have one thing more to do, and then I am going to disband my people. That one thing is good instead of evil — I'll explain it to you later. And I'm going to give my ill-gotten gains to certain charities and retain just enough to live on. Silvia will marry you — and be happy. Go to her now, John Warwick, and leave me alone with my happiness."

Warwick unbolted the door and hurried out. He almost rushed down the stairs, to where Silvia was waiting for him in the big living room. She laughed as she saw the expression in his face.

"Was it all right?" she asked saucily.

"Dear lady, suppose that you give me some sort of an explanation," he said.

"Regarding what?"

"Your jolly old uncle has just told me that I sent the locket up to him by you — thanked me for it. Knew nothing about it, I assure you! Imagined that thug fellow had it — sent Togo chasing after Marlowe to watch the chap —"

Silvia's laugh interrupted him.

"I told you that perhaps I could help, John," she said.

"My word! Can't understand it at all!"

"Why, John Warwick! When the lights went out and those men came over the railing, I suspected that it was a trick to get the locket. I slipped to one side and finally got right behind that man Marlowe I heard him whispering to the other men as they were using the chloroform. He took the locket himself, John, at that moment. There was a hit of light from the arc on the corner, and I could see by crouching against the wall. He took the locket and slipped it into his waistcoat pocket."

"But that was dangerous —"

"Silly! If there had been a search, he would have pretended that he had just picked it up."

"I suppose so. But how did *you* get the locket?"

"I got it while I was dancing with him, John — picked his pocket, you see."

"My word!" Warwick gasped. "You picked a chap's pocket?"

"Yes. It wasn't at all difficult, John. Remember, you foolish boy, I have a strain of The Spider's blood in my veins. It was that Spider strain that called upon me to do it. I wanted to help you — and it was a sort of adventure —"

"See here!" Warwick exclaimed. "You were deuced lucky, and you must never do such a thing again. Suppose he had felt in his pocket afterward and found the thing gone? He would have suspected you at once."

"Oh, he did feel in his pocket!"

"But —"

"But, you see, John, when I took the locket. I slipped in its place a small portière ring that I had taken from the draperies in the hall. He merely felt the ring and thought that it was the locket. See?"

"My word!"

"And then, John —"

But she did not finish the sentence. She could not with his lips pressed against hers.

THE STOLEN STORY

TEMPTATION often had come to John Branton, in one form or another, as it comes to the best of us, and generally he had turned his back upon it and gone on his way a law-abiding and self-respecting citizen, if not an affluent one.

Four years out of college, John Branton found that he was not getting along very well. In common with most college graduates, he once had possessed ambitions that were comprehensive. Buffeted by what he believed was a cruel fate, Branton had failed to achieve any of the things that once he had believed possible.

Because he liked to read, and because he wished to associate with people who really were doing things — the creators — John Branton, during his college career, had decided to become an author. He had applied himself faithfully to the study of English and the classics, and after having been graduated, he had demonstrated to his satisfaction the fact that a man may not create himself merely because he appreciates and understands the creations of others.

John Branton was long on technique and short on ability to stir human emotions or touch the human heart. His English was without a flaw, yet he could not drive home a point when he wrote. He had studied books to the exclusion of humanity — and it is humanity that successful authors write about.

Now, four years out of college, he was holding down a humble clerkship that served to keep him in food and clothing, and still trying to write. Regularly his compositions were returned to him by magazine editors who appreciated his command of English, but who knew that their readers never would get beyond the first paragraph. The ambition of John Branton was low at times, and then it would flare forth again when he read of some other man's success. Ungratified ambition may prove to be a treacherous thing. It was so in the case of Branton; it led him into temptation.

Branton lived in a house where there were bachelor apartments. He had a tiny kitchenette and cooked some of his own meals. Each evening he tried to write. He gave little attention to the other persons in the house. He hated the clerk's job; he wanted to see his name in print; he wanted to be somebody.

Then there came an evening when he heard a knock at the door. John Branton hurried across the room and opened it. Before him stood a peculiar individual, a man some six feet tall, with broad shoulders and an enormous head, with long thick hair that was unkempt, with small glittering black eyes that looked evil — a grotesque figure of a man.

"My water faucet's being fixed," said the grotesque one. "I live in the front, this floor. Let me get a pitcher of water, please?"

John Branton always was courteous. He asked the grotesque one in, filled the pitcher for him, and handed it back with a bow.

"Help yourself until they fix you up," Branton said.

The other had been glancing at Branton's desk.

"Newspaper man?" he asked.

"No. I am a clerk for a mercantile agency," Branton replied bitterly. "But I try to write a bit now and then. I always wanted to be a writer, but the road is a hard one."

"Um! I haven't found it so."

"You are a writer?"

"In a way. I have had some success in a small way. Anything I write seems to sell readily enough, but I don't like to write."

"Don't like to write?" Branton queried, gasping. "I should think you'd love it."

"A man always likes to do what he cannot, and seldom likes to do what he can do well. My name is Marmaduke Loughtry. Silly name, but mine own."

"I — I'm glad to meet you," Branton said.

"I'm sure I don't know why. Come in and see me some time, if it pleases you."

Branton did. He cultivated Marmaduke Loughtry to a certain extent. Unable to write successfully, he felt that the next best thing was to associate with a man who did. And Branton thought it possible that he might pick up a few ideas that would put him on the right track.

Almost from the first he felt disgusted with Marmaduke Loughtry. The man could write and sell almost everything that he wrote, yet he did not seem to care for the talent that was his.

Marmaduke Loughtry wrote only now and then. He spent a great deal of time and money indulging in liquor. He disappeared for days at a time, and returned ill and seedy.

"I'd work my head off if I could write like that man," John Branton told himself.

Branton began to feel bitter about it, too. Why should such a man as Loughtry have this heaven-sent gift when he abused it so? Why should Marmaduke Loughtry have his name in print, and have editors writing him for stories, when a decent fellow like John Branton had no success whatever?

"If I could get one story printed — just one!" Branton thought.

Loughtry took no pride in his work. He did not keep copies of his stories on file, kept no records of their publication, scarcely remembered what they had been about. One night Branton read a paragraph in one of them and commented on its beauty.

"I forgot I wrote that," Loughtry said. "Half the time I don't know what I'm writing about; it's the booze, I suppose."

The following day Loughtry disappeared, and he was gone for almost a week. Branton saw him the evening of his return in Loughtry's rooms. Loughtry had been working, there was a finished story on his desk.

"Turn out a new one?" Branton asked.

Loughtry was maudlin. He picked up the manuscript, glanced at it, tossed it aside.

"Forget — wh-what it's about," he said.

He seemed to be in a sort of stupor. John Branton undressed him and put him to bed. Then he went to his own room and took the story with him.

He had no intention at first of committing a literary theft. He merely wanted to read the latest work of Marmaduke Loughtry and find wherein was the spark of success. It was a short story of ordinary length, badly written, yet with the human note striking through it. John Branton, almost unconsciously, sat down before his desk and began to rewrite it, correcting mistakes in English, changing a name here and there. It was almost dawn when he had finished, and he read it over.

"That's the way I'd have written it," he told himself. "Now it is in decent English, and it also has 'punch'."

And then Temptation whispered in his ear. Why not send

out that story as his own? He had changed the names and a few of the minor incidents. And it was probable that Marmaduke Loughtry had forgotten it. If he had not he would think that he had lost it while under the influence of liquor.

Branton could send it to some magazine that Loughtry did not honor with his work. Loughtry never would see the story, perhaps, if it was printed. For Loughtry did not read the work of others, nor did he watch the market.

Branton changed the title, put his own name and address on the manuscript, sealed it in an addressed envelope, and walked to the corner and mailed it. As he heard the envelope strike the bottom of the letter box, he realized what he had done. He had stolen somebody's brain-work. He had committed one of the unpardonable crimes. There was only one worse literary crime — selling to an editor of a magazine a mutilated copy of a story that had been published in another.

But John Branton shrugged his shoulders and tried to tell himself that he was justified. Loughtry would not care; he would not know. He had no pride in his work. And, if Branton could sell this one story, it might serve to aid him in selling others. Perhaps Marmaduke Loughtry was but helping him to get near the editorial chieftains.

HE SAW Loughtry the following evening, and Loughtry said nothing about the story. His desk was in a mess, and Branton doubted whether Loughtry knew for certain that there had been a story. In fact, Loughtry seemed to be puzzled about something.

"Can't remember whether I mailed it or not," he told Branton. "I believe I wrote one. Must have mailed it, I guess. Doesn't make any difference anyway."

Branton felt a little safer after that, especially since Loughtry started on another spree. The days passed swiftly, and now and then Loughtry disappeared, to return more shaky and seedy than ever.

Then there came a day when John Branton received from the editor of the magazine a letter and a check. The story had been accepted. The editor would like to see more of John Branton's work.

Branton cashed the check and then went out upon the

streets and walked for two hours as if stepping on clouds. It was almost as if he had accomplished the thing without help. He ceased to think of Loughtry. He told himself that the story would not have sold if he had not polished it up. He knew that was a lie, that it was the ability of Marmaduke Loughtry to touch the human heart that had sold the story, yet he strove to convince himself.

He planned more stories, and worked hard each night at his desk! Loughtry had said nothing more about the story, and Branton knew that Loughtry believed he had lost the manuscript. Loughtry was working on another, too.

Branton had sold the story to a weekly publication, and it soon was published. He saw his name in print at last, for he had not used a pseudonym. It was his name in print that Branton wanted, more than the money.

He read the story half a dozen times, and his fears disappeared. Surely Loughtry would not see the magazine; if he did he would not read it. The title had been changed, the names of the characters, the formations of sentences here and there, and the introductory paragraph was new, entirely the work of John Branton.

As a murderer returns to the scene of his crime, so Branton went to the rooms of Marmaduke Loughtry that evening. He was eager to see whether Loughtry had any suspicions. He found that Loughtry was not at home. His desk was a mass of mussed-up papers, his door not even locked.

"He went out late last night," the landlady told Branton. "I suppose the poor man is drinking again. Where he gets the stuff, I don't know. He must have some great sorrow in his life, Mr. Branton, and perhaps we should not blame him. I do not worry about it; his rent is paid months in advance."

So John Branton felt secure. Even if Loughtry saw the story, Branton would declare it to be his own, would say that he had told the plot to Loughtry while he was intoxicated, and he probably had thought afterward that it was one of his own.

"I'll take care of him when I am rich and famous," Branton told himself. "All that I wanted was a start."

That seemed to be true, for he had sold another story. He did not know that the editor had bit his lip when he purchased it, and had put it aside — probably never to be published. The editor was experienced, and knew that new writers generally make a fizzle of their second story, but may "come back" strong with the third; and the editor, believing that he had discovered John Branton, naturally wanted his magazine to profit by the discovery.

So Branton continued to work at his clerk's desk by day, and wrote during the evenings, and wondered what had become of Loughtry, who had been gone for four days now.

Then one evening, just at dusk, as Branton was walking home and trying to think of a new plot, two men stepped from behind a clump of brush in a little park and confronted him.

"We want to see you," one of them said. "You'll just take a little walk with us. Thought that you could get away with it, did you? You've sent up the river a better man than you'll ever be. Your double cross worked all right, but we're not done with you. Step lively and make it quiet!"

John Branton felt the muzzle of a revolver jammed against his ribs.

"Wh-what's the matter?" Branton queried, gasping. "I — I don't know what you mean. You're making a mistake."

"You call yourself John Branton, don't you?"

"Yes."

"And you wrote a story called 'Seven Times Seven,' didn't you, which was printed last week in a magazine?"

"Yes. But what has that to do —"

"That's all we want to know," the spokesman told him. "And now let me drop a little hint in your dainty ear — we're going away from here, down where we can talk things over, and the first break you make, at the first sound out of you, you're going to get a portion of red-hot lead through an important part of your system. Get that? And don't think we won't do it."

"But, what —"

"And we are starting right this minute, so no more talk out of you unless you are ready to be shuffled off. This dark little park is a fine place for a murder."

John Branton shuddered at the whispered words of this man, at the feel of the revolver muzzle against his ribs. He seemed unable to make a defense of any sort. They guided him along one of the narrow paths, cut across a clearing, skirted a group of trees, and so came to a side street where there was in waiting a taxicab with the curtains at the windows drawn.

John Branton was forced to get into the cab, and it was driven away swiftly. Branton could not even guess at the direction after half a dozen turnings. A man sat on either side of him in menacing silence, and the muzzle of the revolver was still jammed against his ribs. He tried once to speak, tried to ask for an explanation, but they ordered him to remain silent, threatening dire things if he did not hold his tongue.

Branton never had been a courageous man and he felt genuine fear now. He could not understand this. What did the story have to do with it? These men were not officers of the law arresting him for stealing Marmaduke Loughtry's story. They had said something about him "double crossing" them.

While he was trying to solve the puzzle for himself, the taxicab stopped, and he was forced to get out. The cab was driven away immediately. John Branton found that they had brought him to a dark place near the bank of the river in the warehouse district. There was little light; no human being was in sight save his two captors. It was a dismal place, made more so by the constant lapping of the water against the piling and the hissing of the river breeze.

Fear clutched at John Branton's heart again as they grasped him by the arms and forced him to walk along a wharf. Near the end of it was a rowboat. They forced Branton to get in, and while one of them held the revolver against his side, the other took up the oars and began to row.

It was so dark that Branton did not know where they were going, except that it was upstream. Twice he tried to talk, to ask for an explanation, and always he received a whispered threat and a command to remain silent.

Finally the boat bumped against some obstruction, and the man who had been rowing gave a peculiar whistle. Light flooded the scene. John Branton saw that they had reached a little houseboat.

They forced him inside. He blinked his eyes for a moment at the bright lights. Two other men were in the houseboat, evil-looking men, thugs in appearance and reality.

"So you got 'im," one of them snarled.

"We got him," declared the man who had been holding the pistol against John Branton's ribs. "It was a lot of trouble, but I guess we can make him pay for it, all right."

Branton collapsed into a chair and looked up at them.

"You — you've made a mistake," he said.

"I guess not. You keep your trap shut. We'll give you a chance to talk after we are done — not that it will do you any good to tell a stack of lies."

"But what have I done?"

"Shut up! You know what you've done. But no man ever will say that this gang didn't give a fellow every chance in the world. I'll tell you what you've done, and I don't want a word out of you until I have finished. Then you can say your piece — and little good it will do you.

"The boss has been caught with the goods, and he goes up the river for a ten stretch; you did that. Another good man goes with him, you did that. The gang has been scattered, and we're all in danger; you did all of that. And you're going to pay — understand? There's only one price.

"Silence — until I am done. Where the boss picked you up I don't know. I never saw you before tonight, neither did any of the others here. All we know is what the boss told us, that he had picked up a man with brains, a man who could gather information for us that no other man could get, and could get it to us in a way the police would never discover.

"Oh, you were an odd duck! You wouldn't associate with the others, you only met the boss once in a great while; said it would be dangerous, and might fix it so you couldn't do your work. You'd spot a crib and make the lay, and then you'd write a story and have it printed in a magazine; and the boss would read it, and in it you'd tell him just what to do. We'd do it, and you'd meet the boss and get a slice of the profits, and booze it up.

"It was a pretty plan, but I've been a little uncertain about you from the start. I'm always a little uncertain about you brainy guys. And you boozed, too. It didn't look good to me, but you certainly delivered the goods for a time.

"And then you met the boss and said that you were planning the biggest stunt of all. When you had it planned, you'd write another story and tell us what to do. You told the boss that the story might be printed in any one of a dozen magazines that had agreed not to change your stuff without permission — giving him the list — and that it might be under another name because you were getting scared.

"That was all right, of course. All we knew was that the story would have a certain plot — something to do with seven criminals. In the story you were going to make the criminals do exactly as we were to do as soon as we had read it. We couldn't mistake the story, even though we didn't know what name you'd write it under. The personal descriptions of some of your characters resembled what the boss told you about some of us too closely to be mistaken. We knew the crib to be cracked, of course. There remained one thing: you was to let us know in the story what night of the week the regular watchman had off and his nephew — a youngster easy to handle — was to be in his place. We were to know that from the name of your hero. If his name began with the letter A, it would be Sunday night, B would be Monday, and so on to G for Saturday night.

"Well, you named him Covington. That meant Tuesday night, didn't it? And you double crossed us. The regular watchman was on duty. He put up a great fight. He made such a fuss that the boss and one of the boys got nabbed with the goods, and we got away by making a run and a scrap out of it. You double crossed us, and I suppose the cops paid you to do it. You stool pigeon!"

John Branton was gasping in fear and wonder now. Of course, when he had stolen Marmaduke Loughtry's story, he had changed the names in it. The name of the hero had been Datton, and he had changed it to Covington. And, if what this man said was the truth, that change had sent two men to jail and had scattered a band of criminals.

"Well, you got anything to say?" he was asked.

"I didn't do it," Branton screeched. "I didn't write that story in the first place."

"Going to try to lie out of it, are you? Small good it will do you, you stool pigeon! The boss told us he didn't know what name you might be going under. He supposed you had changed it, especially after the double cross. He just had a chance to whisper to us as they took him from the courtroom back to jail. 'Get that writer man!' he told us, and we have."

"I didn't do it! I — I stole that story."

"I suppose so," the spokesman said.

"I stole it from a man named Loughtry, who lived in the

same house. He was drunk all the time. I stole it, and sent it to the magazine. I'm a clerk."

"You admitted, when we first got you, that you wrote the story, and that's all we need to know. Don't try to lie out of it now. I don't know anything about Loughtry; you might have used that name once. I do know that you're the man we want. One of the boys got your address in the magazine office, though he had a deuce of a time doing it. And we watched for you and picked you up. I know you work as a clerk, but that's a blind."

"I'm innocent; I changed that name, but I didn't know it meant anything."

"We don't care to hear any more, I guess. We'll finish you, and then we'll scatter. You'll tip nothing more off to the police. We're going to finish you right here."

"I tell you, I didn't —" Branton began shrieking.

The spokesman made a sign, and they fell upon him. In an instant, almost, he was bound and gagged. They lashed him to the chair, and lashed the chair to a corner of the houseboat.

"We've got to scatter, so we don't need this ship any more," the spokesman said. "And we're not making a present of a houseboat to anybody, and so we'll destroy her, and you along with her. You stool pigeon!"

John Branton mouthed the gag and tried to speak, but only choked himself.

He worked frantically at his bonds and found that none of the knots would give. He was utterly helpless.

From a box in one corner of the boat one of the men carried half a dozen sticks of dynamite. He placed them on the table, within two feet of John Branton's face, and connected them with a small black box. From the box came a ticking sound. Branton knew what that meant; he was face to face with an infernal machine.

"You'll have about ten minutes to think about it," the spokesman said, sneering into his face. "You've tipped off your last man to the police, you stool pigeon!"

They stood before him, grinned at him, then scurried through the door like so many rats, and were gone. John Branton, helpless, was alone in the houseboat. On the table was the dynamite, and the little black box that ticked. Beside it the lamp flickered.

Branton was almost insane with terror now. He hoped that the lamp would not go out; it seemed safer with it burning. The terror of death was upon him. He wanted to fight, and he could not. He could only wait, listening to that sinister ticking.

Shots, oaths, the sounds of a struggle! Feet pounded on the deck of the houseboat. The door was thrown open, and two policemen stumbled in. One grasped the little black box and the dynamite, ran to the door again, then hurled the things far out into the stream. There came a gigantic explosion. But John Branton did not hear it, he was insensible of the wave that rocked the houseboat. He was in a dead faint.

"— don't know what we've got against you, unless it was stealing that story." The voice seemed to come from a distance. Branton opened his eyes and saw that it was a sergeant of police speaking. "I suppose we should thank you because your theft helped us break up a gang that's been terrorizing the city for almost a year. Lucky thing for you. We'd been watching that chap Loughtry. The other day he drank too much and stepped in front of a truck. And before he died yesterday afternoon he called us and told all that he knew. He explained how he had tipped off things by means of stories.

"We didn't know anything about you, and neither did Loughtry know you had stolen his story. We came down here to land the rest of the gang and overheard their little conversation with you. Feel like standing up now? Can you walk? Better get home then."

EVERY year, new writers — honest, hardworking men — are achieving success. Names never seen in print before become well known. But among them is never found the name of John Branton.

Branton is a clerk in a mercantile establishment. And he will tell you that the man who steals a story little knows what he may be doing.

"THE MOUTHPIECE
WILL KNOW!"

Fear came to Dan Mork — a clutching, horrible fear — the fear
that paralyzes a man at one time and at another endows him
with more than twice his usual strength.

He was caught like a rat in a trap, caught in a narrow alley
where the light was fitful and uncertain. There was just enough
light for him to see the gleaming brass buttons ahead of him.
Behind him, he knew well, was the terrible "Bloodhound" Kelly,
the detective most feared by those in this particular corner of the
underworld. No way of escape was open.

From Dan Mork's throat there came a single, dry sob of
despair. Was the great career he had mapped out for himself to
come to such an ignominious end? Was this to be the finish of all
the big things he had planned?

Back in the little Indiana village, where he had been reared,
Dan Mork had been something of a butt for jests. Nobody had
taken him seriously. An old uncle had cared for him, and, after
the uncle had passed away, Dan Mork found that he did not
have a relative remaining in the world. And, what was worse, he
did not have a single friend. His few acquaintances were friendly
on occasion and contemptuous at other times — they were not
to be depended on.

Dan Mork did not have a particularly brilliant mind. Perhaps in any line of endeavor he would have been a failure. But,
taking up some common, honest pursuit, probably he would
have made a living and have filled his proper niche in the
scheme of things.

However, because his brain was not all it should have been,
Dan Mork made a mistake common to many. He allowed his
ambitions to follow the wrong trail. He read intermittently, and
there grew in his mind the conviction that master criminals
rolled in wealth, outwitted officers of the law continually, had
excitement and adventure to spice their lives, and attained a
certain amount of notoriety.

Dan Mork of the poor brain determined to become a master
criminal, much as another man might have decided to become a

77

carpenter or painter. He intended to become rich and notorious. Later he would return to the little Indiana village to display his wealth and despise those who had despised him.

A few minor crimes, such as would have caused any regular criminal of standing to curl his lips in a sneer, were accomplished by Dan Mork without detection. They yielded a bit of profit and a great deal of encouragement. In time, working his way across the country and, by some streak of good fortune, avoiding arrest even for vagrancy, he reached New York, his Mecca. Here Dan Mork was to rise to riches through nefarious work.

And now, on his first really big attempt, was he to meet with disaster? Dan Mork had an instant when there came up before him the vision of a term in prison, the deadly monotony of it, the sense of liberty lost. The first term would be light, he knew — but that was not the point. His career would be ruined. He would be a marked man. His photographs and fingerprints would be on file in every police department in the country, He would be merely another common criminal instead of a master crook who was the despair of the police!

Dan Mork waited, and then he seemed to realize his predicament. He knew that Bloodhound Kelly was creeping up behind him. He glanced ahead again and saw that the patrolman was coming slowly and cautiously down the narrow alley. On one side of him was a high wall that could not be scaled. On the other side were buildings, their doors closed and locked and bolted. And there was no window handy, except one protected by a network of steel bars.

Dan Mork glanced around like a cornered beast. His fear gave him strength and cunning for an instant. He showed his uneven teeth, his eyes narrowed, and his hands suddenly became fists. The odds against him were great odds, but still he could fight!

He crouched and darted quickly across the alley to the wall of the nearest building. Behind him a revolver barked, but Dan Mork did not hear the whistle of the bullet. Kelly had fired high, he guessed, for fear of hitting the advancing patrolman, had fired in an effort to frighten the quarry and cause him to make a move that might result in his capture.

"Stop, you — and put 'em up'!"

Bloodhound Kelly voiced the command in a tone of voice that carried terror to the hearts of wrongdoers. It seemed to send a chill up and down the spine of Dan Mork. He crouched against the wall of the building in the darkness and looked above him. But there was no window he could reach.

Along the wall through the black night, careful not to cross a light space, he crept. There was no deep doorway to offer shelter, not so much as an empty packing case to hide behind or give him cover during a fight. No help was offered on any side!

Well, he could go down fighting, Dan Mork decided! He could make a dash for it and be prepared to take the consequences. If he could reach the mouth of the alley safely and get into the side street he would have some chance.

Why had he turned into this alley like a fool — merely because it was in semidarkness? It was strictly his own fault that he had been caught in such a trap, for he knew the district fairly well. He had lost his head for a moment, that was all. A pretty thing for a future master criminal to do!

"Put 'em up and walk out!"

The voice of the terrible Bloodhound Kelly reached Dan Mork's ears again, and again it struck terror to his heart. He knew that he should be making some sort of a move, that it availed him nothing to remain there, crouching against the wall, but he seemed unable to come to a decision. He was trembling again, and his moment of courage and strength was over. Perspiration was on his face and hands — the cold perspiration of fear.

Suddenly he darted along the alley toward the advancing patrolman. Behind him a revolver cracked again, and this time Dan Mork could hear the whining cry of a bullet overhead. Detective Kelly gave some command, and the advancing patrolman quickened his stride. They were closing in!

Dan Mork saw a dark doorway and darted into it. It was no more than two feet deep, and he knew that they could corner him there. And what could he hope to do against them with his bare hands? He did not carry a weapon. He had learned what that meant — to be caught armed and without a permit to carry a gun.

Blind rage seemed to paralyze him now. Through his brain flashed a picture of the big prison up the river. He was afraid to remain in the dark doorway, knowing that they would have him out of it in a minute — afraid, also, to dart toward either end of the alley, afraid of the bullet he feared would crash into his body if he made a move. Surrender! That seemed to be the only thing to do. It was a horrible thought, too. He, who had intended to outwit the police of two continents, to surrender to almost the first officer who took his trail!

He feared Kelly, and he hated him. He did not know whether he feared or hated the more. And they would laugh — that would be the worst of it. Kelly would not even consider this an important case. Dan Mork, to Kelly, would be a novice crook, a man to be sent up the river and taught his lesson.

"Come out — or I'll come in after you!"

There was Kelly's voice again, and again it struck terror to Dan Mork's heart. He drew a deep breath and prepared to step out and accept what Kelly and the others might see fit to give him. He was a failure!

The door behind him opened softly. Before Dan Mork realized it, somebody had grasped him by the collar and jerked him inside. Here it was even darker than it had been in the alley. Dimly Dan Mork realized that the door had been closed again, cutting off the reflection from the distant streetlights, and he heard a bolt shot into place.

"What —" Dan Mork began.

"Keep quiet, you fool! Here — take my hand if you want to make a getaway. Of all the fools — letting yourself get caught in that alley!"

There was no more talk just then. Dan Mork could not imagine who was helping him, but gratitude filled his heart. He grasped the other man's hand, and they hurried through the darkness up a flight of stairs, through a room, and along a hall.

"What —" Dan Mork began again.

"Shut up until we're out of this!" his rescuer commanded. "Of all the fools —"

Dan Mork did not try to speak again. His escape from Bloodhound Kelly was almost unbelievable. He could not understand it, scarcely could understand or realize the all-important fact that he had escaped. He was not safe yet, of course, to speak strictly, but at least he was out of that alley trap, and something seemed to tell him that all would be well.

Down a flight of stairs they went, through another dark hall, and finally they came to a stop against a wall.

"Pull yourself together and try to act natural!" the rescuer commanded. "Don't breathe so hard! I'll bet your face is white, too. Pull yourself together!"

"I'm — all right!" Dan Mork declared.

"Steady, then!"

A door was opened slowly in the wall before them. Dan Mork looked into the rear room of a little, greasy restaurant. He slipped inside behind his rescuer, and the door closed behind him.

"This table here! Sit down — be quick!" said the voice of his rescuer again.

Dan Mork had sense enough to know what that meant. He was to sit at table with this man, as though they had been eating. If an officer came into the restaurant everything would have a natural look. He dropped into the nearest chair, and the other man sat across the table from him. A dirty waiter rushed up, got an order, rushed back again with food and placed it before them.

"You — you are —" Dan Mork began.

"Not yet — no talk yet!" the other warned in a whisper. "Bolt some of that grub."

Again Dan Mork understood. He gulped some of the food, messed the remainder on his plate, swallowed half the cup of coffee. The man across the table did the same. Now let a cop come in! To all appearances these two men had been there for some time.

"Now —" Dan Mork tried again.

"Silence, you boob!" the other protested. "Kelly is coming in from the street. Buck up and act natural! Do they know who they're after?"

"No. They didn't get a good look at me."

"Just act natural, then. I'll do the talking. Kelly knows me well. You be careful!"

Dan Mork glanced around and saw the terrible Bloodhound Kelly approaching them. He looked down at his food and started eating once more. Kelly came to a stop beside the table, and both Dan Mork and the other man glanced up. Kelly, his fists planted against his hips, glared down at them.

"Evening, Tubb Lane!" Detective Kelly said in greeting. "Who's your friend?"

"Hello, Kelly! My friend's name is Mork. He just got in town — looking for work."

"Let him be careful what kind of work he finds," Kelly answered. "We just lost a man in the alley, Lane."

"I didn't know you ever lost a man, Kelly."

"Not after I once get my hands on him, Lane. But I never got my hands on this one. I don't suppose you've noticed anybody rushing in here?"

"Would I tell you if I had?" Tubb Lane asked.

"All right," Detective Kelly said. "I know you weren't the man, because he wasn't as fat as you by half. I suppose it wasn't this new friend of yours."

Detective Kelly had glanced at the table and the half-devoured meal, but he did not base his decision on those things. They would not have fooled Kelly.

"We came in here for chow and not for trouble," Tubb Lane told the detective. "You'd better look somewhere else for your victim, Kelly."

The detective grunted and turned away to survey the others in the little restaurant, many of whom squirmed under the close scrutiny of the officer. Bloodhound Kelly had a very disconcerting way of gathering evidence on old crimes and grabbing a man when that man least expected it.

Dan Mork and Tubb Lane ate more of their food, though neither craved it. Detective Kelly made the others in the place feel uncomfortable and then departed. Dan Mork bent across the table, wonder and admiration in his face, and spoke in whispers. "You — you're Tubb Lane!"

"I am!"

"The great Tubb Lane!" Dan Mork exclaimed.

"Just cut out that 'great' stuff," Tubb Lane replied.

Dan Mork's eyes glowed. He had been saved by Tubb Lane! Tubb Lane, the acknowledged king of that section of the underworld, the man to whom other crooks gave homage!

"And you — you saved me!" Dan Mork said. "And you knew my name, too!"

"I make it my business to learn the name and habits of every new gun who shows up in these parts," Tubb Lane said.

"And you saved me! I'll never forget that!"

"You'd better forget it, you poor hick — you poor, would-be crook! Do you suppose that I saved you because I felt sorry for a boob who couldn't take care of himself? I did it to get even with Kelly. If it had been any other cop he could have taken you in and welcome! But I throw a wrench into Kelly's works whenever I get a chance. That's the explanation!"

Dan Mork gulped. "But you saved me," he said, "and I'll remember it, and if ever I get a chance to do anything for you —"

Tubb Lane's laugh rang out. "I think I can take care of myself, you boob!" he said. "You hand me a plate of merriment when you suggest that you ever could help me."

"But maybe I can, some day," Dan Mork persisted. "If you ever want anybody to do anything —"

"If I do I can find a real gun who knows better than to get himself caught in an alley," Tubb Lane assured him, "I don't know what sort of a bum play you made to get the cops after you this early in the night, but it must have been some sort of a childish affair. Got any money?"

"Yes. If you need —"

"Forget it! I don't happen to need anything just now. I meant money enough to pay the check for this grub. It'd look funny if I paid it. You leave a dollar on the table for the waiter — he's wise, and you may need him again some day. We'll walk up front, and you pay the check, and, when we get outside, you go north — I'll travel south."

"All right," Dan Mork replied. He slipped a dollar bill beneath the plate on the table before him. "But I want you to know that I'm grateful. Maybe I can do something for you some day. I ain't a big gun yet — but I'm goin' to be."

"I doubt it!" Tubb Lane said. "If you're grateful just forget what happened. That's my advice. Remember that I didn't do it for you — I did it to keep Bloodhound Kelly from nabbing a man and getting credit. Come along now."

They got up, and Tubb Lane led the way through the maze of tables toward the cashier's cage.

II.

In the days that followed Dan Mork was like a dog at his master's heels. For the first time in his life somebody had done him a service, and he rewarded it with a loyalty that surpassed understanding.

Tubb Lane did not notice it at first, because the great Tubb Lane was busy with certain plans having to do with a contemplated act of burglary. Dan Mork approached Tubb Lane whenever there was an opportunity. He listened when Tubb Lane talked, though Lane never spoke to him. His face glowed whenever a man said words of praise concerning Tubb Lane.

Presently the underworld began to take notice and to remark about it. They called Mork Tubb Lane's shadow. An educated crook, noticing how Tubb Lane was annoyed by Mork's loyalty and devotion, called Mork an incubus.

Tubb Lane ascertained what the word meant, and his anger flamed. He met Dan Mork in a pool hall and spoke his mind. "I want you to quit hangin' around me, Mork," he said. "You ain't in my class, and you'd better know it!"

"I don't mean any harm," Dan Mork replied. "You saved me, and I haven't forgotten that. And, if ever you need help, I want to be near."

"You poor boob, a precious lot of help you would be to me! Forget what I did. I told you I did it to keep Kelly from nabbing a man, not to rescue you."

But Dan Mork continued his loyalty and devotion. Tubb Lane scorned him in public, but that did not cause Dan Mork to turn his face away. Now and then he committed a minor crime and managed to get enough to pay for a poor room and food. Tubb Lane's shadow and incubus persisted.

Dan Mork's knowledge of things in the underworld was growing rapidly. Professional criminals considered him a half-wit when it came to crime, but they recognized him as one of themselves — a man outside the law.

There came a day when Tubb Lane and two companions began planning an event that would result in much loot. Dan Mork got some inkling of it. He approached Tubb Lane while that worthy was sitting alone in the rear of a cigar store. "I — I'd like to ask you somethin'," Dan Mork said.

"You here again?" Lane asked. "I thought I told you to keep away from me."

"But I don't want to do that," Mork persisted. "I won't harm you any. What I want to ask is this — take me in with your gang."

Tubb Lane tossed away a half-consumed cigarette. For a moment anger was plain in his face, and then his countenance cleared, and he laughed. "Poor boob!" he commented. "If I needed help — which I don't — there isn't a gun in this part of town who wouldn't be ready to help me. I'm talkin' of regular guns, men who know how to do things and don't let themselves get caught in alleys. So why, you poor fish, should I take you on? Tell me that!"

"I'd be square," Dan Mork said, "And I'd do anything you wanted me to do, I — I just want to work with you."

"I'm about fed up with you," Tubb Lane declared. "You've been followin' me around like a dick. You stop it, or I'll make you! I'm sorry I kept Kelly from gettin' his paws on you. If I hadn't you'd be in stir instead of pesterin' me. Get away from here!"

Some who heard laughed, but Dan Mork did not show any anger. The master was out of sorts, that was all. Tubb Lane was the great Tubb Lane, and as such was entitled to have his moods. Dan Mork left the cigar store and walked down the street and stood at the corner. He seemed unable to tear himself away from the vicinity of Tubb Lane.

"Some incubus you've got!" said the educated crook to Tubb Lane after Mork had gone. "Some little shadow! It's the laugh of the town, Tubb."

"Is it?" Lane asked.

"Regular little bodyguard, this fellow Mork! It's a good thing you've got him around to protect you, Tubb."

Tubb Lane snarled his sudden anger. "If the boob doesn't stay away from me, I'll send him home in an ambulance."

An hour later, as he left the place, he came face to face with Dan Mork who had been waiting. "Here's a pack of cigarettes I got for you, Tubb," Mork said. "If you like 'em —"

Tubb Lane took the box of cigarettes, wrecked them in his great hands, tossed the wreckage into the gutter, and strode up the street without a word. Half a dozen men laughed. Dan

Mork's face went red for an instant, and then he hung his head and went up the street still following Tubb Lane.

There came another day when Tubb Lane was infuriated because one of his lieutenants had failed to obtain certain needed information. Tubb Lane could be a beast when he was infuriated. At such times his particular friends remained away from him.

He paced the rear end of the poolroom like an enraged lion. His fists were clenched, his eyes flashed, his breathing was heavy. There was murder in his glance, and his heavy rage demanded an outlet.

At this inopportune moment Dan Mork put in his appearance. He had heard something of what had happened. He had a vision of Tubb Lane's great plans going astray because some member of the gang had failed in the work set aside for him.

"I wouldn't go near Tubb now, if I were you," somebody told Dan Mork, "He's a good man to stay away from when he acts like that. No tellin' what he might do."

But Dan Mork failed to take the advice. He went to the rear of the room where Lane was pacing back and forth and shaking his fists at the walls.

"Tubb!" Dan Mork said in a hoarse whisper.

Tubb Lane stopped his pacing and stood with his fists against his hips and his legs spread far apart. "Well?"

"If — if there is anything I can do for you, Tubb —"

Tubb Lane's two hands shot out and caught Dan Mork by the shoulders and jerked Mork toward him. Tubb Lane had found an object upon which to expend his wrath. "I told you to stay away from me, you boob! Have everybody sayin' I've got an incubus, will you? You good-for-nothing little rat! You little, half-portion crook!"

"Why, Tubb, I only —"

Retaining his hold on Dan Mork with one hand, Tubb Lane drew back the other and struck. The blow hit Dan Mork on the side of the head. He tottered backward, an expression of surprise and bewilderment in his face.

Tubb Lane was upon him like a maniac, striking, kicking at him, hurling him halfway across the room to a corner, following and striking at him again. Not once did Dan Mork seek to defend himself. He could not have done so in any case, since Tubb Lane had almost twice his size and strength and was used to fighting.

Down upon the floor in the corner went Dan Mork, and Tubb Lane kicked at him, voicing loud maledictions. A man rushed forward and risked a blow to speak.

"Careful, Tubb! You'll kill the little rat! Want to go to the chair for a thing like him?"

Tubb Lane stepped back panting, his face suddenly white. His fury was at an end. His rage had been expended. Dan Mork, the faithful dog who would have served him, was a senseless heap in the corner, his clothes torn, his body bruised, his face cut.

One look Tubb Lane gave his victim, and then he turned toward the door. "Maybe he'll stay away from me now."

III.

Even a lowly character such as Dan Mork may have friends. Dan Mork did not have friends exactly, but there were a few men who admired his gratitude to Tubb Lane, and they believed that Lane had treated him badly.

Two of these picked up the unconscious Dan Mork, bathed his face and restored him to consciousness, and finally managed to get him to the poor room he called home. Dan Mork had a little money, and a doctor was called. For two weeks Dan Mork kept to his room, sending out now and then for food.

At the end of the two weeks he crept forth like a rat from its hole. His body still was sore, his face discolored. There had been a bad cut under one eye, and the cut had healed imperfectly.

He met those who sympathized with him, but he quickly lost their sympathy. For they discovered immediately that Dan Mork did not live for revenge, that the rat had not come from its hole to fight.

"Tubb didn't know what he was doin'," Dan Mork said. "He was mad at something, and he just took it out on me. I don't hold any grudge."

There were some who scorned him for the speech, and there were others who thought Dan Mork was playing a deep game, that he wanted to give Tubb Lane the impression he had forgiven, and in reality would await his opportunity. He came face to face with Tubb Lane that first afternoon, and Lane sneered at him and passed by. Dan Mork said nothing. He looked after Lane as though the man who had beaten him was the king of the earth.

"The poor boob!" Lane grunted to a companion. "Doesn't know when he has enough. If he pesters me any more I'll be liable to go to the chair for him."

Dan Mork did not trouble Lane. He remained strictly in the background, but he remained Lane's shadow for all that. Lane did not bother much about him. Tubb Lane was completing arrangements for a crime that would startle the city. Here and there in the underworld a little was known concerning that contemplated crime. And those who knew anything at all knew that it was to be a war between Tubb Lane and Bloodhound Kelly. Lane wanted to do the thing under Kelly's nose and in such a manner that Kelly would know he had done it, yet would find no evidence that would be strong enough to warrant an arrest.

Dan Mork lived these days by sneak-thief work, the lowest of the low in the world of crime. He ate when he could, paid his room rent, smoked cheap cigarettes. And always he watched Tubb Lane.

Others noticed it, of course, one of Lane's lieutenants in particular. "I'm afraid of that guy, Tubb," the lieutenant said. "I don't care what kind of talk he makes, he's got it in for you. He's just watchin' for his chance. He'd turn you up in a second. I wouldn't be surprised if he was Kelly's stool pigeon right this minute."

"I guess not," Lane declared.

"He's watchin' you too close to suit me. You'd better keep an eye peeled for that boob, Tubb."

That evening Lane entered a poolroom and met Dan Mork coming out. He clutched Mork by the coat and thrust him back against the wall. He spoke in a hoarse whisper, so that none of the others could hear. "You cur!" he said. "So you're a stool pigeon, are you?"

"Whoever told you that lied, Tubb," Dan Mork answered.

"You've been snoopin' around me since you got on your feet. Tryin' to get an earful, are you? Want revenge, do you? I'll give you something to want revenge for, you rat! I'll send this incubus of mine to a hospital —"

He struck out, and Dan Mork did not have time to dodge. The old cut under the eye was reopened. But before Tubb Lane could do anything more, the proprietor of the poolroom interfered. Tubb Lane withheld further blows, and Dan Mork went out to the street.

"It's all right," he told an acquaintance. "Tubb ain't himself, that's all."

"You poor boob!"

Dan Mork remained farther in the background after that. He seemed to have sensed, finally, that Tubb Lane did not care for his companionship. He lived his pitiful life, denied even the pleasure of showing his gratitude to the man who had saved him from arrest and prison. And Tubb Lane forgot him, for the time of the big event was drawing near.

There came a night when Lane crept through an alley and met two other men in the rear of a warehouse. A motor truck crept noiselessly through the alley after him, its lights extinguished, and stopped in the deep shadows near the warehouse wall.

There was a short consultation, and then Tubb Lane used a key which he had prepared and let himself inside. The other two men followed, and the driver of the truck crouched in the darkness beneath it.

Inside the warehouse a watchman was overpowered and rendered helpless. And then Tubb Lane and his two assistants began their work. Bales of valuable silks were carried swiftly to the alley and loaded into the truck. The work was done silently, accurately, for every detail had been planned and every arrangement perfected by Tubb Lane.

But in every so-called perfect arrangement there may be a minor detail overlooked, some little thing forgotten, or fate may step in and take a hand and wreck well-formed plans, chuckling the while. Tubb Lane and his associates, after loading the truck, were about to make away with their loot when they found themselves confronted by half a dozen officers. The struggling night watchman, before being overpowered, had touched with his toe a button that had given an alarm.

There were hoarse commands. There was an immediate show of resistance. Tubb Lane and his men were not the sort to submit to capture without a fight. Revolvers barked, flashes of flame illuminated the alley. An officer fell wounded. The truck was deserted. Tubb Lane and his men scattered, each to make his own getaway if he could.

Lane had had many narrow escapes. Getaways were his specialty. He knew how to take advantage of every bit of cover. And now he exerted his skill to its utmost, for fear was upon him. Another conviction would mean that Lane would be termed an habitual criminal — the next incarceration would be for life!

As he ran he bent forward, his elbows glued to his sides, an automatic held in one hand. After him came one of the officers, a man who could not be shaken off easily. Tubb Lane heard a revolver crash, heard a bullet sing by within a few inches of his head, heard a command for him to halt.

"Kelly!" he exclaimed as he ran.

The thought of Kelly caused both fear and rage. Was he to be captured by the very man whom he had belittled? Was Bloodhound Kelly to get more glory by bringing in Tubb Lane?

Over a fence he went, and Kelly followed. Lane turned and fired a single shot and ran on. But he could not shake off the human bloodhound. He began to sense that he was cornered. Kelly was not human, Lane told himself. Every trick he tried was understood by Kelly, Every artifice met with failure. The man who pursued was as wise as the man who ran. Tubb Lane was racked with rage and fear. To be captured would be bad enough, but it would kill him to be captured by Kelly. Down another alley he darted, and suddenly he found another man running beside him.

"Keep ahead until we come to that dark spot," he heard a whisper, "then you duck aside, and I'll lead Kelly on." There was no time for further talk. Tubb Lane saw that the other man was running close to the wall, knew that Kelly could not see him. It was a good trick. Kelly thought he was pursuing but one man.

Tubb Lane was gasping for breath. He was not in good physical condition, and Bloodhound Kelly always was. He took the advice, but he did not know the man in the dark, had been unable to identify his voice. When the big black spot was reached, Tubb Lane sprawled behind a pile of empty packing cases, and the other man ran on. He made a great deal of noise about it, too.

Tubb Lane, his chest heaving, his breath coming in gasps,

realized only that Bloodhound Kelly had charged past him and was firing wildly at the other man. Tubb Lane felt a rush of gratitude to the unknown who had helped him in his extremity. Some loyal member of his band, he supposed.

The sounds of the chase died away in the distance. Tubb Lane had an alibi prepared, of course, and now he had to connect with it. The alibi would have availed him nothing if Bloodhound Kelly had caught him, but now he had only to reach a certain poolroom, and there would be several persons ready to swear that he had been in a back room playing cards for hours. The card game was there, his chair waiting for him.

Lane crept from the alley, reached a side street, and hurried toward his destination. He slipped through another alley, let himself through a door, entered a tiny room, and dropped into the chair waiting for him. He tossed his hat to a corner of the room and picked up the hand of cards that was ready.

His heart was pounding at his ribs. The other men at the table said nothing, but continued the game, just as though they had been playing for hours. Fifteen minutes passed without disturbance, and Tubb Lane, between deals, rolled and lighted a cigarette. His hands were still shaking.

"All right?" one of the others asked.

"No. The bulls jumped us, and we scattered for a getaway," Tubb Lane answered.

"Everybody make it?"

"I don't know. Kelly almost had me, but one of the boys helped to fool him. I don't know which one."

The game continued. There was a knock at the door a quarter of an hour later, and the educated crook stepped into the room. There was a peculiar look in his face.

"Evening," he said.

A couple of the men growled at him. The educated crook smiled and sat down at Tubb Lane's shoulder.

"Nasty little affair," he offered.

"What?" Lane asked.

"Common report has it that a gang of thieves made an attempt, about an hour or so ago, to lift a truckload of silk from a warehouse. Nothing small about their intentions."

"Well?" Lane demanded.

"A gang of cops interrupted the party. The silk thieves

immediately scattered."

"Any caught?" Lane asked, pretending indifference, yet waiting impatiently for the answer.

"One. Bloodhound Kelly caught him."

"Who — who was it?" Lane asked.

"That's the funny part of it, Kelly chased one of them down an alley and finally plugged him. Didn't cash him in, but brought him down."

"Curse you, who was it?" Lane demanded.

"That's the funny part, Lane, as I said. Who on earth would have expected the chap to be in with a gang of high-class cracksmen? It was your incubus, Lane."

"What's that?" Lane asked, springing from his chair.

"Your shadow, Lane. It was Dan Mork. Kelly brought him down, and after the hospital will come the jail. Most peculiar! Who would have thought it?"

Tubb Lane sank back in his chair. Conflicting emotions mirrored themselves in his countenance. Dan Mork had saved him! Dan Mork, the despised, the man whom he had beaten for being grateful and loyal, the man whom he had charged with being a stool pigeon! Dan Mork who, instead of showing enmity such as Lane might have expected, had remained loyal to the last. Dan Mork had saved him from Kelly! And, because he had done so, Dan Mork was in a hospital with a bullet in him, and he would come from the hospital to go to a cell.

There was silence in the little room. The others watched Tubb Lane and waited for him to speak. Suddenly he spoke.

"Bailey," he called, "you get busy! See our mouthpiece and tell him the sky's the limit! That boob must be got out of this! He was the man who ran beside me in the alley and carried Kelly past while I dropped in the dark. Every cent I've got — every cent the gang's got — goes to get him out! Bail — stall! The mouthpiece will know! Innocent man shot by mistake — all that stuff. Go out and get busy, Bailey!"

"All right, Tubb." Bailey hurried from the room.

"Incubus, eh?" Tubb Lane asked. "Hereafter Dan Mork is my friend, and every man better know it. And when he gets loose — and he will — he's my right-hand man — even if he makes some bum play that lands us all in stir! Stikes!"

"Here, boss!" responded another of the gang.

"You get to Dan Mork some way tomorrow. See him in the hospital. You can fix it some way. Just get a word to him while the cop guard is called into the corridor, or something like that. And you tell him for me, Stikes, that Tubb Lane is sorry. Get that? Tubb Lane is sorry, and he's goin' to make it up to Dan Mork!"

"But, boss —"

"You heard me!" Tubb Lane snapped. "Incubus, eh? Any man who's got an incubus like that is lucky — he's mighty lucky!"

Tubb Lane rolled another cigarette, and the educated crook, still smiling, held a flaming match to its end.

HOOKED

I.

Quarrels and Threats.

Striding slowly and noiselessly across the deep carpet of velvety grass, Mr. Stanley Smead suddenly stepped around a huge clump of brush and came upon a sight that astounded him. He beheld his daughter Lucy in the close embrace of his private secretary, Christopher Flane.

Stanley Smead stopped abruptly and gasped, then exploded in a rash jumble of words that were almost incoherent. The pair before him separated and whirled to confront him. Lucy Smead's countenance was flushed; the face of Christopher Flane suddenly went white.

"So!"

Stanley Smead stood before them, his fists planted firmly against his ample hips. His voice rolled through the woods and out over the lake, rang back from the nearby crags, and echoed from the mouth of the tiny canyon not far away.

There was a moment of deep silence while Smead gathered the forces of his wrath, and the pair before him waited anxiously for him to speak. Then the verbal storm broke upon the heads of the culprits, and Lucy Smead and Christopher Flane seemed to bend before it like trees before the brutal strength of a tropical hurricane.

"So!" Smead cried again. "How long has this sort of thing been going on? I warned both of you months ago, when you first seemed to be showing interest in each other, that it had to stop! Are my commands nothing to either of you? Into the cabin with you, and we'll talk!"

He drove them before him along the forest aisle and toward the cabin. What Stanley Smead called the "cabin" was, in reality, a splendid house that had been constructed at his direction on the shore of the Maine lake he owned — a place to which he journeyed from the city for a couple of weeks each summer, to get away from the world of big business.

Stanley Smead was regarded as one of the foremost figures

in the "Street." He had smashed many financial combines and had formed others in his time, and he always seemed to be on the right side of the market. His fortune was estimated at several millions.

Smead loved to pose, too. When he traveled, it was like royalty. Here, when he pretended to live in the wilderness for two summer weeks, he really lived with all the comforts of civilization around him. His cabin had electricity, hot and cold running water, and a big ice machine.

With him this season he had brought from the city his motherless daughter and her maid, his private secretary, his pet cook — a young Italian named Antonio Maleno — and Dr. Frederic Jargell, a physician in whom Smead had great confidence, and who had attended him for many years. Dr. Frederic Jargell, it was well known, could command Stanley Smead and he obeyed when other men could do nothing with the financier.

Smead drove his daughter and his secretary before him as though they had been two children caught playing a prank. Lucy, who had inherited a great many of her father's characteristics, held her head high, and her eyes glistened brightly in her flushed face. She knew that a verbal battle was coming, and she was prepared to take an active part in it.

Christopher Flane appeared to be somewhat frightened. He was a tall, not unhandsome man of about thirty, adept at his profession, known to be silent and loyal. Stanley Smead had great confidence in him, such as a great financier must have in a private secretary who knows a lot about his business secrets and plans.

Flane walked with his head held high, like the girl at his side, but his face remained white, and his hands were clenched until the knuckles showed white, too. He dreaded the scene that he knew was coming, yet he was determined to stand up for his rights.

Without another word being spoken, they reached the house and went directly into the big living room. Lucy Smead sat down on a divan without looking at her father. Christopher Flane remained standing until Smead imperiously gestured for him to be seated.

"Now I want to know what this means!" Stanley Smead shouted. "I told you two months ago that this foolishness had to stop! It's been going on since without regard to my commands, has it?"

"You cannot command love, father," Lucy Smead said.

"Love?" Smead sneered. "It's rank nonsense and nothing else! When the proper time comes for you to have a husband, my girl, I'll get you some substantial man of the world who has ample funds. I can understand your silly sentiment, of course — you are just at the silly age. And I can understand Flane. Oh, I can understand Flane! He isn't the first fortune-seeker —"

"Sir!" Christopher Flane thundered, his face flushing with sudden anger. "I — I love Lucy, Mr. Smead — and that it all there is to it."

"You love the money she'll have some day, too, don't you?" Stanley Smead sneered nastily. "How do you expect to keep her on five thousand a year? And especially if you happen to stop getting the five thousand?"

"So that is it?" Christopher Flane asked, his voice calm now. "I'm to be kicked out of my position because I have dared love your daughter? Very well, sir! I can resign!"

"Resign?" Smead thundered. "Quit your job? Not a bit of it! I need you, with that big deal coming on next month. You'll not resign, and you'll not quit! You'll stay on the job, but you'll cease paying your attentions to my daughter. I'll show you that I am strong enough to command my own affairs! You dare resign! I'd break you and put you down in the gutter —"

"Father!" Lucy implored. "Please listen to reason! I love Christopher, and he loves me. Why not let it go at that? I'm not afraid that Christopher cannot support me. You didn't have much when you married mother."

"I had brains and ability," Smead declared, "and they make an excellent capital. I wasn't working for another man for five thousand a year."

"No; you were working for yourself and earning about twenty dollars a week," his daughter told him. "And mother used to tell me, before she died, what fun it was growing prosperous. Those were her happiest years."

Stanley Smead stopped her with a roar. "I am master here!" he declared, as though somebody had questioned the fact. "You two young fools listen to me! This thing must end! I'm going to find out why it hasn't ended before this. I had my eyes on you two for a time, so there must have been treachery somewhere. Ha! I've got it! I understand now!"

He strode angrily across the room and rang. One of the servants appeared immediately, looking frightened. "Send me Miss Smead's maid!" the financier ordered.

"Father! If you make Marie angry —" Lucy began.

"Silence! I am handling this affair now! I'll see whether everybody can go against my orders!"

He paced back and forth for a moment, and then the maid appeared.

Marie Bazin was a dainty little French woman who had been attached to Lucy Smead for about three years, a very satisfactory servant in every way. She stopped just inside the doorway, knowing well that there was something amiss, and guessing what it was. Everybody in the house had heard the roaring of the master's voice, and it was nothing new to them.

"You!" Smead thundered at her. "You've been helping these two young fools, haven't you? Did you know that they were skylarking around?"

"I — I —" the maid stammered.

"Answer me, confound it! Have you been carrying notes for them, and all that sort of rot?"

"I — I didn't see the harm in it, sir," Marie Bazin said. "If they are in love —"

"Bah! You're a fool too!" Smead shrieked.

"Sir, you have not the right to speak to me like that!" the maid snapped. "I'm a human being, if I am a maid!"

"Get out of here!" Smead cried. "And if I find you taking part in any more of this affair, off you'll go, without recommendation! Remember that!"

Marie Bazin's head went up angrily, and her eyes flashed.

"No man can talk to me like that!" she exclaimed.

"Get out of here!"

The maid glared at him, then stumbled through the doorway and disappeared. But she was not in tears nor on the verge of hysterics. Her eyes still were flashing, and there was a dangerous expression on her face.

Smead whirled toward his daughter and Flane again.

"Understand me well!" he cried. "This thing must stop at once! Flane, you'll attend strictly to business and forget my daughter. And you, my girl, will do as I command, or I'll plant you in some school where there is strict discipline. And I can do it, even if you are twenty-three!"

"I think that you are going a bit too far, father," Lucy Smead retorted.

"No back talk!"

Christopher Flane cleared his throat and spoke nervously. "What is your particular objection to me, sir?" he asked.

Smead whirled toward him. "As a private secretary, you leave but little to be desired," the financier replied. "As a son-in-law, you'd be a rank failure. You'd better remember your place, and keep it!"

"I do not like that sort of talk, sir!" Flane cried angrily. "I may not have a few millions, but my birth and breeding are as good as yours — and possibly better!"

"You puppy!" Smead shrieked. "I could break you in less than forty-eight hours. And I'll do it, if you raise your voice against me again! You attend to business, and nothing else!"

Then there came an unexpected interruption. Through the doorway hurried Tony Maleno, the cook. His face was alight with enthusiasm.

"Meester Smead!" he cried. "I have, at last, perfected the new sauce! Et es magnificent! Et weel teekle your palate! Et has a flavor ze gods would luf! Et —"

Stanley Smead interrupted the enthusiastic young cook with a roar of anger.

"What are you doing in here?" he cried. "How dare you come into the living room like this, you cook? By Heaven, the whole world must be going mad! Out of here, you cur!"

Antonio Maleno came from a country where red blood flows hot through the veins at times. In an instant he had changed from an enthusiastic human being to a snarling, dangerous beast with red eyes and heaving breast.

"So! Et es a cur you call me now?" he cried angrily. "I, who haf done ze best to please —"

"More back talk, eh?" Smead roared. "And this time from a cook! I've got a notion to manhandle you — and I can do it, too! Back to your kitchen!"

"For thees ensult —" Tony Maleno began.

"Out of here!" Smead thundered, making a quick start

toward him.

The cook disappeared rapidly, angrily, muttering his threats. Smead whirled once more to face his daughter and his secretary. Christopher Flane was standing now, his face white again, his eyes narrowed.

"Mr. Smead —" he began.

"Not another word!" Smead cried. "Let us hope that you two understand the situation, and can be sensible. No more of this nonsense! I won't have it! My orders must be obeyed in this as in everything else! If there is any more of it —"

There came another interruption, and this time it was Dr. Frederic Jargell who stepped swiftly into the room and confronted the raging millionaire.

"See here, Smead!" the doctor broke out in commanding tones. "What have I often told you about these fits of temper? Do you want to get flat on your back and let your business enemies have a chance to strip you? Do you want to have apoplexy and pass out years before your time? You stop this nonsense, Smead, and come right along with me! I could have heard your shouting half a mile away. You'll kill yourself, man!"

"Now, doctor, I —"

"You'll do exactly as I say, Smead, or you'll suffer the consequences, for which I refuse to be held liable. You come right along with me! Come down to the lake and catch a fish. I've got a new lure that I made myself, and I'll give you the honor of trying it out. That should be inducement enough for you! Come along, catch a fish, and eat it for your luncheon."

Stanley Smead sputtered angrily for a moment longer, then hung his head in token of utter defeat, thrust his hands deep down into the pockets of his coat, and stalked from the room after the doctor.

Christopher Flane followed them at a short distance, for it was Stanley Smead's standing order that his secretary always be near him.

Lucy Smead remained behind, seated on the divan. Now that the verbal battle was at an end she experienced a depressing reaction. She seemed to sense a tragedy, something that would change the entire course of her life. Dry-eyed, white of face, she sat quietly and stared through the window before her.

II.

Sudden Death.

Stanley Smead was like a wayward boy going toward the woodshed to receive an application of the rod at the hands of an irate parent. Dr. Jargell, the financier knew very well, had a nasty tongue when he wanted to rebuke a patient, and Smead expected a tirade such as he often had received, and, in truth, relished a bit at times.

But Dr. Jargell, it appeared, was inclined to be merciful this day. He was a tall, thin man of about fifty, an eager student, and he had made rapid strides in his chosen profession until he found that a few wealthy patients were demanding all his time. Then he had attended to those few, had played the social game, and also had attempted to "play the market," with somewhat disastrous results to his bank balance.

Dr. Frederic Jargell, said those who knew him best, had ice water in his veins instead of blood. He was skilled in medicine and surgery, had made some wonderful cures and was credited with some wonderful operations, yet to him a mere human life was as nothing. Dr. Jargell looked upon a human body as a machine, to be perfected or repaired or corrected when some important part of it happened to run amiss.

"Smead, I am downright ashamed of you!" the physician said as they left the veranda and started toward the shore of the lake. "What is a love affair, more or less? Is it anything to cause a man of your ability and importance to get all fussed up and make you carry on in this way?"

"I want my girl to marry some big, important man!" Stanley Smead answered.

"In my opinion, this is nothing more than one of those puppy-love affairs," said the doctor.

"I do not think so. The youngsters are serious about it. And I'll not have it! I'll —"

"You'll manage to forget about it for the time being, and not give away to your passion again!" the physician broke in sternly. "I'll bet your heart is pounding this minute. What did I tell you? Stop your silly rage and save your strength for your financial battles. You've hinted to me that there is some big deal in the wind. Therefore, save your heart and nerve and sinew, as the poet says."

"Now, doctor —"

"No more talk, Smead! No argument! Come on out here and hook a trout and have it cooked for your luncheon. That'll get you over your fit. Smead, you insulted young Flame, raised blazes with your cook, made your daughter's maid angry, and Heaven knows what else! And all in a few minutes! You create enemies by the score. Try to behave yourself."

The shore of the lake was but a short distance from the corner of the veranda of the house. Just here there was a deep pool shaded by overhanging trees.

Dr. Jargell's fishing rod was leaning against the bole of a tree near the shore, the new lure already fastened to the leader. This lure was nothing more than a small spinner with an arrangement of peculiarly colored feathers attached. But the doctor handled it as carefully as though it had been a great treasure.

"Go after a trout, Smead!" the doctor directed. "There should be some good ones in that pool. Show me whether you are a real fisherman!"

Stanley Smead grunted his assent, took the rod, and prepared for a cast. Christopher Flane had approached and was standing within a few feet of him. Smead turned and glared at Flane without speaking, and Flane looked away quickly, as though he did not wish for a continuance of their quarrel.

Tony Maleno came swiftly from the rear of the house and started toward the shore of the lake. Stanley Smead saw and glared at him, and Maleno turned his head and hurried on toward the shore. He was going to the live box, to get some fish to prepare for luncheon. The live box was anchored only a short distance from the pool where the financier intended to cast.

"Stop him!" the doctor grunted.

Christopher Flane hurried toward Tony.

"Wait a moment, Tony!" he commanded. "Mr. Smead is going to try for a trout. Don't go near the live box until after he casts."

"Ver' well, Meester Flane," Tony replied. And then he edged a bit closer. "Meester Flane," he whispered so that the others could not hear, "I know all about et — and et es a shame. That he should talk so to you and Mees Lucy, and say such things to me —"

"Hush!" Flane warned him. "I understand, Tony. You were eager to tell him about some new sauce you have invented. You were probably enthusiastic about it. But you happened to strike him at the wrong time."

"He call me a cur — me, who hez try so hard to please heem! He say to me —"

"Hush!" Flane commanded again. "You must not speak in that way, Tony! Mr. Smead, unfortunately, makes many enemies."

"Yes! And some of these days one may strike back!" Tony declared.

"Yes — some one may strike back!" repeated Flane.

They turned, then, to watch the others.

Stanley Smead hesitated a moment, then made his cast. No more had the lure hit the water than a trout struck the lure. The line grew taut, switched from side to side, the rod bent almost double.

"Hooked!" the doctor cried; and Stanley Smead began playing the prize like a master fisherman.

A few minutes later the trout had been landed.

"Only about a pounder, but he fought like a veteran!" Stanley Smead exulted.

"Eat him for luncheon," said Dr. Jargell.

"Tony!" the financier cried. "Come and get this trout! Let nobody else have a bite of him! Give him to me for luncheon!"

Tony Maleno hurried forward and took the trout from Smead, and Smead handed the rod back to the doctor. The cook did not glance toward his employer as he hurried away with the fish. He carried it directly into the house, and a few minutes later he emerged again and went toward the live box to get more fish for the luncheon.

Christopher Flane drifted back into the house, too, while Smead and Dr. Jargell walked slowly toward a bench in the shade near the shore of the lake. The doctor methodically unjointed his rod and reeled in his line.

Smead seemed to be in better spirits now, but the doctor had the appearance of being tired. His face was pale, and he closed his eyes and leaned back his head after they had seated themselves on the bench.

"Well, I got my fish!" Smead exclaimed, "You can boast about it at your club when you get back to town. Lie a little, and make him out a five-pounder!"

"I may not have a club before which to boast," Dr. Jargell said in a peculiar voice.

"Huh! You're hinting at that market affair again, are you?" the financier asked. "Don't you talk to me about it! Every man to his own business is my motto, I'd sure make a great mess of it if I started doctoring — just as you certainly made a rich mess of it trying to play the market."

"I sure made a mess of it!" the doctor replied. "But you could have saved me."

"Yes, I could have lent you twenty thousand dollars and saved you. But that is against my principles, and you know it. I thought that it would do you good to be taught the lesson. Now you'll forget the market and attend to your doctoring. You aren't going to starve, you know. I'll shuffle off one of these days — and you are in my will. You're probably in the wills of several other men you have been doctoring, too."

"Oh, well, Smead, there is no sense in talking about it now!" Dr. Jargell said.

"You're right. Not a bit of sense in talking about it," Smead agreed.

Suddenly a twig cracked behind them, and they turned to see another man making his way toward the bench. He was less than ten feet distant.

"The old professor!" Stanley Smead exclaimed. "We'll have him take lunch with us, doctor." The newcomer approached, wiped the perspiration from his brow, and finally came to a stop before them, removing his hat respectfully.

"Greetings!" he said in a thin voice.

"How is Professor Ellis Darlew today?" Smead asked, chuckling a bit.

"Can't complain," the professor answered.

"Then, sit down and make yourself comfortable, professor. You must have luncheon with us. I just landed a dandy trout."

"Yes, I heard the fuss when you made the catch."

Professor Ellis Darlew was a character, peculiar in many

ways. Smead knew him in the city, so also did Dr. Jargell. He
was an eccentric old fellow who had acquired quite a reputation
as a scientist some years before. Then he had undertaken the
study of man and his methods and motives, and so had achieved
a second enviable reputation aiding the authorities in running
down criminals.

More than once a puzzled chief of police had called on Ellis
Darlew. He was a small man, dressed in inconspicuous clothing.
His gray hair was thin, his eyes small and watery. But he had a
massive and well-ordered brain.

"Thanks, Smead!" Professor Darlew said. "I'll sit down, and
be glad to take lunch with you."

"Then I'll call Flane and tell him to command Tony to have
an extra fish prepared. Flane! Confound it, where's Flane? He
has orders to stand by."

"But not half an hour before mealtime," the doctor said
soothingly. "Give the man a chance to wash up once in a while."

Christopher Flane suddenly appeared on the veranda, as
though he had been summoned by royalty.

"Flane!" Smead ordered. "Tell Tony that Professor Darlew
will have luncheon with us. Tony must get another trout out of
the live box."

Christopher Flane nodded his head in assent and disappeared. A few moments later Maleno hurried from the house
once more, got another trout from the live box, and hastened
back to his kitchen.

"Smead," said Professor Darlew, "you should stay out here
for two months every summer, instead of a measly two weeks. I
wouldn't take a lot for the two months that I get out here. And I'll
never be able to thank you enough for letting me build a little
cabin on your land."

"Forget that!" Smead replied. "It gives the place tone to have
you on it, professor. Only I wish that you'd be my house guest
while I am here."

"Nope!" the professor responded. "I am a funny old duffer,
and I like to live according to my own habits. I'm all right in my
little cabin, but I'd feel cramped in your big house, I'd have to be
nice and polite and clean all the time, because of Miss Lucy. A
meal now and then is about as much of your high-toned civilization as I can stand, Smead!"

The financier laughed and got up. "Let's go inside and tackle this luncheon," he said.

Professor Darlew and the doctor followed him. Christopher Flane was waiting on the steps of the veranda. They went to the dining room, where Lucy Smead joined them.

Everything was informal in Smead's "cabin." These fish luncheons were always the same — a fish to a guest, and that fish flanked with hot biscuits and honey and a variety of side dishes. Down they sat, and the meal was served. Tony Maleno came from the kitchen himself and put before Smead the trout he had taken from the pool.

Lucy Smead said nothing beyond a few kind words to the professor, and the meal began. Christopher Flane's face was still pale because of the earlier scene and his consequent emotion. Professor Darlew gave his attention entirely to the food before him — eating being a sort of ceremony with him. Dr. Jargell, looking pale and tired, fussed with the trout that had been served him.

A sudden exclamation from the old professor caused all to glance up quickly.

"What's the matter, Smead?" the professor cried in his thin voice. "Are you ill, man?"

There was a chorus of exclamations. Stanley Smead had dropped his fork and was clutching at his breast. And now he struggled to get out of his chair before any of the others could assist him. His hands caught at his collar and ripped it off as though it had been choking him. His eyes bulged, his face began to turn purple, a light froth suddenly appeared on his lips. And just as Lucy Smead gave a cry of fear for him, just as the men sprang to their feet, Stanley Smead whirled halfway around and crashed to the floor.

"Fish bone!" the old professor shrieked, trying to get around the end of the table. "Do something for him, doctor! Be quick about it!"

Dr. Jargell already was kneeling at the side of his patient. Now he glanced up at the others. But it was not to issue a volley of orders.

"It is too late," said Dr. Jargell softly. "I regret to say that Mr. Smead is dead!"

"Dead!" they cried in chorus.

"And it was no fish bone!" the doctor declared. "Look at the froth on his mouth. He has been poisoned!"

"Poisoned!" Lucy shrieked, trying to get to her father's side. "But how?"

"The fish!" the doctor gasped, "He made Tony angry a short time ago —"

In the sudden silence they heard a new voice from the open doorway.

"Need any help?" it asked. "I was passin' by and heard all of you yellin'."

It was Rills, the local constable, who always happened by the Smead place when he got the chance. He liked to talk of "the big Wall Street man, my friend, Stanley Smead."

III.
Bits of Evidence.

Constable Rills, blinking his eyes rapidly, hurried into the room when news of the tragedy was shouted to him. He was a man of medium size and medium age, a fellow of no particular ability, a minor official content to draw a small and sure salary and have an easy time earning it.

Constable Rills had a high regard for his authority. He believed in wearing a large badge of office in a conspicuous place. He had managed to arrest several tramps during his term of office, and one of them had been wanted for a minor crime, hence Constable Rills firmly believed that, as an officer of the law, there were several things that he could teach the fellows at New York headquarters or even Scotland Yard.

"Reckon that I'd better take charge here!" he said now, clearing his throat impressively. "I'll telephone the coroner."

Dr. Jargell gave him scant attention. "Don't touch the remains of that fish!" he commanded. "And none of us shall leave this room just now except Professor Darlew. Professor, you get the servants together in the hall, please, and keep them there — particularly Tony Maleno."

"I can do that," said Christopher Flane.

"We'll let the professor do it," said the doctor. "The professor, for one, cannot be under suspicion."

"Meaning that I am?" Flane flared.

"It's only fair, Flane. We want to get at the bottom of this quickly. Kindly assist Miss Smead to a chair. Cover the body with that rug, constable."

"Seems to me you're tryin' to run things around here," Constable Rills said haughtily. "I represent the law in this here locality, and don't you forget it."

"We must all work together," said the doctor. "Let's get busy now. If you solve this, constable, it'll be a big feather in your cap."

Christopher Flane led the weeping Lucy to a chair in one corner of the big room. Constable Rills covered the body, after Dr. Jargell had made another rapid investigation. The doctor looked at the dead man's eyes, at his mouth, at the face that was rapidly changing color, then stood up, wiping his eyeglasses.

"I know the poison," the doctor announced. "I'll name it at the proper time. It is deadly — a product obtained from the South American jungles, and often used by the natives there."

"By gosh, how did it come here?" the constable demanded.

"I presume you'll have to discover that," the doctor replied, trying to wither the other with a look. "I suggest that we all retire to the living room and go into the details of this affair. Professor Darlew can have the servants in there, too. We can do nothing more for poor Mr. Smead. Constable, will you kindly telephone the coroner?"

Five minutes later they were all in the big living room, Lucy Smead weeping softly while Flane tried to comfort her. The servants were terrified. Tony Maleno's face had gone white. Marie Bazin's eyes were bulging. The other two, housekeeper and maid, seemed on the verge of collapse. Those were all the servants. Stanley Smead had left the others at his city residence.

"I see that there is a safe in one corner of the room," said Dr. Jargell. "Flane, do you know the combination?"

"Yes, sir," answered the secretary. "It is an old safe in which we keep valuable papers sometimes."

"Unlock the safe, please," directed the doctor. "Professor, you kindly come with me, and we'll get the remains of that trout and lock it in the safe. We may want an analysis later, to satisfy the coroner. But there is no doubt in my mind that the fish was poisoned — or the butter sauce."

"Not the sauce!" Tony Maleno cried. "The sauce es good — jus' butter melted, and herbs."

"The sauce you poured for this particular fish may not be good," said the doctor pointedly.

Tony Maleno collapsed into the nearest chair. The doctor and Professor Darlew went back into the dining room and got the fish. Flane opened the safe for them, and the deadly trout was put inside it and the safe locked again.

"Now, let's get to business!" Constable Rills exclaimed.

"An excellent idea!" the doctor said. "Allow me to suggest, constable, that you handle this case with Professor Darlew. As you perhaps know, the professor has quite a reputation for solving affairs of this sort."

"I don't need any city help, I reckon!" rejoined the constable. "But I'm willin' to work with him."

Professor Darlew wiped his glasses, adjusted them on his nose, cleared his throat, and glanced quietly around the room.

"Where shall we start, constable?" he asked.

"I reckon we'd better arrest that cook," Constable Rills said. "I never did like an Eyetalian, anyway. He gives Mr. Smead a trout that's poisoned, and Mr. Smead eats a part of it and dies. I reckon there ain't much of a case to this!"

Tony Maleno sprang to his feet. "I deed not poison!" he cried. "I deed not keel!"

"Sit down, young man!" Professor Darlew commanded. "Constable Rills, let me conduct the first part of the investigation. It is a bore to ask questions, you know. And you sit there quietly and take in all the answers and sum up when I am done."

"Suits me!" the constable said. He got out pencil and notebook. Professor Darlew glanced once at him and turned away.

"Dr. Jargell," said the professor, "Mr. Smead caught that fish?"

"He did, professor."

"Sure it's the same fish?"

"Yes. There was none like it in the live box, for I looked in there this morning. And this is a rainbow, and we seldom catch those in the lake."

"Who was with you when the fish was caught?"

"I was standing near Mr. Smead. Mr. Christopher Flane and Tony Maleno were a short distance away. Flane had stopped

Maleno from going to the live box until after Mr. Smead had made his cast."

"How did Flane happen to be there?"

"Mr. Smead's orders were that his secretary should always be near him."

"I understand," said the professor. "Go ahead."

"Mr. Smead cast and hooked a trout. The three of us saw it."

"That right, Flane?" the professor asked.

"Yes, sir."

"Right, Maleno?"

"Yes, sir," said Tony.

"Then what?" the professor demanded.

"Mr. Smead landed the trout and called Tony. He handed the trout to Tony and told Tony to cook it for his luncheon. He said the fish was to be served to him alone."

"So," said the professor, "Tony had reason to believe that only Mr. Smead would eat of that fish?"

"Certainly," Jargell replied. "A fish to a person was Mr. Smead's standing order."

"And so Tony wouldn't be afraid of poisoning somebody other than Mr. Smead."

"I deed not do et —" Tony was screeching again, but he grew quiet when the professor turned and looked at him sharply.

"But why," asked the professor, "should Maleno wish to poison his employer?"

"They had a quarrel a short time before, and Tony was furiously angry at Mr. Smead," the doctor explained. "Mr. Smead was having a conference with his daughter and Mr. Flane, and Tony rushed into the room without ceremony. Mr. Smead happened to be angry, and said some hard things to Maleno."

"He call me a cur, but I not keel him!" Tony declared.

"What did you do when you took the fish?" the professor asked him.

"I take that fish into kitchen and prepare him for to cook," Tony replied.

"Did you leave the kitchen from that time until the fish was served?"

"Yes, sir. The first time I go to the live box to get fish for others. The second time I go to live box again, when Mr. Flane tell me that you, sir, would be for luncheon, to get another fish for you to eat."

"How long did each trip take?"

"Maybe ten minutes," said Maleno.

"Anybody else in the kitchen either time you left it?"

"No, sir."

"Find anybody there either time you came back?"

Tony Maleno hesitated for a moment, and then: "'No, sir!" he replied.

"Why did you hesitate before answering me just now?"

"I stop to theenk," Tony explained. Constable Rills cleared his throat and spoke. "I reckon that I'd just better take this cook to the lockup," he said. "It's plain to me that he's guilty!"

"Let us not be too hasty," the professor begged. "We want to be fair to all. When Tony Maleno was gone from the kitchen somebody else could have poisoned the fish. Who, besides Tony, knew that Mr. Smead, and no other, would eat that fish?"

"Mr. Flane heard Mr. Smead say so to Tony," the doctor replied. "And Tony knew, naturally."

"I tell other servants, too!" Tony put in. "I say et was a beeg feesh, but Mr. Smead could eat it."

"So practically everybody knew about it," the doctor concluded, turning toward the professor again.

The professor twisted his thin lips and squinted up at the ceiling.

"Anybody besides Tony Maleno have a motive for killing Mr. Smead?" he asked.

There was silence after his question, and the professor opened his little eyes wide again and looked around quickly. Finally Dr. Jargell spoke.

"Mr. Smead," he said, "had one of his temper spells this morning. I was forced to remonstrate with him about it. He had them frequently, as you know, professor."

"Yes," the professor replied. "I have seen Mr. Smead in several fits of temper. But what got him started this morning?"

Lucy Smead spoke up promptly. "Mr. Flane and I are — are quite interested in each other," she said. "Father was opposed to it. This morning he accidentally discovered that we were — were growing fonder of each other, and it made him angry."

"I understand," Professor Darlew said. "What did he do?"

"He was very angry with Mr. Flane, and with me, and said

that we must cease to have interest in each other. My maid —
Marie Bazin — was called into the room, and father rebuked her
because she had — had been aiding Mr. Flane and me."

"Did he make you angry?" Darlew demanded of the maid.

"Yes," Marie Bazin answered promptly. "He — he was terrible. He had no right to speak to me the way he did, and I told
him as much."

"French woman, aren't you?" the professor asked. "Yes, sir."

"Inclined to grow furious and lose control of yourself — um!"
the professor grunted. "And where does Tony come in?"

"Tony came into the room while father was talking to Mr.
Flane and me," said Lucy Smead. "Father rebuked him, and
made him go out."

"Then Mr. Smead angered Flane, this maid, and Tony
Maleno in the space of a few minutes?"

"Precisely," said the doctor, getting into the conversation
again. "I heard the uproar and rushed here to get Mr. Smead to
be quiet."

"Did he quarrel with you, too?"

"We quarreled every now and then," said the doctor, smiling
a bit, "but our quarrels never amounted to much. Mr. Smead always recognized that I was his physician, speaking for his own
good. I tried to hold him down as much as possible, though it
was difficult sometimes when things were going badly on the
market."

"So Mr. Flane had trouble with him, and Miss Bazin, and
Tony Maleno," the professor mused. "Enough to make suspects
of all three of them."

"Surely, Professor Darlew, you do not think that Mr.
Flane —" Lucy Smead began.

The professor stopped her with a gesture. "My dear young
lady," he said, "we are only considering every possibility and trying to arrive at the truth through the process of elimination.
Until we know the truth, we must suspect everybody."

"I presume that I am eliminated already?" said Dr. Jargell. "I
never touched the fish. Mr. Smead caught it and handed it to the
cook. Then Mr. Smead and I sat on the bench until you joined
us. The three of us came into the house together. I had no opportunity to touch the fish."

"So much for you," said the professor. "Let us consider the

more pressing possibilities. Who could have entered the kitchen while Maleno made his trips to the live box?"

Nobody seemed to have a reply, so the professor continued:

"Any of the servants could have done so," he said, "including Marie Bazin, whom we still consider a suspect. Marie Bazin, enraged because of the scene she had had with Mr. Smead, and having heard Tony say that Mr. Smead was going to eat that trout, could have slipped into the kitchen during the cook's absence and poisoned the fish. Is that poison easy to apply, Jargell?"

"Yes, professor," the doctor replied. "A drop of it would be enough to impregnate a dog in a few minutes. It is lasting, too, in any form, liquid or dry."

"Um! I think I know the poison to which you refer. Very well! Marie Bazin could have done it. Were you in the kitchen, Marie?" Professor Darlew shot the question at her suddenly.

"I — I didn't go near the kitchen," she faltered.

Lucy Smead suddenly sprang to her feet, "Marie Bazin, that is a falsehood!" she cried. "I sent you to the kitchen to tell Tony to make me some strong tea for luncheon — because I had a bad headache after the scene with father — and you must have done so, for Tony made me the tea, Marie Bazin! Did you, in a fit of anger, kill my father because of the way in which he had talked to you?"

IV.
Some Facts Come Out.

Lucy Smead's ringing voice died out in a sob, there was a moment of silence, then Marie Bazin rushed across the room and threw herself at the feet of her mistress.

"I did not! I did not!" she screeched. "I could not have done such a thing as kill him, no matter how he talked to me. I was very angry — yes! But I could not have done that! Please say you don't think I did it!"

Dr. Jargell stepped forward, lifted her gently and forced her to return to her own chair on the opposite side of the room, then nodded to Professor Darlew. The professor had been regarding Marie Bazin carefully, now he polished his eyeglasses again, put them on his nose, and looked at her in a close scrutiny that made her face go white again.

"Young woman," said the professor, "we must get to the bottom of this deplorable affair. If you tell falsehoods, if you hide any facts that you may happen to know, it will only be so much the worse for you in the end. Were you in that kitchen?"

He thundered the last question at her in his peculiar voice, and the maid looked up at him quickly and fearfully, to meet his piercing eyes fixed squarely upon her own.

"Answer me," the professor cried.

"Y-yes, sir," the maid faltered.

"Ah! Now we are getting at it? Why did you lie when I asked you the first time?"

"I — it was because I was afraid of getting into trouble," the maid sobbed. "I never did anything wrong. I was afraid that they might arrest me —"

"When you went into the kitchen, was Tony Maleno there?" the professor interrupted.

"Not — not at first."

"He returned soon?"

"Yes," Marie Bazin replied. "He had been down to the live box to get some fish for luncheon. When he came back, I told him about the tea for Miss Smead."

"Um!" Professor Darlew grunted. "One lie opens up another every time! Tony Maleno, I asked you whether, on your return, you found anybody in the kitchen. You hesitated, then said that you had not. Why did you lie to me?"

"Et was because I was afraid you would blame the little Marie, and I know that she have nothing to do with et," Tony Maleno replied quickly.

"So you call her the little Marie, do you? Have we another love affair here?"

Tony Maleno's eyes flashed. "Yes!" he declared boldly. "The little Marie and I — we love! We do not care if the whole world know et. Es et a crime?"

"Certainly not, under the proper circumstances," Professor Darlew observed. "So you lied because you thought I might bother the girl? And she lied for the same reason. Um! Now, Maleno, suppose you tell me what happened in that kitchen!"

"I return from the live box with the feesh," Tony replied, "and

I find Marie waiting in the kitchen for me. That es all."

"You didn't even speak to each other?" the professor demanded. "You'd better tell me the whole thing, Maleno. If you are innocent, there is nothing for you to fear. I want to know what happened in that kitchen."

"Ver' well! I am innocent, and so es the little Marie," Tony declared. "She tell me that Mees Lucy has a headache and want strong tea at luncheon. Then I see that Marie have been crying and ask her about et. She tell me, then, that Meester Smead have said cruel things to her."

"And that increased your anger against Mr. Smead?"

"I love the little Marie," Tony explained. "I tell her that Meester Smead say hard things to me, too. I say that I get me another job when we go back to the city, and she quit, and we get married. I kees her once, and then she hurry back to the front of the house. That es all."

Constable Rills, who felt that he was not playing a part quite important enough, sprang to his feet and waved his notebook and pencil toward Maleno.

"It's as plain as the nose on your face!" the constable declared. "Tony Maleno, your gal told you how she'd been treated by Mr. Smead, and you raved about how Smead had treated you mean, too. And then the both of you — both darned foreigners — poisoned that fish and killed him! You're both guilty! I reckon that I'll just haul the two of you along to the lockup!"

"I did not do et!" Tony Maleno shrieked. "And the little Marie did not, either!"

Professor Darlew raised a hand for silence.

"Constable, wait a moment!" he begged.

"All right! Anything to oblige. You go ahead and plague 'em with your question. But when you're done, I'm goin' to take 'em in! My good gosh, professor! What more do you want? Them two folks had motives and the opportunity. And that's what detectives always looks fer, ain't it? What more do you want?"

"We want some real evidence, enough to convict, Mr. Rills," the professor said wearily. "It is quite true that Tony and Marie Bazin both had motive and opportunity. But possibly there are others who had both, also. Maleno, was anybody else in that kitchen besides Marie?"

"I not see anybody," replied Tony.

"Miss Bazin, was there anybody in the kitchen when you entered it?"

"No, sir. I had to wait for Tony to come back."

"Did you see anybody coming away from the kitchen as you went toward it?" the professor demanded. "Have you any reason to believe that somebody besides yourself and Tony was in that kitchen at any time after the trout was caught?"

Marie Bazin started to speak, but hesitated.

"Well?" the professor snapped. "Why don't you give me an answer? Trying to hide something else now, are you?"

"I — he could not be concerned, sir," Marie said.

"He? Of whom are you speaking?"

"It — it doesn't make any difference, sir."

"It happens to make a lot of difference," the professor said. "Of whom were you speaking? Answer me!"

"Mr. Flane," the girl replied.

"Ah! So Mr. Flane was in the kitchen?"

"He was coming through the rear hall, from the direction of the kitchen, when I was going toward it," Marie Bazin confessed. "He hurried past me, and I did not speak to him, only bobbed my head as he passed."

"So!" Professor Darlew sat back in his chair and removed and polished his eyeglasses once more. "This is interesting. What about it, Flane?"

"What do you want to know?" Christopher Flane asked, his face suddenly white again.

"I want to know what you were doing in the kitchen — want you to explain your presence there. Let's see! You left the shore of the lake and returned to the house right after the trout was caught, didn't you?"

"I did."

"Why?" the professor demanded.

"I wanted to clean up before luncheon, sir," Christopher Flane replied. "And, to tell the truth, I wanted to get away from Mr. Smead for a time, because of the trouble we had had, and because I saw that Dr. Jargell was quieting him after his flare of passion."

"I see. And Mr. Smead was compelled to call for you when he wanted to have you tell Tony Maleno that I'd be an extra guest for luncheon, didn't he?"

"Yes, sir."

"Tony Maleno went out to the live box soon after he carried the trout into the house. You were in the house then," the professor said. "You went into the kitchen while Maleno was gone to the live box. And you were coming through the hall, returning to the front of the house, when Marie Bazin, going toward the kitchen herself, passed you!"

"I — I suppose so," Flane admitted.

"And why did you go into the kitchen, Flane? Have you been in the habit of doing it? Did you have any particular business there at that time?"

"Does it matter?" Flane asked.

"It matters a lot!" Professor Darlew declared. "You had the motive and opportunity that our friend, the constable here, talks so much about. Mr. Smead had objected to your attentions to his daughter. With Mr. Smead out of the way —"

"Sir!" Flane thundered.

"I'm just trying to show you how it looks to an outsider, Flane. With Mr. Smead out of the way, possibly you could get the girl. Also, the fortune that she inherits."

"Professor Darlew, you are heartless!"

Lucy Smead cried. "Is it necessary to suggest such a diabolical thing?"

"My dear Miss Smead! I am not at all heartless, and I have no intention of turning so," the professor replied. "I am trying to look at this affair from every viewpoint. That is the only safe method to use if we are to arrive at the truth. And allow me to remind you that Mr. Flane has not yet told us why he went into the kitchen and tried to keep the fact a secret."

He stopped speaking, and looked toward Christopher Flane, and Lucy Smead looked toward him also.

"Explain to them, Christopher," she said. "I am quite sure that you can explain."

"I — I have nothing to say," Flane replied.

"Christopher!" There was agony in the girl's cry. "Surely, you want to show them that you could not have done this dreadful thing! Do you not wish to spare me?"

"Do you think that I did it?" Flane asked.

"No!" she cried, "I know your nature too well. I know that

you are not guilty. But, tell them why you went into the kitchen — convince them, also."

"Very well!" Christopher Flane lifted his head and looked the professor straight in the eyes. "I — I used to drink a bit now and then," he confessed. "There were times when I felt that I needed a stimulant, and I started it while I was in college. Never to excess — I never was really intoxicated in my life. But Mr. Smead found it out one day after I started working for him, and he warned me to stop. The private secretary of a big financier, you understand, must not drink. He might overindulge, let some valuable office secret slip out —"

"I understand," the professor interrupted.

"However, knowing that I never would drink liquor to excess, I always kept some handy, to use as a sort of bracer. With all due respect to Mr. Smead, he made a man feel that he needed a 'bracer' at times. He was very exacting in business relations, as all his associates know. He was able to work for a long time without rest or sleep, and he seemed to believe that all other men should be like him in that respect."

"I know," said the professor.

"I — well, I had a bottle of liquor hidden in the kitchen — old liquor that I have had for years. I had not touched it since we came to the summer camp. But after the scene this morning I felt the need of it, and when I got a chance to come into the house I slipped into the kitchen to take a drink. The bottle is still there as proof of what I say — I can tell you where to find it."

"How did you happen to hide it in the kitchen? Why not in your own room?" the professor asked.

"I just happened to put it in the kitchen the first day we came. With it in my own room, and handy, I might have been tempted to take a drink when I really did not need it. I can tell you where it is hidden."

He told, and Constable Rills, looking very important, left the room, and presently returned with the bottle.

"Nevertheless, Flane, you had a chance to poison that fish," Professor Darlew reminded him.

"My heavens, sir, do you think that I am the sort of man who would do such a thing?" Christopher Flane cried. "I admired Mr. Smead very much. I love his daughter, and I hoped, in time, to win his consent to my marriage with her. Lucy, do you believe I could do such a thing?"

"Certainly not!" the girl cried. "Oh, this is dreadful! Who could have done it?"

Constable Rills cleared his throat again.

"I reckon that it is an easy thing to see who did it, miss," he declared. "Tony, that cook, did it, and maybe this Marie girl, his sweetheart, was in the deal with him. You can't fool met Eyetalians and other foreigners —"

"May have hot blood in their veins, and be inclined to resent insults quickly," the professor interrupted, "but they are not necessarily murderers."

"Well, I'm goin' to take them two to the lockup!" the constable declared. "The coroner will be here soon, and he'll side in with me, I reckon. It's the only thing to be done."

"Suppose, Constable Rills, that we step aside and discuss this affair," the professor suggested. "Nothing more, I feel sure, can be gained through questioning at this particular time."

"And while we're discussin' it, these here folks might make their getaways," the constable protested.

"We need fear nothing on that score, Mr. Rills. An attempt at a getaway would be equivalent to a confession. And they couldn't get far without being recaptured, as you know. Maleno and Miss Bazin will remain in that little room across the hall; the other servants may go to the rear of the house. Mr. Flane and Miss Smead may do as they please as long as they do not leave the premises. I presume that Dr. Jargell will want to order Miss Smead to bed and give her something to quiet her. She has had a terrible shock."

Professor Darlew had his way, and his orders were being carried out before Constable Rills could form an objection. Dr. Jargell read a command in what the professor had said, and prevailed upon Lucy to retire.

Then Professor Darlew grasped the constable by the arm and led him slowly out on the veranda, where they occupied seats far from doors and windows. There they could talk without danger of being over heard.

V.

Developments.

Constable Rills was trying to look important again. He leaned back in his chair, crossed his legs, cleared his throat in an impressive manner, and glanced over at the professor.

"Well?" the constable asked. "We've done about all the talkin' and investigatin' necessary, seems to me."

"What do you think of it?"

"I think that the cook did it, and maybe the girl helped — anyway, she knows a lot about it."

"They had motive and opportunity — but we have no direct evidence, constable," the professor reminded him.

"There's one thing that puzzles me. Where did that poison come from, and is there any of it left? Is that poison easy stuff to get?" the constable asked.

"It is very difficult to obtain," Professor Darlew explained. "It comes from South America, and is rarely used as a medicine, hence there is no regularly established trade in it. The natives in a certain section of South America use it to remove their enemies, and it can be purchased now and then, of course, from certain unscrupulous dealers."

"Then, which one of these folks could have got that poison?" the constable demanded.

"I see your line of reasoning, and it is a very good one," the professor observed. "But I am inclined to believe that it will get us nowhere. Tony Maleno, as I happen to know, once worked in South America. However, Mr. Smead had extensive business interests down there, and last year he cruised to South America in his yacht. At that time Mr. Flane went with him. Miss Smead also went, and her maid, Marie Bazin, accompanied her. So either Tony, Flane or Marie Bazin could have procured the poison down there."

"Gosh!" the constable breathed. "Begins to look like a tangle. But I'd say that the cook did it."

"Christopher Flane had a chance also, please remember, and a strong motive."

"Yeah, I know that! But he doesn't look like a murderer to

me. I reckon that if I took in the cook and the maid, and gave 'em the third degree, one of 'em would cave in mighty quick. I'll have to do that, I suppose."

"Have you anything else to suggest?" the professor asked. "I am not entirely satisfied with the progress we have made. We have motives for our suspects, but none of the motives seems quite strong enough for cold-blooded murder, in my estimation."

"The coroner ought to be here pretty quick, and we can put it up to him," replied the constable. "He's a doctor, too. He can examine the body and have it removed to the village, and he and this Doc Jargell can analyze the rest of that fish."

"Thus establishing the cause of death beyond the shadow of a doubt, but not pinning the guilt on the guilty person," said the professor.

"Well, what else can we do?"

"I intend to continue the investigation," Professor Darlew replied. "As I have said, I am not entirely satisfied. Possibly we are far from the right track."

"My good gosh!" Constable Rills exclaimed. "Mr. Smead catches a fish and hands it over to the cook, doesn't touch it again. The cook takes it and cooks it, and Mr. Smead eats it and dies. Doc Jargell is out of it. And that puts it up to the cook, Marie Bazin, and Mr. Flane. They all had a chance to poison that fish. Maybe somebody else had a chance to get into the kitchen, too. That's the only thing I can see that would change matters. Here comes the coroner now!"

As he finished speaking, the coroner stepped up on the veranda, followed by two other men, and the constable and the professor got up to greet him. The coroner was an ordinary country official, but he was more sensible about it than Constable Rills. He sat down and listened patiently while the constable told the story, with a word put in here and there by Professor Darlew.

"I'll examine the body, and then have it removed to the village," the coroner announced when the story was done. "We have come prepared for that. The roads are very poor, or we'd have been here a lot sooner. I never did understand why Mr. Smead didn't have the road to his property improved."

"Because he wanted to hide away here for a couple of weeks without having a horde of friends pestering him," the professor explained. "He didn't want an automobile on the place. As you perhaps know, he always came by train and drove out in a rig from the village, leaving his cars and chauffeurs in the city."

The coroner nodded. "It seems to me that suspicion rests on the cook and the maid," he said. "And there is this man Flane to be considered, too. But we can leave that end of it in your hands, professor."

"Thank you," the professor rejoined. "I'd like to have Mr. Rills work with me, however. He is the man who must make the arrest if there is one to be made. And I think, Mr. Rills, that I'll let you take Tony and Marie Bazin to the village and put them in jail — arrest them on suspicion. Then we'll have them safe while we continue to search for evidence."

"That's the ticket!" Constable Rills exclaimed. "I always knew you was a brainy man, professor."

"Thanks!" Professor Darlew said innocently. "Mr. Coroner, how about the sheriff?"

"He's up at the other end of the county, and won't be back until some time tomorrow. I've notified him, of course. Maybe you'll have time to complete your investigation before he arrives."

Dr. Jargell stepped out on the veranda and walked toward them. The coroner treated him with great respect because of his reputation as a physician.

"Dr. Jargell, is there anything of importance that you care to tell me about this affair?" the coroner asked.

"I can name the poison," said Dr. Jargell, "and will do so at the inquest. I suppose you have been told everything — about the fish, and all that?"

"I believe so. Mr. Smead caught the fish, handed it over to the cook to prepare, and afterward, eating of it, died of poison."

"Precisely," said Dr. Jargell. "Professor Darlew can solve the mystery for us, I feel sure. There are two or three possibilities. It is a very sad affair. I have been associated with Mr. Smead as his personal physician for years, and to have him taken off in this way —"

Dr. Jargell seemed to betray emotion, the first time since the tragedy.

"I understand," said the coroner. "We'll look at the body now, please."

Constable Rills led the way into the dining room, but the coroner's examination of the body was short. He ordered his two men to superintend its immediate removal to the undertaking establishment in the village.

"Has Miss Smead any wishes?" the coroner asked.

"I believe not at this time," replied Dr. Jargell. "I ordered her to retire. She is suffering acutely from the shock, naturally. I have asked Mr. Flane to write telegrams to Mr. Smead's legal representatives, and they undoubtedly will come here as soon as possible and assume charge."

Christopher Flane entered the room at that moment, holding the messages in his hands.

"Professor Darlew, will you see that these telegrams are sent?" Flane asked. "Under the circumstances, I presume that you do not wish me to go to the village myself."

"I'll be glad to see that they are forwarded at once, Mr. Darlew," the coroner offered.

"Thank you. But there need be no extreme haste. The news of Mr. Smead's violent death must not reach the city before the market closes, or there may be a panic and certain securities smashed. Given all night in which to work, his brokers may be able to protect the Smead interests."

The coroner looked at him in surprise. "I am afraid that the news has leaked out already," he said. "When the constable telephoned, one of my assistants received the message. The news was all over town in no time, and there's a newspaper correspondent, too."

"But the news hasn't been verified," Flane rejoined, "and let us hope that the report will be considered a hoax until these official messages get through."

"But the telegram!" the coroner exclaimed. "The station agent spoke to me just as I was starting here. He said somebody had telephoned a message right after I had got the news. It was a message to New York, he informed me, to some broker, and he made the remark that he'd bet the market would be upset."

"Telephoned a message!" the professor gasped.

"Yes. I asked him about it, of course — even compelled him to show me the message. I have forgotten the name of the broker. But the message said that Mr. Smead had died suddenly, and was signed by some crazy code name. It was ordered charged to the Smead account, too."

"Who could have telephoned that message?" the professor cried. "And what did it mean? Was somebody deliberately trying to smash the market?"

"I fail to see who could have telephoned," Flane declared.

"You could have done it, sir, while the servants were being rounded up and before we started questioning in the living room," the professor suggested.

"But I did not!" Flane declared indignantly. "I certainly would do everything to protect the Smead interests, not smash them. And that message, you may be sure, got to the city in time to start something of a grave nature on the market."

"Who else would be interested?" the professor demanded.

"You can find that out by makin' that city broker say who the message was from," Constable Rills suggested.

"You don't know city brokers very well," the professor replied. "If he was in some shady deal with a man here, he'd admit that he got the message, but declare he did not know the code signed to it, didn't know who had sent it, or why. We'll certainly have to look into this message matter."

"That's your work," said the coroner, "and I have mine. I must get back to town. And I think that I'll take along the remains of that poisoned fish with me. It won't hurt any to have an examination of it made by some outsider, you know."

"Mr. Flane will get it for you," Professor Darlew replied. "It is locked in the safe in the living room. I'll have one of the servants get a basket and some heavy wrapping paper, so you can carry the thing safely."

"Gruesome thing to handle!" the coroner exclaimed. "Dangerous, too, isn't it?"

"One bite of it might kill a man," the professor admitted. "It's a thing to be guarded and handled carefully, you may be sure."

They went slowly into the living room, where Christopher Flane knelt before the safe and started working the combination, while the others stood back and watched. Finally Flane pulled open the door as the others bent forward — then gave a little cry and staggered to his feet.

"Look! Look!" he cried.

The poisoned fish was gone!

VI.

To Wait for Dawn.

Up to this time Professor Ellis Darlew had been a quiet, rather unusual type of investigator. But now he changed in an instant. His eyes opened wide and blazed, his nostrils distended, he breathed deeply, and his stooped shoulders seemed to straighten suddenly and broaden.

"So!" he thundered, and even his voice became deeper, more commanding. "We are going to have a real case here, after all, it appears! Mysterious telegram! Missing fish! It is possible that we are facing something not so simple as we believed it to be at first."

"Gone! Gone!" Christopher Flane was muttering.

"That's a fine bit of acting, Flane!" Dr. Jargell sneered, stepping a bit closer to the secretary. "You are the only man, I believe, who had the combination of that safe. Certainly nobody has had the opportunity to work at the thing and open it except in the regular manner, for that would take time. It seems to me, Flane, that you're playing some sort of deep game. The mysterious message — and now the missing fish —"

Christopher Flane whirled toward him angrily. "Are you trying to insinuate that —"

"Wait!" Professor Darlew commanded. "Sit down, all of you! I am handling this end of the affair, kindly remember, and with the help of Constable Rills I believe that I can handle it properly."

They sat down. Constable Rills was blinking his eyes rapidly and looking important again. Christopher Flane dropped into the nearest chair. Dr. Jargell, still looking angry, glared at the secretary once, then stalked across the room and sat on the divan.

"Flane," the professor began, "who had the combination to that safe?"

"Mr. Smead and myself," Flane replied.

"And no other?"

"I cannot swear to that. The safe was used only to guard papers in case of fire. Generally, there was little of real importance in it. The combination has not been changed for three years or more. Mr. Smead might have given the combination to somebody else at some time, but I do not know that."

"To whom could he give it?"

"I do not know, professor. I do not see why he should have given it to anybody, to be fair about it. As far as I know, Mr. Smead and I were the only ones who knew the combination."

"That fish was removed from the safe after the constable and I went out on the veranda," the professor said. "At that time the servants had retired from this room. Tony Maleno and Marie Bazin had gone to the room across the hall, as I directed — and they are there yet. Dr. Jargell took Miss Smead to her own room and ordered her to bed. Didn't you do that, doctor?"

"Yes, sir. I left Tony alone in the room across the hall for a short time and had Marie Bazin aid Miss Smead to disrobe. After that the maid returned to the place where Tony Maleno had remained, and I gave Miss Smead something to quiet her, then came downstairs and went out on the veranda, to find the coroner there."

"And what did you do, Flane?" the professor demanded.

"After the doctor took Miss Smead to her room I went to my own for a moment."

"Why?"

"No particular reason," Flane replied. "I — I felt a bit shaky because of what had happened. And I knew that Miss Smead was suffering —"

Flane waved his hand languidly to show that he had nothing more to say.

The professor looked at him closely.

"How long did you remain in your room, Flane?" the professor asked.

"For quite some time. I do not know exactly how long. I came out and met Dr. Jargell in the hall. He suggested that I write the telegrams to Mr. Smead's attorneys. I agreed that it was the proper thing to do, so went back into my room and wrote them."

"You had a chance, however, just after the doctor took Miss Smead to her room, to open the safe and remove the fish," the professor said, "and ample time to hide it."

"But why should I do such a thing?" Flane cried. "I did not kill Mr. Smead. And, had I done so, what good would it do me to remove the fish? The doctor already has said that Mr. Smead died of poison."

"A man does peculiar things sometimes, when there is a burden of guilt on his soul," the professor replied. "Tony Maleno, too, had a chance to remove the fish while the rest of you were upstairs. But Tony certainly did not have the combination to his employer's safe. Likewise, Dr. Jargell had the opportunity when he came downstairs. But we assume that he did not have the combination either. And why should the doctor, even if he had it, remove the fish?"

"It — it is bewildering," Flane admitted.

"Constable, search Mr. Flane's room well!" the professor ordered suddenly. "If you do not find the fish there, search the entire house. It cannot be far away, for whoever removed it from the safe did not have time to carry it any distance. That fish must be found — it is a dangerous thing."

Constable Rills lost no time in hurrying up the stairs. This was something important, the constable thought. He began the search in Christopher Flane's room, while, on the floor below, the professor had Tony Maleno come across the hall and into the living room.

"You were alone, Maleno, while the maid was attending Miss Smead?" the professor asked.

"Yes, sir."

"Did you stay in that room across the hall all the time?"

"Yes, sir."

"Hear anybody moving about in here?"

"I hear people going up and down the stairs, sir," Tony replied. "But I do not hear anybody in here. I stand at the window most of the time, looking at the lake and worrying about thees."

"You sure you didn't leave the room?"

"I not leave him one minute!"

"All right. Go back now."

Tony hurried back across the hall gladly, and Professor Darlew faced Flane once more.

"Flane," he said, "it certainly looks as though you opened that safe and took away the poisoned fish!"

"I give you my word that I did not, sir!"

"Who else could have done it?" Dr. Jargell cried. "You had the combination."

"But why should I do such a thing?" Flane demanded.

The professor cleared his throat and adjusted his spectacles once more.

"I intend to get to the bottom of this affair," he declared. "I am going to have Constable Rills take Tony and Marie to the village and jail them on suspicion. If they are guilty, we don't want them escaping, and I'll be too busy to guard suspects. This theft of the fish I do not understand — nor do I understand that mysterious telegram to the brokers in New York. Flane, did you send that message?"

"Certainly not, sir! Why should I?"

Dr. Jargell sneered openly. "It would not be the first time in the history of the world that a private secretary had betrayed his employer for gain," the doctor said. "Mr. Smead's sudden death accomplished, and the news of it received by his financial enemies, those enemies could make a million dollars in a few hours. And, if they had promised you a big slice of the million —"

Christopher Flane sprang to his feet, but the professor and coroner stopped what would have been his wild rush across the room toward the doctor.

"Don't you dare suggest such a thing again!" Flane shrieked. "I have always been loyal to Mr. Smead and his affairs. Long ago his business enemies discovered that they could not corrupt me. If you dare suggest such a thing again —"

"That will do! Sit down, please!" the professor commanded. "Dr. Jargell, kindly refrain from making such remarks. Naturally, you are angered because of the diabolical murder of your old patient, but let us get at the bottom of this thing properly, and without the heat of passion."

Constable Rills came hurrying back.

"Well?" the professor asked.

"Can't find the fish!" the constable reported. "I've searched every room but this one, and I've searched good."

"We'll let the matter drop for the present," said the professor. "Constable, you may take Tony and Marie to the village and put them in jail on suspicion. That'll keep them safe for the time being. And we'll continue the investigation, and I have something to say to you before you start."

"All right, professor."

Constable Rills squared his shoulders and stalked across

the hall to do his duty. There came shrieks from Marie Bazin and wild lamentations from Tony Maleno. But Constable Rills handcuffed them together, despite their protests.

"You're arrested just on suspicion," he informed them. "But it'll be more than that, I reckon, in time."

He walked them out into the hall, and glanced toward Professor Darlew, who had not left his chair.

"Mr. Flane, you will kindly remain in the house," the professor was saying. "Dr. Jargell will attend to Miss Smead, if she needs his attention. Tony and Marie will be gone, but the other servants can handle things here for tonight. I intend to continue the investigation, and I do not wish to be disturbed."

He got up, walked out into the hall, and beckoned Constable Rills aside.

"Put your prisoners in jail, make arrangements for them to be cared for properly, then return here after nightfall, constable," the professor whispered. "I'll meet you by the bench down by the pool. You are to wait there until I come for you, no matter how late it happens to be."

"I understand, professor," the constable whispered in reply, "But we've got the right birds here, I'm thinkin'. One of 'em will probably confess."

"It is conclusive evidence that we want, in case one does not confess," the professor said, smiling slightly. "Get back as soon after nightfall as you can."

"Yes, sir."

"The net of evidence is forming, constable. And when it has been all formed, perhaps you are going to be surprised. There may be some more arrests to make, so you be sure to return as quickly as possible. And send this telegram for me, and tell the agent to stay up for the answer and telephone it out."

"Yes, sir."

Professor Darlew scribbled a message on a sheet of paper he tore from his notebook, and handed it to the constable. And Constable Rills, piloting his two prisoners before him, followed the coroner out to the vehicles that were to carry them to the town.

The professor turned back into the room where Christopher Flane and Dr. Jargell were scowling at each other.

"We have had a very trying afternoon, gentlemen," the professor remarked. "We have faced tragedy and mystery, and on some of us the dark shadow of suspicion has fallen. It is almost nightfall, and we can do nothing more today. I presume that I am to remain here for the night?"

"I'll have them prepare a room for you, sir," Christopher Flane said. "And the other servants can manage, surely, to get us up some sort of a meal without Tony Maleno's aid. The housemaid, afterward, can be at Miss Smead's service in place of Marie. Is that satisfactory?"

"Good!" exclaimed the professor. "Then, suppose that we eat, rest for a time, and retire. Each of us can think on this puzzle, but let us cease talking about it to one another until tomorrow. I am tired of asking questions. I want to rest my head for a few hours, and possibly attack the problem from some other angle tomorrow. It is possible that the real culprit is now on the way to jail. But we want to gather evidence that will be strong enough to insure conviction."

"I suppose I remain under suspicion?" Flane asked.

"Yes, sir!" the professor retorted, flashing him a quick glance. "That missing fish affair, you know —"

Dr. Jargell cut into the conversation. "I think that the professor has the right idea," he said. "Flane, if I said some hard things to you a short time ago, perhaps it was because, this tragedy has rather shaken me, and under such conditions a man is inclined to suspect everything and everybody. Let us keep our minds off it as much as possible, and see what the night brings forth."

"Yes," the professor agreed, "let us see what the night brings forth."

Christopher Flane said nothing.

VII.
Events of the Night.

Lucy Smead did not come down for the evening meal. The sorrowing girl remained in her room with the housemaid in attendance. She was told of the arrest of Tony Maleno and Marie on suspicion, but said nothing regarding it. She seemed to be stunned by the tragedy.

Dr. Jargell gave her a sleeping powder, and then went down to the dining room. The three men ate, for the greater part, in silence, now and then talking a bit on ordinary topics, and after the meal they adjourned to the living room to smoke.

Professor Ellis Darlew's eyes had narrowed again, and he appeared to be thinking deeply, though he replied instantly to remarks of the others. Christopher Flane's face was pale, and there was a queer expression in it. Dr. Jargell puffed languidly at a black cigar and talked of city affairs.

"Mr. Flane," the professor said after a time, "I have your word that you'll not leave the house during the night?"

"My word of honor, sir."

"Then let us retire. Doctor, kindly hand me a glass of water from that carafe."

Dr. Jargell poured out the glass of water and handed it to the professor, who drank a bit and remained with the glass in his hand, sipping from time to time.

"In the morning we must solve this riddle," the professor said. "We can't hold Tony and that maid in jail unless we can gather some real evidence. Perhaps questioning in prison might break them down."

"I am inclined to believe that the cook did it," Dr. Jargell observed. "He has a vicious temper, and he certainly had the opportunity to poison the fish."

"Please!" the professor begged. "Let's speak no more of it until morning."

The telephone bell rang, and Christopher Flane answered the call.

"Somebody in the village wants you, Professor Darlew," he said.

"Ah, yes!" The professor got up and stepped to the telephone, spoke, listened. His eyes grew more narrow, and he seemed satisfied about something as he put the receiver back on the hook and turned away.

"Well, let's retire," suggested the doctor.

They ascended the stairs and went to their several rooms, calling their "good nights" to one another. The doctor and Christopher Flane had regular rooms in this summer "cabin," and the professor had been given one at the end of the hall.

Professor Darlew entered, locked the door, and snapped on

the lights. He moved around the room for a time, then sat by the hall door and listened intently.

Half an hour later he turned off the lights, went across to the window, and slowly and carefully raised the shade, making not the slightest noise. Then he lifted the window, an inch at a time, stopping now and then to listen.

Just outside the window was a little rustic balcony. Professor Darlew had noticed it often. Now he crept out on this little balcony and along it to one end. Here there was a rough log post, with large knots in it. The balcony had been constructed for artistic effect more than for use.

Professor Darlew went down the post like a young athlete, waited on the ground beside the house for a moment, then hurried toward the shore of the lake. As he had hoped and expected, he found Constable Rills waiting.

"I put them folks in the jail, sent 'em a meal and let it go at that," the constable whispered. "I tried to talk to 'em, but they wouldn't talk. That Eyetalian whispered to the girl to keep her mouth shut, I reckon."

"We can attend to them tomorrow," said the professor, "if it is necessary. Sleepy, constable?"

"Nope! Why?"

"Because," the professor went on, "I want you to remain awake all night. I want you to do something for me inside the house, and you must carry out orders faithfully."

"I don't see any sense in it," the constable replied, "but I'm willin' to do anything to help."

"Come along, then — and be quiet about it!"

The professor led him to the end of the veranda. One window was unfastened there, for the professor had made sure of that. He whispered his instructions, then opened the window carefully and let the constable slip inside. Then he closed the window again.

Around the side of the house slipped the professor, and up the rustic post he went to the little balcony again. There he stopped for a moment to let his breathing return to normal, for climbing that post noiselessly had been no easy task.

Safe inside his room again he lowered the window and the shade and crept across to the door. This he unlocked, listened intently a moment, then slipped into the hall and closed and locked the door behind him. Without making the slightest noise, he went to a place midway the length of the hall, where there was a closet.

Professor Darlew got into the closet, but he allowed the door to remain open about an inch. He made himself as comfortable as possible on the floor, curling up like a boy, his right ear near that crack in the door.

There was silence in the house, except that now and then he could hear the housemaid doing something in Miss Smead's room. And after a time even those sounds died away. The rustling of the breeze through the treetops, the swish of the lake as the wind stirred its surface — those were all the sounds that came to his ears now.

He shifted his position, made himself comfortable once more, and continued listening, watching, waiting. Suddenly he stirred, for there came to his ears a slight creak. Somewhere along the hall a door was being opened cautiously.

The moon was shining now. The hall was in darkness except for the faint light of the moon that entered from a window at one end, just enough to show a deep shadow moving swiftly and silently along the corridor.

The professor did not leave his post. That deep shadow, he knew, was a man, and the man was going toward the stairs, intending to descend to the lower floor. Well, Constable Rills was waiting down there.

Fifteen minutes passed. Once more Professor Darlew heard a soft creak. The person was coming up the stairs again.

Professor Darlew opened the door a few inches wider, and got to his feet. There was deep silence for a moment; then there came a sudden tumult. A light flashed on in the hall. Professor Darlew sprang out of the closet.

Dr. Jargell stood in the hall, clad in his pyjamas. Before him was Christopher Flane, fully dressed, except that he wore slippers instead of shoes. They were confronting each other angrily, fists clenched, eyes blazing.

"What's the meaning of this, gentlemen?" Professor Darlew demanded.

They whirled to face him. Both tried to speak at once. The professor held up a hand demanding silence. Then he noticed something else. On the floor was a platter, and on the platter —

the remains of the poisoned fish.

"Flane, well hear your story first," the professor said.

"I made up my mind to see what was going on," said Flane. "I heard somebody go into the hall, and I opened my door and listened. I heard somebody come up the stairs, and when I snapped on the light I saw Dr. Jargell, carrying that fish."

"What about it, doctor?" Darlew asked.

"I still had suspicion of Flane," the doctor replied, "I knew that he must have taken that fish from the safe for some reason. Then I remembered that there was a tiny closet on the lower floor, and that the constable had not searched there. I expected that Flane would try to get the fish out tonight, and get it away. I watched for a few minutes, but he did not come to the closet, so I took the fish out. I was intending to carry it to you, professor, tell you were I had found it, let you keep the fish in your room, and go with me to watch the closet and catch Flane when he showed up. He came from his room as I was passing, and snapped on the light. I thought he intended attacking me, and put the fish on the floor. He was just starting down to get it, I suppose."

"You seemed to know where that fish was," Flane accused him. "You must have put it there when you took it from the safe."

"The professor knows I could not have taken it from the safe. According to your own words nobody had the combination except Mr. Smead and yourself."

The professor took charge of the situation immediately.

"Gentlemen," he said, "let us have no more of this now. I ask you both to return to your rooms and remain there for the remainder of the night. Do so immediately, please. I'll take charge of the fish."

They glared at each other and returned to their rooms. Professor Darlew heard the keys turn in the locks. He unlocked his own room, carried in the fish and put it in a closet, then slipped from the room again, locking the door as before.

Down the stairs he went noiselessly. Constable Rills crept from his hiding place and whispered a report. The professor gave more instructions, and Rills ascended the stairs to where he could watch the hall. The professor then went into the living room.

He was busy there for a few minutes. Then he went back up the stairs and met the constable.

"Remain at the end of the hall and watch until morning," the professor instructed him. "Call me if either man tries to leave his room. I'll be awake — thinking."

The professor let himself into his room and locked the door on the inside. For fifteen minutes longer he was busy. Then he relaxed in an easy chair, put the tips of his fingers together, narrowed his eyes, and thought!

VIII.

"Hooked."

The dawn came. Professor Darlew left his room and greeted the constable in whispers. Then he went out into the cool air and walked toward the shore of the lake, breathing deeply, getting the sleep out of his eyes.

He went down to the edge of the pool where the trout had been hooked. He walked around the vicinity, around the clumps of brush, searching. When he returned to the house a short time later, his face was stern.

Christopher Flane and the doctor got up, refusing to speak to each other when they met for breakfast. Constable Rills partook of that breakfast also. When it came to an end the doctor ascended to pay a professional visit to Miss Smead.

"Kindly ask her to keep to her room for an hour or so longer, doctor," the professor said. "We don't want her shocked more than is necessary. I have something to say to all you gentlemen in the living room immediately."

When the doctor returned to this apartment Professor Darlew faced Christopher Flane.

"Now open the safe, Flane!" he commanded.

Flane stared at him, then knelt before the safe, worked the combination and pulled the door open. He stepped back, and the professor knelt before the safe, a magnifying glass in his hand. He looked over the interior for several minutes.

Flane had sat down near the others across the room. The body of the professor blocked sight of what he was doing. But presently he closed the safe door without locking it, and got up. He polished his spectacles, sat down facing them, put the tips of his fingers together again.

"Gentlemen, the case is solved," he said. "It has been very interesting, too. Poor Tony Maleno and Marie Bazin! They have had to spend a night in jail for nothing."

"They did not do it, then?" Dr. Jargell asked.

"No!"

"Then —" The doctor suddenly turned and looked straight at Christopher Flane.

"Bear with me, and I'll explain," the professor went on. He flashed one look at Constable Rills, and got a nod by way of reply.

"In Heaven's name, professor," cried the doctor, "let's get the guilty person behind bars!"

"In due time," the professor said. "Are you so eager, doctor?"

"Naturally! Stanley Smead was my friend and patient —"

"Patient, possibly," the professor interrupted. "But a man does not kill his friend."

"What do you mean?" the doctor cried.

Professor Darlew made a quick motion. So did Constable Rills. Handcuffs snapped on the wrists of Dr. Jargell before he realized what was occurring.

"What do you mean by this outrage?" the doctor shrieked. "I'll sue you for this! Are you in with Flane? Going to get a slice of money from him?"

"Calm yourself, and listen to some facts," the professor said, smiling slightly. "Dr. Jargell, yesterday noon as I approached you and Mr. Smead, while you were sitting on the bench after Mr. Smead had hooked the trout, I overheard a part of your conversation. I learned that you had met with disaster in the market, that Smead had refused to lend you money, and that you were in Smead's will for a goodly sum if he died before you. So much for that!

"Now, we come to Mr. Smead's sudden death. You were not cautious enough there, doctor, else you did not give me credit for having much intelligence. You were too quick to say that he was dead. I know something of doctoring, remember, and I have seen many men die. You also were too quick to say that he was not choking on a fish bone. Also, you knew at once that he had been poisoned, and you identified the poison as a South American one, and you did it instantly. As a matter of fact, there are several poisons that would act the same. How could you tell instantly what poison it was by the froth on a man's lips and the condition of his face and eyes?

"You suggested, remember, that Mr. Smead catch a fish and eat it for his luncheon. You wanted to kill Stanley Smead for two reasons — because you were mentioned in his will, and because you had been conspiring with his financial enemies!"

"Are you insane?" the doctor cried.

"I scarcely think so, doctor. Pay close attention, please, for you are vitally interested in all this. After Smead's death, after the constable had telephoned the coroner, and while we were rounding up the servants to be questioned, you slipped to the telephone and sent that message to the city, to a broker confederate, and at once the hammering of the market began. You and your associates must have cleaned up yesterday, and may this morning — but you'll all be in jail soon.

"I sent a message to the city myself last night, to the chief of police, who happens to be a good friend of mine. He turned half a dozen good men loose on the case, and they gathered me a lot of important information. I know the persons with whom you have been dealing, doctor. They expected Smead's sudden death and were prepared to act when news of it reached them — but the million it got them will do them little good!"

"But —" the doctor began.

"You pay attention to me," the professor snapped. "Now we come to another phase of the case. You evidently became convinced that I did not believe deeply in the guilt of either Tony or the Bazin girl. Christopher Flane was under suspicion also. And you took the fish from the safe to throw more suspicion on him, to make me believe that, in a panic, Flane had stolen the fish."

"Now I know that you are insane!" the doctor screeched. "Constable, take these handcuffs off me and put them on that maniac. How could I steal the fish?"

"You had the combination of the safe!" the professor continued. "Possibly Mr. Smead at some time gave it to you so you could put papers or medicines in the safe, since it was used only as a sort of fire protection affair."

"But —" the doctor protested.

"Don't lie to me!"' Professor Darlew thundered. "Listen! Do you mean to tell me that you've never been inside that safe?"

"I certainly have not!"

"I can prove that statement a lie! Last night, doctor, just before we retired, I asked you to hand me a glass of water. You were kind enough to do so. You handed me your fingerprints, on the glass, at the same time. I examined those prints. A few minutes ago, when the safe was opened, I found your prints inside it on the end of the strong box."

"That's a lie!"

"Oh, no, it isn't! They are there, properly chalked, and there they will remain until needed. I'll show them to you after a while, then we'll lock the safe and guard it — unless you are prepared to confess.

"And now let me tell you something else. Last night Constable Rills was on guard down here. He saw a man slip down the stairs and open the safe and take a slip of paper out of the strong box. That man was in pyjamas, doctor — that man was you!

"That man, also, went to the tiny shoe closet and got out the poisoned fish. He tore up the slip of paper, rolled the pieces into a ball, and tossed the ball into a corner of the closet. Didn't know what else to do with it, being in his pyjamas and wishing to hurry back upstairs. Expected to pick up the ball of paper later, I suppose.

"That man was you, doctor! The paper was a note that you had given Stanley Smead for five thousand dollars. I have it now. Even wanted to save that five thousand, didn't you? Whole hog!"

"Of all the preposterous —" the doctor began.

"Aw, I saw yer!" Constable Rills grunted.

"I sent Tony and Marie away," the professor continued, "because I wanted as few persons as possible around here last night. I rather expected some movements during the night, and I wanted to pin it down to two men. You see, I had my suspicions of you, doctor, all the time."

"Well, are you all done?" the doctor sneered. "I still think that you are insane, professor. As a matter of fact, I did know the combination of the safe and I took the fish, thinking that it would puzzle Flane and make him give himself away. For I think that Flane killed Smead! And because I was trying to aid you, working a bit in the dark, I find myself accused!"

"You are guilty!" the professor said.

"Please try to be sensible," the doctor begged. "Come right

down to the facts. Granting everything that you have said, except that about my guilt, please tell me how I could have killed Stanley Smead. He caught that trout and handed it to Tony Maleno, who took it immediately into the house to cook it. I sat down on the bench with Smead, and, as you know, sat there until called to luncheon. I never touched that fish. Now, use your sense!"

"Oh, I have used it — I have, indeed!" the professor replied. "I never said that you touched the fish."

"Then, man, how could I have poisoned it?"

"It was poisoned when Mr. Smead handed it to Tony."

"Why, that is preposterous!" the doctor cried. "Constable, can't you see how absurd that is?"

"I reckon that the professor is handlin' this case," the constable retorted, looking at Darlew in admiration.

The professor sat forward in his chair.

"Dr. Jargell," he said, "where is the lure you made, and with which Mr. Smead caught that trout?"

"I — I am a bit superstitious about such things," the doctor replied. "I believe a lure is no good after one fish has been caught on it. Plenty of men will testify to my belief in that. So I threw that one away immediately after Mr. Smead caught his trout."

"Where did you throw it?"

"Tossed it over the bank into the lake."

"You thought you did," said the professor. "You tossed it around the clump of brush and toward the edge of the water. There was a tiny weight on it, and you expected the lure to sink. But the bit of leader still attached to it struck a twig, and the lure dropped to the ground. I found it, doctor."

"Well, what about it?" Jargell asked, licking at his dry lips.

"I went down to the rabbit pens and scratched a rabbit with one of the hooks of the lure. The rabbit died instantly! That lure was poisoned, Jargell! Your scheme was a good one. You were particular not to touch that fish. Suspicion might be thrown upon anybody but your self. An excellent plan, you cold-blooded monster, but it didn't work!

"You planned the murder deliberately to get money from the estate, and to get it through the market deal with your crooked associates when they, ahead of everybody else, were notified that Smead was dead. There is no way out of it for you, Jargell

You showed that lure to several persons, so it can be identified. And we can show, I believe, that you had that particular poison in your possession. We've got you every way, Jargell!"

The face of Dr. Jargell had turned white, and his eyes were bulging. For a moment he breathed heavily, then he laughed like a fiend.

"Professor Darlew, I'd lift my hat to you if I had one on," he said. "You're one great little man when it comes to solving a crime. And to think that a bit of leader caught on a twig —"

"I am to take that as a confession?"

"If it so pleases you to do," Jargell said. "You see, I don't go in for sentimental mush and religion and all that sort of thing. The human body is merely a machine, and, being broken, it merely stops running. Life is pleasant — but death is nothing!"

"You beast!" Flane cried.

Dr. Jargell laughed again, and stood up slowly. And swiftly the fingers of one manacled hand dived into a pocket of his waistcoat. Professor Darlew gave a cry — but Constable Rills had been watching. He seized Jargell's hands, fought him, held him secure. Then the professor reached into the waistcoat pocket, and took out a tiny phial filled with a dark brown, thick liquid.

"Going to kill yourself, were you?" the professor said. "We can't allow that, doctor. The law has a little collection to make from you. Um! A phial of the same poison, eh? More evidence than necessary, even if you had not confessed. Constable, we'll take him to the county seat and put him in jail. He's booked for the extreme penalty!"

PODDIN'S MISTAKE

Crouching in the darkness Poddin rubbed one hand over his bullet-shaped head, on which the hair was clipped close. Then he put on his dirty cap and pulled it down over his eyes, slouched forward, and continued down the street.

Poddin snarled as he walked, snarled like an angry wolf, and for no special reason except that he was betraying his true disposition. Years before, Poddin had caused himself to believe that it gave him courage to snarl at the world in general.

He was slipping along through the shadows cast by giant trees at the edge of the boulevard. The night before he had cached his revolver at a certain spot in front of a vacant lot, beneath a hedge that had not been trimmed for some time. He had been working at the other end of town the night before, but he reached the room he called home in a roundabout manner, and so had a chance to hide the gun. Poddin knew better than to carry a revolver except when it was absolutely necessary. A man of his ilk caught with a gun on his person was as good as on his way to prison.

It was almost midnight, and the section of the city which Poddin graced with his nocturnal presence was that of the better class of residences. Poddin was in new territory, and did not know whether he would have good fortune or not. He was killing time, after a fashion. He knew better than to be in another part of town where there had been several holdups recently, for the police were watching there. So he would strike here, if he got the opportunity. If he gained anything, it would put him so much ahead; he could not work at the other end of town for a time, anyway.

After a while, Poddin reached the spot where he had hidden his revolver. He made sure that there was nobody near, and then he took the gun from beneath the hedge and slipped it into his pocket. He knotted a black silk handkerchief around his neck in such a manner that it could be drawn up quickly over his face to the eyes, thus making an effectual mask. He was prepared.

There appeared to be a dearth of pedestrians. A few automobiles dashed by, but that was all. Poddin sat down in front of the hedge and began thinking that it was a fool stunt to be in this section of the city. Men did little walking at night up here. Those who were abroad were in their limousines.

To pass the time while he waited for a victim, Poddin began considering his past life, his present circumstances, and what the future held for him. He had been reared in the gutter, and at an early age had become the companion of crooks. He was without high standing, however, even in crookdom. For Poddin had been too shiftless to learn a crook's trade in the proper way. He hated mental exertion and a game of wits. Poddin's character was such that he deemed it the correct thing to step from a shadow, poke a gun under a man's nose, take his money and his watch, and make a getaway. That did not call for brainwork. A sinister, treacherous thug was Poddin.

Twice he had done time, and at his previous appearance in court he had been warned that, if convicted again, he would be put away for life as a habitual criminal. Poddin's nature was such that he had no pals to aid him in case of disaster. He stood alone, and on insecure ground.

Take the present, for instance. The police were after him, and he knew it. They suspected him, rightly, of several highway robberies that had occurred within a month. He had seen a certain detective he knew loitering in his vicinity. The city was getting dangerous for him, and yet he did not want to go away and seek new fields.

Poddin thought that it would be an excellent thing if he was assured of bed and board and spending money for a time without doing anything nefarious to get them. If he only could avoid law breaking for a while, if he had money enough to be honest until the police forgot him to an extent and began watching others! But Poddin had not saved money. His holdups never netted him great sums. He had but a few dollars in his pocket, and that was all he had in the world.

If he could hold up a man in this section of town, he might get something besides small change, he thought. But it was midnight now, and there was nobody in sight. Poddin did not even see a policeman or a watchman. He thought for an instant of robbing a house; and then he dismissed that idea from his mind.

For Poddin knew nothing about burglary; he never had

taken the trouble to learn the tricks of the trade, and so he feared it. It took nerve to enter another man's castle, facing probable death if discovery came, and Poddin did not possess nerve of that sort. Why, he did not even know how to enter a window without making a noise! And, once inside, he would not know how to protect himself or how to obtain articles of value.

No, he could not attempt to rob a house. It was highway robbery or nothing for Poddin. He was not clever enough to be a pickpocket, and he knew none of the tricks of other branches of crime. He was an ignorant holdup man, and that was all.

Poddin looked down the boulevard again, and then, far down the street, he saw a pedestrian approaching. For an instant a corner arc light flashed on a glistening shirtfront. The man who approached Poddin was in evening dress.

"A swell," Poddin thought. Probably he would have a goodly sum on him, and an expensive watch, and a diamond ring of three or four carats. Poddin, you understand, was not well acquainted with the usages of polite society; he judged that any man who had the price would wear a diamond of three or four carats. He believed, with a certain man known to fame, that "them as has 'em, wears 'em."

Silently Poddin gave thanks that the enemy was delivered into his hands, If he could manage to get a good roll, he could take it easy for a time and let the police watch in vain, he told himself. So Poddin drew back farther into the shadows, pulled up the handkerchief to screen the lower part of his face, and took the revolver from his pocket and held it ready.

II.

Wallace John Walkins, scion of the wealthy and socially prominent Walkins family, did not usually walk home at that hour of the night. But a man in love may do peculiar things, as Poddin learned that night.

Wallace John Walkins had been at the home of Gertrude Sanleigh for dinner. He had been paying particular attention to Gertrude for more than a year, and everybody in their social set said it was a match. Walkins, however, had not been sure, for Gertrude seemed to give him hope one moment and dash him upon the rocks of despair the next.

On this evening, however, Wallace John Walkins grew bold and asked the question, and Gertrude replied in the way he had hoped, and so they spent several hours out on the veranda, as lovers will, disregarding all other persons and the flight of time.

It was midnight when Walkins decided that it was certainly time for him to return to his father's house. Gertrude offered to send him in one of her father's cars, but Walkins decided that he would rather walk, since he would be walking on air, so to speak, and would not be fatigued. So he swung off down the boulevard, humming a song, dreaming of romance, and thinking not at all of the possibility of a holdup man stopping him and putting the muzzle of a gun beneath his nostrils.

Wallace John Walkins was twenty-eight. At the university he had been a leader in the more strenuous forms of athletics. He had been taught to act quickly in an emergency, to preserve his presence of mind, and he never had known the meaning of fear. It was reasonable to expect, then, that there would be a lively time when Poddin held him up.

Turning a corner Walkins made his way quickly along the tree-bordered boulevard toward his father's mansion. His hands were swinging at his sides. His overcoat was open. His hat sat on the back of his head, and that head was in the clouds.

Walkins came to the untrimmed hedge before an old estate, and went on inside the shadow it cast. Suddenly another shadow darted forward and stopped before him, there was a flash of the distant streetlight reflecting from the nickeled barrel of a weapon, and a gruff voice demanded:

"Hands up, bo! Elevate 'em, and don't try any funny business! Understand?"

At the command Wallace John Walkins elevated his hands and stopped humming the song, for he was startled — not afraid, but startled. Poddin stepped forward, still covering his man, and ran a hand into the inside pocket of Walkins' coat. He clutched a wallet, transferred it to one of his own pockets, and fumbled to see whether Walkins carried a watch. The victim had not spoken a word, and Poddin supposed that he was badly frightened.

Then Wallace John Walkins went into action with a suddenness that disconcerted Poddin to an extreme. He swerved to one side, knocked the muzzle of the revolver away, caught Poddin behind the ear with his fist and almost knocked him flat, and then giving one more spring forward, hurled Poddin into the prickly hedge, yanked him forth again, slapped his face, and then held him with his arms pinioned at his sides.

"Trying to rob me, you rat?" asked Wallace John Walkins pleasantly. "Trying to hold me up on a night like this? It can't be done!"

Poddin gasped, but had nothing to say. He realized that he had made a mistake, that a white shirtfront did not mean lack of courage and strength. He began to whimper.

"I suppose you'll give me over to the police," he said. "Well, I can't help it."

"Why go around trying to rob people?" Walkins asked.

"It's the first time," Poddin lied. "I couldn't get work, and I was hungry, I sneaked the gun from a friend, and thought I'd turn bad. A man's got to eat."

Now Wallace John Walkins was a peculiar young man in some ways. It had been said of him that, during the usual trip around the world following his graduation from the university, he had consorted with all sorts of persons. He hauled Poddin forth into the light and looked him over.

"You have the appearance of a professional thug," Walkins said, "and I believe that you are, but I am willing to give you the benefit of the doubt."

"Then you'll let me go?" Poddin asked thankfully.

"You are not going to get off as easy as that," Walkins said. "Something of a scrapper, aren't you?"

"I guess I can take care of anybody in my own class."

"Ever been in a real home? Know how a gentleman lives, and all that?"

"I don't know much about such kind of things, sir."

"Well, you're due to learn. I fired a valet yesterday because I caught him stealing. I'm going to take you home with me and give you the job. You certainly are not a professional valet, and so you should be refreshing."

"Thanks, sir; but I'm afraid that I couldn't fill the job," Poddin replied. "I wouldn't know what to do."

"I'll explain all that to you. And this isn't an offer of a job you can turn down," Wallace John Walkins informed him. "I am insisting that you take it. Understand? I'm going to give you a chance to go straight — and, believe me, you'll go straight, too! If I ever catch you stealing — you can guess what'll happen! Do you doubt that I can handle you?"

Walkins shook Poddin again.

"I guess you can handle me, sir," Poddin said.

"We don't want any guessing — understand? Are you sure that I can handle you?"

"I — yes, sir."

"Very good! I'm going to take you home right now, see that you take a bath and clean up, and then give you proper clothes. You'll probably frighten everybody else around the house into fits — for you do look like a thug — but they are used to these little fancies of mine. You will not be a prisoner — understand that! There'll be all sorts of things around that will be worth picking up — but the Lord help you if you pick up any of them without permission. I've got all kinds of money. If you stole from me and made a getaway, I'd drop everything else and take after you. I'd get you, and I'd do more than hand you over to the police — I'd handle you myself! That is understood? Come along, then!"

Grasping Poddin by the shoulder Wallace John Walkins forced him along the street at a rapid rate. Poddin found his brain working at top speed for the first time in his life. This wouldn't be so bad, he decided.

As valet to Wallace John Walkins — Poddin did not know his name as yet, but he realized he was a gentleman of means — he would be able to keep away from the police for some time to come. He could play at being honest and grateful to Walkins for giving him a position, and then, at the proper time, he could take things of value from the Walkins house and seek other climes, there to live on the fat of the land for a time.

He continued to whimper, however, until Walkins commanded that he cease. They walked for several blocks, and finally turned in at a magnificent mansion and went to the front door. A butler opened it, though it was almost one o'clock in the morning.

"I have brought home a new valet," Walkins told the butler.

"Very good, sir," the butler replied. But he did not look as if he thought it was very good. His nose curled toward the ceiling when he caught sight of Poddin, and then and there warfare was declared between the two.

Walkins took Poddin to his own suite, forced him to bathe, gave him some clothes, showed him the little room where he was to sleep, and instructed him as to his first duties in the morning!

Poddin looked around the suite in amazement. He saw many things that he considered worth stealing.

"I'm to sleep in there, without anybody watchin' me?" Poddin asked then.

"You are," Walkins answered. "I explained the thing to you, didn't I? I've got to have a valet, and you're elected. It's difficult to get a good one in these days, and so I have decided to train you from the ground up. If you feel like stealing things and making a getaway through one of the windows, help yourself. But you know what'll happen if you do!"

Walkins glared at him, and Poddin retired to the other room. He had no idea of stealing things and making a getaway so soon. He wanted to impress upon Walkins that he was grateful for the chance to go straight. He'd wait for some time, until he had gained the confidence of his employer, until he had discovered the things most worth stealing, and then he would make plans and get away with a big haul.

Poddin was further instructed in his duties the following day, and soon became a fixture, despite the fact that the rest of the Walkins family regarded him as a dangerous crook, and the other servants would have little to do with him. He learned his work well, and attended to it. And gradually he learned things about the Walkins household.

The family was very rich, he found. Wallace John Walkins was engaged to Gertrude Sanleigh, who also came from a family exceptionally rich. Moreover, it was a love match. There was considerable entertaining being done already, and the marriage was to be consummated within four months.

The Walkins family had a fortune in jewels, and Poddin learned that the gems were kept in a special safe in the wall of the library. That safe was electrified heavily; the man who touched it died, and alarms were sounded in half a dozen places at the same time. Poddin knew that it would be no easy task to get into that safe, but he thought that it could be done, if he bided his time and watched.

Two months passed. Poddin knew a great deal about the house now. He knew that, any time the members of the family were out, he could go through certain rooms and pick up articles worth several thousand dollars. But Poddin wanted bigger game.

He pretended to be grateful to Wallace John Walkins, and he did his work as well as he could. Poddin was playing the game. In reality, he hated Walkins for forcing him to be an honest man. Walkins had missed a roll of bills once, and the way in which he had looked at Poddin was enough to make Poddin's flesh creep. Poddin was glad when Walkins found the roll of bills in the library, where they had dropped from his pocket.

The jewel safe fascinated Poddin, for that was his goal. Now and then he had a chance to get downtown to his old haunts, and he made arrangements with a "fence" to buy jewels of value when he should be able to deliver them. Poddin was doing a great deal of thinking these days. Two things he had to know — the combination of that safe, and the location of the switch that turned on and off the deadly electric current.

For Poddin was going to do it all by himself; he did not care to call in a professional cracksman. It was ridiculously easy, Poddin decided. When he learned the two things he had to know, he would have only to await his opportunity, turn off the current, open the safe, take the jewels and make his getaway. Then he would laugh long and loudly at his employer.

III.

Very much in love was Wallace John Walkins, so much so that he was not his normal self. His father and mother, his sister and his young brother worshiped his fiancée, too. It was a happy household as the time for the wedding approached.

Then Poddin began to fear that he would fail, that Walkins would get married and dismiss him, and that he would have to leave the Walkins house without securing the jewels, and with only his wages as reward for his service there.

He succeeded in developing a sort of cunning, and he put forward his best efforts to keep from using his usual snarl. He felt sure that Walkins trusted him now, though Walkins looked at him peculiarly now and then.

"Well, how goes it, Poddin?" Walkins asked upon a certain morning, looking at Poddin closely.

"Very well, sir."

"Glad that you're running straight?"

"Yes, sir. I have peace of mind, sir," Poddin said.

"Um! Don't revert to type, Poddin, if you want to keep that peace of mind. I'm not quite sure of you yet. I think you'd like to run away. I'm to be married soon, as you know, and shall be gone on my honeymoon for three months, and I'm not sure what I'll do with you. I'll decide it later."

Poddin snarled after Walkins had left the room. He knew what he intended doing. He hated Walkins. He'd show Walkins that he wasn't to have his comings and goings bossed by any man!

He redoubled his efforts to learn the combination of the safe. Now and then he got a chance to enter the library, but seldom when there was nobody else in the big room. But there came a day when Walkins' mother was entertaining for the bride-elect, and all the servants were called upon to prepare the rooms on the lower floor for the event.

Poddin maneuvered so that he was assigned to the library. He betrayed a particular adaptability for banking flowers and ferns in that room, and Mrs. Walkins, who considered that Poddin was grateful to her son and worshiped him and wanted to see him happy, left Poddin alone in the library to finish the work while she took the other servants to the other rooms.

Poddin seized his chance. He arranged mirrors so that there was a continued reflection from the safe in the wall to a corner of the veranda outside. It took him some time, but it was not a difficult task after all. And when he had finished, he aided in the work to be done in other rooms, and finally went up the stairs to his master's quarters.

Walkins left to conduct this fiancée to the house. Poddin slipped out of the house and made for the veranda, for he had listened at the door of Mrs. Walkins' room and knew that she had about finished dressing. She would then descend and get certain jewels from the safe, Poddin knew, for that was her habit.

Poddin reached the veranda and made his way along it

slowly. In time he reached a spot near the railing. He could not see the safe in the wall directly, but he could look into the corner of a mirror that reflected another mirror that showed the safe.

With a stub of pencil and a card in his hands Poddin waited. Through the mirror he saw Mrs. Walkins enter the room and speak to her husband, who got up and went immediately to the safe. Now Poddin bent forward and watched closely.

It was even better and easier than he had dreamed, He saw every move of Mr. Walkins' hand; he read the combination as easily as if he had been standing beside the master of the house. Five minutes later Poddin was back in his proper place, and in the pocket of his waistcoat was a card upon which had been written the combination of the safe in the library wall.

The first part of his work was done, and for that Poddin felt glad. But the electrification of the safe puzzled him a great deal. He knew how dangerous it would be to touch the strong box if the current was turned on. And he did not know the location of the switch.

Poddin watched closely for another week, but could not discover it. There were more entertainments for Gertrude Sanleigh, and Poddin made the discovery that the valet of a young gentleman of means about to commit matrimony has work to do.

Then came a day when he was obliged to help the other servants. Poddin made himself generally useful, so much so that he was given more downstairs work. Mrs. Walkins was going out that afternoon to a tea, and Poddin supposed that she would wear a few of her jewels. So he watched carefully, managing to keep near the library.

He observed Mrs. Walkins talking to her husband, and then, hiding behind portières, Poddin saw Mr. Walkins go along the hall to an innocent-looking panel, press against it, saw an aperture, and an electric switch within a secret wall box. Walkins threw the switch, and then went to the library and got the jewels for his wife. Then he returned and put the switch back again.

Poddin had all the knowledge he required now. He had but to perfect his arrangements with the "fence," await an opportunity, and commit the crime he contemplated. He would be in no hurry about it. Within a few days the house would be in a turmoil because of the approaching wedding; he would not be watched so closely by Wallace John Walkins — and that would be the time.

He had only to press back that panel, throw the switch and thus turn off the current, work the combination of the safe, take the jewels, close the safe and throw back the switch — and he would have a fortune in his hands.

He had another reason, too, for waiting. Wallace John Walkins had let it become known that his present to his bride would be a diamond necklace worth more than fifty thousand dollars. Poddin wanted to get that necklace, if possible. Then he could live as a man of means for the remainder of his life.

For he had his getaway planned perfectly. He would commit the robbery at night and at a time when it would be easy to get away from the house. He would go immediately to the "fence," who would be notified beforehand and would have money ready to purchase a part of the jewels. The money and the remainder of the jewels in his possession, Poddin would hurry to a suite of rooms he had rented, his landlady believing that he was a traveling man away from home a great part of the time. There he would change clothes and alter his appearance as much as possible. Having done that, Poddin would take a local train to a small station up the river. There he would engage an automobile and drive to a certain resort not far away. After that, he had two plans, depending upon what day the robbery was committed. One was to catch a steamship for a South American port, and the other was to go to Halifax and ship from there to a European city.

"She's sure some plan!" Poddin told himself. "That holdup of mine's goin' to turn out pretty good at that! Grateful to him, am I, because he helped me go straight? I'll show him!"

Poddin remembered that he had heard a man say once that ingratitude always is punished. The remembrance startled him for a moment, and then he laughed at his fears. He'd show Wallace John Walkins! If the bride was to have a diamond necklace, Wallace John Walkins would have to buy a second one. But he could afford it.

IV.

It was two days before the wedding when Poddin's chance came. Upon that evening there was a reception at the Walkins residence in honor of the bride-elect. And Poddin knew that the diamond necklace had arrived and had been placed in the safe in the library wall.

He helped Wallace John Walkins with his greatest skill that night.

"I think I'll leave you here, Poddin, while I'm on my honeymoon," Walkins told him. "My father will give you your wages. When I return, I'll need you again in your old capacity. While I'm gone, you just behave yourself and keep my rooms in order. Run away if you like — but remember what'll happen if you do!"

Poddin smiled sinisterly after Walkins had left the room. So Walkins thought he was afraid, did he? He'd have the laugh on Walkins before long. For this was the night Poddin intended to make his move. He had informed the "fence" and everything was in readiness.

He remained upstairs during the early evening, but he watched as the guests left, and he knew that Gertrude Sanleigh had remained to spend an extra hour with the family, and that Wallace John Walkins would take her home.

Poddin managed to get down the stairs and secrete himself in a position where he could watch the library.

"I'm going to give you a glimpse of it now," he heard Walkins saying to Gertrude Sanleigh.

The unwilling valet dodged back behind the portières. He watched Walkins go into the hall, open the panel, and throw the electric switch. He saw him return to the library and open the safe, and take from it a jewel box.

Poddin almost gasped as the diamond necklace was held up to the light. The little bride-to-be clapped her hands like a child to express her delight. For a moment they looked at the necklace, and then Walkins returned it to the safe. Poddin hurried noiselessly up the stairs. An hour later he helped Walkins prepare for bed.

Until about two o'clock in the morning Poddin waited, and

then he dressed quietly and went out to slip down the stairs. He had an electric torch in one pocket, a revolver in another pocket. He was snarling once more; he was his old self now. He did not fear the consequences of ingratitude. He wanted that fortune in gems. He'd teach Wallace John Walkins not to take a holdup man into his home and force him to do honest work!

It was all so simple that Poddin felt like leaving a note for Walkins, telling how easy it had been. But he knew better than to do that. He stopped at the bottom of the stairs to listen, hiding behind the portières. There was no sound in the house.

Poddin had discovered much since taken into the house. He knew, for instance, how to disengage the electric burglar alarm that was attached to the doors and windows. He disconnected it now and raised a front window cautiously.

Then he hurried back to the hall and stood there for a minute or so, listening intently. He heard nothing to alarm him. He went down the hall noiselessly and stopped before the proper panel in the wall. He flashed his electric torch now, and pressed around the edge of the panel until he touched the spring. The panel slid back. Poddin flashed his torch again, quickly, for he did not like to make too much light. He saw the big electric switch before him, and quickly swung it up. Then he closed the panel again.

Poddin almost chuckled now. Force him to go straight, would they? Ingratitude be hanged! They could only blame themselves, he decided. Wallace John Walkins was to pay the price for trying to turn a criminal into an honest fellow.

Back through the hall Poddin went, making not the slightest noise. He stopped now and then to listen, and finally he came to the door of the library and opened it cautiously. He closed it behind him, stood against it to listen once more, and then went across the room cautiously to the panel behind which the safe rested.

Poddin had a touch of nervousness now, and he hesitated long enough to make an attempt to shake it off. He fumbled in his pocket and got the card upon which he had written the combination. But he would not need it unless nervousness caused him to forget, for he had memorized that combination long ago.

He flashed his torch and opened the wall panel before the safe. The door of the jewel safe was before him, and again Poddin almost chuckled because the theft was going to be so easy. He remembered how he had obtained the combination, how he had watched Wallace John Walkins betray the hiding place of the electric switch.

Once more he flashed the torch, and caused the light to play on the dial of the safe. He glanced at the card upon which he had written the combination, chuckled again, and then looked up at the dial. His hand went out carefully, and he grasped the knob.

And then it seemed to Poddin that a million lightning bolts struck him at the same time, that his life story flashed before him in an instant, that he took leave of a familiar country and came upon a new one in the twinkling of an eye!

A gong sounded, an alarm rang. Servants, suddenly awakened by the clamor, armed themselves according to orders and rushed toward the library.

Wallace John Walkins was one of the first persons to arrive on the scene. Stretched on the floor before the safe, lay Poddin, dead.

He had made his plans well, and he had made, also, one fatal mistake. He had neglected to take into consideration the fact that a young man very much in love, and to be married within forty-eight hours, is likely to be rather forgetful.

Wallace John Walkins, having given his bride-to-be a glimpse of the magnificent necklace, had taken her home afterward — forgetting to turn on again the current that protected the safe.

And so Poddin, the ungrateful, when, he threw the switch and believed that he had made things safe, had, in reality, thrown the current on instead of off, and his life had paid the forfeit.

WOMAN'S WEAPONS

I.

The Subterfuge.

For all of her twenty-two years had Kitty Crade gone merrily on her way, being denied nothing by anybody who loved her, which meant everybody in her sphere of acquaintance.

As a baby she had been the pet of the neighborhood, and as a child her school days were made easy by doting teachers. Girlhood found her the belle of every neighborhood dance, and the despair of lovelorn youths who got nothing but laughter in return for their avowals. She had a way with her, had Kitty Crade — a smile that flashed a vision of dimples, a roguish twinkle in the Irish eyes of her, a hint of soft music in her voice. It was, perhaps, because she had been denied nothing that she almost took the wrong path in life. Having met no resistance worthwhile, it was natural for her to take the path of least resistance when obstacles did present themselves.

There had been a flash of fear when her father died, another when her eldest brother was temporarily out of a job. But fear did not remain long in the vicinity of Kitty Crade. Tears dashed from eyes, a deep sigh, a smile — and Kitty Crade was herself again.

But now she felt fear, and it came from a sense of guilt and a dread of guilt's consequences. Kitty Crade had played on the borderland between right and wrong too long, and had stepped across the line. And Detective Tim Murphy, of all men, had seen her.

She blamed herself, and she blamed Joe Draylon, whom she preferred above other youths of the masculine gender. But most of all she wanted to escape.

"The devil himself must have whispered in my ear," she told herself, "and that same ear must have been ready to listen."

There really had been no sense in it. Of course there were many things that Kitty Crade desired, and which she could not have. There were three younger Crades kicking out shoes at school, and one elder brother to support the lot. Kitty Crade held a job now and then, but not for long. Either she was displeased with the work, or someone made advances that she wouldn't tolerate.

Being twenty-two and pretty, Kitty Crade wanted pretty things. She wanted to be pretty always in the eyes of Joe Draylon, though she pretended to him that his opinion was as nothing to her. It irked her to see less handsome women decked out in the height of fashion, The thought of theft came to her many times, but not as theft, rather as merely helping herself to something she wanted. Kitty Crade, going her way merrily through life, scarcely understood the seriousness of such a thing. It spelled cleverness to her.

Her first offense had been taking a bottle of cheap perfume from the counter of a department store during a bargain sale. She did it by way of a lark, and was thankful that her mother supposed some admirer had given it to her and so asked no questions. Kitty did not care to lie to her mother.

Then it was a half dozen handkerchiefs, taken during another bargain sale. After that stealing came easier. Kitty Crade thought only of the cleverness of it, not that it was wrong, and that it promised shame and imprisonment. She was not a bad girl at heart; she simply had had life made too easy for her, and did not understand. Petting neighbors had forced her to the belief that Kitty Crade could do no wrong without it being forgiven.

And then — today! That very morning, Kitty Crade had read in a newspaper how a well-dressed woman had been arrested in a shop for stealing a waist. Shoplifter, the paper called her! The article went on to say that the police were starting a campaign against shoplifters — "sneaking, petty thieves who are the bane of merchants." Kitty Crade never before had stopped to consider herself a sneaking, petty thief who was a bane to merchants.

Her mother had spoken, too.

"Stole a waist, did she? She ought to be sent up. 'Tis wrong to steal, even food for the starvin', but to steal things she could do without and did not have to have — dirt, she is!"

Kitty Crade had an hour of serious thought after that. And then she dressed and went downtown with the avowed purpose of getting a job. She met Joe Draylon on the way, and he went along. Joe, also, was looking for a job; he always seemed to be looking for a job. He managed to keep himself looking decent and to have a little spending money in his pocket, but he did it more by a certain skill at pool than by honest labor.

Joe remained on the street, and Kitty Crade entered a department store and sought the office of the superintendent. She was informed that there was no vacancy at present, but that one might occur soon, and so she filled out a card with her name, address, abilities, and references. She did not like the manner of the superintendent; he appeared to be a man who had become soured on the world, and he did not prove susceptible to Kitty Crade's smile or the flash in her blue eyes.

Down on the lower floor of the big store again, Kitty walked slowly along the aisles, looking at the goods displayed, watching the rush of bargain hunters, and wishing — always wishing — that she had more money to spend for the things she wanted to possess. There was a special sale on at the jewelry counter, she found. Kitty Crade particularly admired a display of combs studded with brilliants.

To do her justice, she did not really intend to steal. But she wanted one of those combs, and she felt a little downhearted, as she always did when she failed to get a job promptly, and she had decided that she hated the superintendent of this particular establishment. Women were jammed around the jewelry counter, and Kitty Crade found herself hemmed in and thrust forward.

She struggled to get along the counter and to the edge of the throng. Again she was jammed forward, and she saw before her a tray of the combs within reach of her hand. Every saleswoman had her back turned; the shoppers near her were not looking in her direction, but over her head at the clerks.

Kitty Crade's hand darted forward. It was ridiculously easy. She had one of the combs, and had switched it inside the sleeve of her jacket. She backed away, turned around.

And her heart almost stood still! She had been careful as far as the saleswomen and other shoppers were concerned, but she had not taken the trouble to glance behind her. And now she found herself looking into the eyes of Detective Tim Murphy.

Many things flashed through her mind in that instant. Murphy had seen her steal that comb. Though he knew her well, and had known her father, he was a man to do his duty, and so she would be arrested. And the true realization of what that would mean flashed through her mind for the first time. She saw herself disgraced, in prison. Only that morning her dear, old mother had expressed her opinion of shoplifters, and it had not been complimentary.

Panic seized her for an instant, and then presence of mind returned to her even as Detective Tim Murphy started forward. He was still some ten feet away when she managed to drop the comb on the floor and whirl away. Escape was the one thought in her mind. If she could escape now she could declare with every breath that Detective Tim Murphy had been mistaken, that she had not been the girl he had seen steal the comb. If he as much as exchanged words with her, that accusation would be gone forever.

Without seeming to flee she fought her way through the jam in the aisle, through the crowd of bargain-hunting women who were pushing one another in an effort to reach the counters. She won free, and walked rapidly toward the nearest exit, which was on a side street.

Now she dared to glance behind, and saw Detective Tim Murphy following as swiftly as possible. As she looked he beckoned for her to wait. Terror claimed her, and she darted through the exit and made for the nearest corner. She was glad that Joe was on the other side of the building, for she did not want to be stopped now.

Detective Tim Murphy continued to follow. Kitty Crade darted around the first corner and went rapidly toward the next, dodging through the crowds, trying to evade the officer. She reached the corner, finally, just as a surface car was starting. Kitty Crade sprang to the steps and hurried inside.

Murphy caught a glimpse of her and hailed the chauffeur of a taxicab. Kitty Crade was almost in a panic now. She had hoped that Murphy would give up the chase, and that, the next time she saw him, she could declare that he had been mistaken and had seen another girl. She watched through the window, and saw that the cab was following the car. When it stopped the cab drew abreast, and Kitty Crade turned her head away to avoid being recognized.

The car went on, and the cab still followed. Kitty Crade began wondering how she was to escape. They were leaving the retail district now, going toward a section of select homes where there would be but little traffic. Half a dozen times she thought to leave the car, but a glance showed her the taxicab a short distance behind, Murphy leaning through one of the windows and watching.

She didn't dare ride to the end of the line, for he would be sure to come up with her there. And now she grew frightened that he would go ahead in the cab, wait at a comer, and board the car.

"I've got to convince him he was mistaken," she kept telling herself. "It isn't the arrest. I haven't that comb on me, and he has no evidence. But if he's sure he'll tell mother, and that —"

There were scarcely half a dozen passengers left in the car now. Kitty Crade knew that she would have to leave it soon. She watched her chance, watched until Murphy's chauffeur was obliged to slow down at a cross street to dodge other cars. She signaled and left the trolley car at the next corner.

A glance showed her that the taxicab was coming at a higher rate of speed, showed her Murphy leaning out of the window on her side. She came to the corner and turned into the cross street, and the taxicab made the turn also before she had reached the middle of the block.

There was no hiding place in sight, not even a hedge behind which she might get and so double on her tracks. There was only a row of imposing residences on a sort of terrace, with no fences in front, not even large trees or banks of shrubbery.

"He — he'll get me," Kitty Crade almost sobbed.

There was but one way, and she took the chance. She darted up the steps to the front door of one of the imposing residences and rang the bell. Half turning as she waited for her ring to be answered, she saw that Murphy had ordered the taxicab stopped before the house adjoining. She watched him get out, glance in her direction, speak to the chauffeur, and then start briskly along the walk. She had hoped that Murphy would think he had made a mistake and drive on.

They seemed slow in answering the bell at this house. Kitty Crade rang again, waiting impatiently, fear in her heart. She had decided on her course now. Why didn't some one come! Where were the servants, and what were they doing? Didn't they attend to business in a big house like this? Surely somebody was at home, for the shades were not drawn, and one of the front windows was open.

Then she heard a step. Murphy was directly in front of the house now, and she had but an instant. The door opened, a butler stood before her.

"Let me in! Pretend that I belong here," she whispered hoarsely. "That man is following me — annoying me."

II.

Alone With Tragedy.

There was half a second of hesitation that seemed like an age to Kitty Crade. And then the butler inclined his head and she darted past him, into the house. The servitor closed the door behind her in a manner quite natural.

"I — I —" Kitty was gasping.

"Try to calm yourself, miss. You have nothing to fear now, miss, believe me."

"He — he has annoyed me half a dozen times," she said. "I feel sure he will follow me in here. He will try some trick — say that he is a policeman, or something, and —"

Clever Kitty Crade, preparing the butler for a statement like that on the part of Murphy! As a matter of fact she doubted whether Tim Murphy would follow her into the house. Surely he would think that he had been mistaken.

But Tim Murphy thought nothing of the sort, knowing very well that it was Kitty Crade he had seen steal the comb and afterward drop it; that it was Kitty Crade he had followed half way across the town.

"Step in here, kindly, miss," she heard the butler saying. "And should he come to the door, go on into the room adjoining."

She turned to see him holding aside the portières, and she hurried into the big room, glad to be farther from the front door. And as the portières dropped into place again Detective Tim Murphy rang the bell.

The butler braced himself and, going leisurely to the door, threw it open.

"Sir?" he asked.

"That young woman who just came in," said Detective Tim

Murphy. "I want to talk to her."

"I beg your pardon, sir?"

"You heard me. I want to see her at once. Kindly notice my shield."

"Of the police, are you?" the butler said. "Of course, sir, if you insist."

"I know that girl, and I want to talk to her," Murphy persisted. "She is Kitty Crade —"

"Pardon, sir, but there must be some mistake," the butler interrupted. "That was Miss Sellington, sir, niece of my employer, sir. I would suggest, sir, that to annoy her might cause a complaint to be made by Mr. Sellington, sir, in the proper quarter."

Detective Tim Murphy narrowed his eyes and looked straight at the butler.

"Miss Sellington, is she?"

"Yes, sir."

"Um! Well, we'll let it go at that, then. Miss Sellington, eh? Very strange."

"Sir?"

"If she is a Sellington I am surprised that she takes a trolley car home from a shopping trip. What's the matter with the limousines and roadsters?"

The butler glanced behind, then bent nearer.

"A poor relation, sir," he whispered. "A sort of — er — charity guest in the house. A nice lady — but democratic, very democratic. She realizes her position, of course, and —"

"Um!" said Detective Tim Murphy. "So that's the way of it. Well, we all make mistakes."

"Yes, sir."

"All of us," Murphy persisted. "Some of us make them in one way and some in another. It is a mistake, for instance, to imagine that I am easily fooled."

"Sir?"

"Miss Sellington should be above stealing a two-dollar comb. If she is Sellington's niece, I'm willing to overlook a little thing, of course."

"I do not understand you, sir."

"Possibly not. Tell the young lady for me that she should be more careful. The next time she goes to the jug."

Without another word Detective Tim Murphy turned around and went down the steps. He got into his taxicab and drove away for a block, then dismissed it and slipped carefully back toward the Sellington house.

"Now why the devil," Detective Tim Murphy asked himself, "did that butler lie to shield Kitty Crade? Not know her? Miss Sellington, eh? Mighty queer — mighty!"

Kitty Crade, her heart pounding at her ribs, had heard the conversation between the butler and Murphy, and wondered at it a bit. She retreated to a corner of the room as Murphy left the door, and sank into a chair. The ordeal had wrought havoc with her nerves. She was busy making herself promises that she would behave hereafter.

The butler came into the room and walked toward her silently, still stiff and dignified.

"Thanks! Thanks!" Kitty Crade said.

"Always ready to help out a pal," the butler said. "You may call me Bramley, by the way. That man said he was a detective and that he thought you were a girl called Kitty Crade."

"He did? That shows to what lengths he will go," said Kitty Crade. "If he annoys me, or follows me again, I shall report it to the police."

"As a matter of fact," said Bramley, without unbending in the slightest, "the man is a detective."

"Sir?"

"I recognized him immediately. He was here once several years ago, as a guard of jewels during the wedding of Mr. Sellington's only daughter, now deceased."

"A real detective?"

"Just as much as you are a real Kitty Crade," Bramley said. "Do not be frightened, I implore you. I have no intention of surrendering you, I really think I misled the man. He stated, I believe, that he had seen you steal a comb."

"Sir?"

"How could you be so careless, my girl? But accidents will happen now and then, of course. You will have to dodge him for some time to come, I take it."

"I — I don't understand you," said Kitty Crade.

"Do you imagine, young woman, that you fooled me for an instant?" Bramley asked. "I knew immediately that the man was an officer and that you were trying to escape him."

"And you — you helped?"

"Gladly. I did not care to see you taken in charge. My sympathies are always with malefactors rather than with the police."

Kitty Crade looked at him, bewildered. Bramley unbent enough to smile at her.

"Th-thank you! And now I'd better be going."

"Possibly you may walk into a trap," Bramley said. "He acted as if he believed me, but that may have been a subterfuge. Allow me to suggest that you remain here until we are certain that the coast is clear. I told him, you see, that you were a niece of Mr. Sellington, who owns this residence. If you go out now, and he finds that that is not the truth, he may cause me some amount of trouble."

"Oh, I don't want to get you into trouble after what you have done for me. But if anybody should find me here —"

"There is nobody in the house except the housekeeper and cook, besides myself," Bramley said. "Mr. Sellington is — er — gone away. And the chauffeur is out on an errand. You are perfectly safe from discovery."

"But I can't stay here long," she persisted.

"I shall ascertain immediately whether the detective has retired or is waiting without," Bramley said. "I shall go out to the curb as if to look up at the windows —"

"And leave me in this big room alone? Suppose the — the housekeeper should come in? I'd not know what to say."

Bramley smiled again.

"I shall conduct you across the hall to Mr. Sellington's study," he said. "It is dark in there, because the shades are kept drawn in the daytime, but you will be safe from bother. You do not mind the dark?"

"I'm not afraid of the dark."

"Very well. None of the servants will invade the study, you may be sure. And Mr. Sellington will not return. Should he do so, you have but to say that a man annoyed you, and that I placed you in the study until I could attend to the fellow. Mr. Sellington is an aged gentleman, and very kind. This way, please."

Kitty Crade followed him into the hall.

"I must get away as soon as possible," she said.

"I'll investigate immediately and see whether the officer has really gone. Just sit down, and wait."

He came to a door, and opened it. Kitty Crade found herself looking into a dark room.

"Just sit down and wait," Bramley repeated.

He thrust her gently inside, and by the light that came from the hall Kitty saw a chair. She grasped the side of it as Bramley closed the door behind her.

A tiny film of light came in around the drawn shades at the windows, just enough to cause a few ghostly shadows to play around the casements. Kitty Crade saw that much as she sank into the chair. And the next instant she was upon her feet; she had heard a key turned in the lock of the door through which she had just passed.

She sprang to the door, tried it, found it was indeed fastened. A shriek was at the tip of her tongue, but she choked it back. Why be foolish? The butler probably had locked the door and taken the key so that, if Murphy returned and made a search, he could be told that the room was a private one, always locked, or something like that.

She went back to the chair and sat down again, listening intently for sounds in the hall. She thought that she heard the front door closed, but was not sure. Well, she had evaded Detective Tim Murphy. If he approached her now, or spoke to her mother, Kitty Crade could pretend a righteous indignation and declare that Murphy had been mistaken. And it had been a lesson; she realized now that she had been on the road to shame and disgrace. She regretted the few things she had stolen — she called it stealing now. It did not seem as clever as once it had.

Though she strained her ears she could hear nothing. The house seemed very quiet; but Bramley had said that nobody was in it besides himself except the housekeeper and the cook, and probably they were in the rear, she thought. And she supposed that Bramley was out at the curb, making sure that Detective Tim Murphy had gone away. When he came back Kitty would thank him, and then slip from the house and hurry back downtown, and then, go home.

She had forgotten Joe. She supposed that he was still waiting for her near the department store, or that he had believed she had obtained a place and gone to work immediately, and had gone on about his business. She would have to tell Joe that the superintendent had kept her for a long time.

"It'll be another lie — and I'm gettin' sick of them," Kitty Crade told herself. "Me for the straight and narrow after this."

It seemed that Bramley had been gone for a long time, though she tried to tell herself that it had been no more than a couple of minutes. The darkness, the close room, the quiet were getting on her nerves. She sank back in the chair and took a deep breath. There seemed to be a peculiar odor in the room, too.

"Wonder people like this wouldn't give themselves some air," she mused. "In stuffy rooms like we live in we try to get all we can, and here there's oceans of it and they keep it out. I don't get this dark room stuff either. Study, huh? Sunlight hadn't ought to hurt it any. Old man's idea, I suppose. Well, if he's rich he's got the right to have a few freak notions of his own."

She straightened herself in the chair and turned half way toward the door again. She heard nothing.

"And I won't hear a thing until he unlocks the door," she told herself. "How these servants can run around without making a sound is more than I know. I — I wish he'd come back. I hope Tim Murphy isn't hanging around. If ever I get out of this scrape —"

She sniffed the air. She got the peculiar odor again, and tried to place it. It seemed reminiscent, somehow. She had spilled some medicine at home that morning — but it wasn't an odor of medicine. And the office of the superintendent at the department store had an odor that came from heaps of ledgers and papers. Perhaps that was it — books and papers — since this was a study.

No, it wasn't that, Kitty Crade decided. But what could it be — this odor like something she had smelled before, and recently?

She amused herself trying to determine the odor. The street — no! Goods in the department store — no! Let's see. She had been in the butcher shop on her way downtown, ordering meat for her mother — blood! — the odor of —

Kitty Crade gasped, and then called herself a fool. It couldn't be that certainly — the rich Mr. Sellington didn't have a butcher shop in his splendid residence. But now that she had recalled it, the odor seemed stronger. It seemed to stifle her, to alarm her.

"I — I wish that butler would hurry back," she said.

She felt her way to the door again, tried it, and found that it was still locked. She began to feel nervous once more. She rattled the doorknob, but nobody answered.

The odor of blood was in her nostrils, and some other odor, too. She couldn't make it out at first. She tried associating it with different things. And presently she knew. Stale smoke — a shooting gallery! — stale pistol smoke!

She began to feel frightened now, though she could not tell herself just why. The room suddenly was stifling, mysterious, horrible! She failed to convince herself that fear was silly. The darkness seemed closing in upon her, and a sort of premonition came — a premonition of serious trouble, black despair.

Kitty Crade almost screamed. She felt that light was a necessity. She forced herself to listen at the door for an instant, and heard nothing. She beat upon it and listened, still nothing.

She had to get to one of the windows and lift the shade a trifle, she told herself. It would hurt nothing, and it might dispel her fear.

She found her way back to the chair, looked across the room to the film of light that struggled into the room at the bottom of a shade. She would go there, lift the shade a trifle, and let in the blessed light.

She started slowly, for she supposed there were articles of furniture in the study, and she did not care to collide with them. Her hands groped before her. Her knees struck against the side of a couch, and she sank forward, throwing out her hands to prevent herself from falling.

Her hands came into contact with something soft, and she stifled a scream. She knew that she had touched a human being.

There was no movement, no exclamation such as a sleeping man, suddenly aroused, might make. Kitty Crade, now almost beside herself with terror, felt for the edge of the couch and started around it. Again she stumbled, and again her hands shot out to save her. And then she sprang back.

There was something on her hands, something she had touched, something that was sticky. She sprang wildly toward the nearest window, stumbling over rugs, knocking down chairs, groping wildly for the edge of the shade.

She reached it, grasped it, fumbled in an attempt to let it up. And then she discovered that it was an unusual shade, one that opened from the middle, and she felt for the cord that controlled it. Her breath was coming in gasps now, and the perspiration was standing out on her forehead, Never before had she known such terror as this, though she was fighting to tell herself that there was no reason for it, that it was the darkness fooling her.

The odors came to her again. She darted to the other side of the window, found the cord, pulled at it, sent the shade flying.

She saw her hands first. One horrified instant she looked at them, her eyes bulging, trying to comprehend. And then she whirled around and looked back into the room. Her wild shriek rang through the great house.

Sprawled across the couch was the body of a white-haired man. His eyes were open and fixed, his face colorless. One of his hands had dropped to the floor, and the other clutched at the side of his coat as if he had died in agony. His shirt and waistcoat were stained from a wound in his breast. On the floor in the middle of the room was a revolver.

III

The Butler's Story.

Joe Draylon knew from frequent experience that once Kitty Crade was inside a department store she might not emerge for some time. So, after she had disappeared into the building, Draylon crossed the street to a cigar store on the corner, purchased a package of cigarettes, and held conversation with an acquaintance, meanwhile standing at the curb in such a position that he could watch the store exits on both sides and catch sight of Kitty Crade when she came out.

He had just started his second cigarette when he saw her hasten from the side entrance and turn down the street. Draylon excused himself from his acquaintance and started after her. He didn't exactly understand the move. Was Kitty Crade deliberately trying to dodge him after asking him to wait for her?

He knew instantly, from her manner, that she was trying to avoid somebody, and then he saw Detective Tim Murphy. Joe

Draylon marveled a bit at that. He knew Tim Murphy well, as did everybody in the district where he lived. And why should Detective Tim Murphy, who had been a close friend of Kitty's father, pursue Kitty Crade now?

Draylon went after them, following them around the first corner. He saw Kitty take the car, and watched while Murphy engaged a taxicab and followed. Joe Draylon had five dollars in his pocket; he engaged a taxicab himself.

When Kitty Crade left the car and started down the cross street, Joe's taxi was a block behind that of Murphy. When Kitty went into the Sellington house Joe was on the corner below, where he could see without being seen.

The thing was a puzzle to him. What was Kitty Crade doing in this section of the city? Why had she gone into that house? And why was Detective Tim Murphy even now at the door holding conversation with the butler?

Draylon did not care to have Murphy see him at present. He remained at the corner and awaited developments. He saw Murphy leave the house, get into the taxi, and drive to the corner, and there dismiss it and walk back, keeping under cover as much as possible.

Murphy had not been fooled. He knew well that he had been following Kitty Crade, and he wondered at her entrance into that house, and at the lies the butler had told about her. Murphy had been watching Kitty Crade for some time, for the sake of her mother and her dead father, and he began wondering, now, whether he had watched closely enough.

Was the theft of the comb but a minor matter? Was Kitty Crade identified with criminals? What interest could she have in the house of a man like Richard Sellington?

Detective Tim Murphy had determined, of course, to remain in the vicinity for some time in the hope that Kitty Crade would come out; and then he would "give her a talking to." And so he loitered around the corner, from where he could watch the street in front of the house, and the mouth of the alley that ran from the rear of it into the side street. Kitty Crade could not leave the Sellington place without Murphy seeing her.

Joe Draylon observed Murphy's actions, and hung around the corner below. Draylon was as much puzzled as the detective. He thought that he knew Kitty Crade pretty well, and never had he known her to come into this section of the city before. And he could not understand why Murphy was watching for her.

For half an hour they waited, Draylon at one corner and Murphy at the other, and then the latter was surprised to see a police department automobile dash up the street and stop before the Sellington residence. Draylon saw it, too, and saw half a dozen officers spring out and hurry toward the residence. But Detective Tim Murphy knew what Jim Draylon did not — that the half dozen officers comprised the homicide squad.

Tim Murphy had worked with that squad many times. He was a sort of specialist on murders. But recently he had been doing some special work of a political nature. He stood high enough, however, to step in and take command at the scene of any murder. And now, when he saw the homicide squad go to the front door of the Sellington residence, where Kitty Crade had entered, Detective Tim Murphy felt called to action. Waiting on a corner no longer appealed to him.

He hurried along the street and reached the others just as Bramley, the butler, opened the door.

"What's the trouble?" he asked.

"Hello, Murphy; glad you were in the neighborhood," one of the men replied. "The butler telephoned — said that some woman had shot and killed Sellington. That's all I know about it."

Tim Murphy felt something grip at his heart. He had seen Kitty Crade, daughter of his deceased friend, go into that house, and the butler had lied about her. And now it was reported that some woman had shot Richard Sellington!

"Want to handle this?" Murphy was asked.

"Go ahead. I'll hang around behind for a bit," Murphy replied.

The other nodded; it was Murphy's way of working. And they crowded forward to the door.

"This is terrible, gentlemen — terrible," Bramley was saying.

Murphy glanced at him sharply. The butler did look as if he had received a shock. He stood aside as the officers entered, and then conducted them along the hallway.

"I — I don't know exactly what you wish," he faltered.

Murphy crowded past the others and faced him.

"Well, you called for the police, didn't you?" he said. "What, is the trouble?"

"Mr. Sellington has been shot, sir, and killed. In his study, sir. It is a terrible tragedy. He was such a kind gentleman."

"We aren't here to learn about Sellington," Murphy reminded him. "He had a good character that spoke for itself. You have touched nothing?"

"I knew better than to do that, sir."

"Who shot him?"

"A young woman."

"And where is she?"

"Safe under lock and key — in the study with the body, sir, I locked her in there. Listen! You can hear her now!"

A woman's shrieks came to their ears, and they could hear her pounding against the door of the study. A horrible fear gripped Tim Murphy that those shrieks came from the throat of Kitty Crade. He looked at the butler sharply.

"Unlock the door," he commanded, and stepped back.

The butler led the way along the hall and put the key into the lock. He turned it, threw the door open, and a white-faced Kitty Crade stumbled out and into the arms of one of the officers. Murphy, looking on from the rear, glanced past her and saw the body of Richard Sellington sprawled across the couch.

"Take the girl to another room and keep her there," he whispered to one of the other men. "Have the boys round up the servants and let nobody leave the house or enter it. I'll take charge of this."

Kitty Crade, frightened so badly that she did not see Murphy, was hustled along the hall to the front room. Two of the men darted toward the rear of the house. The butler remained standing beside the opened door, Murphy behind him, two other officers at the other side. One of them was the police surgeon; the other was a fingerprint expert.

"All right, boys," Murphy said. "We'll go into the study. The butler will come, too. Close the door and throw up all those blinds."

The shades were lifted and sunshine flooded the room. Tim Murphy went forward and stood beside the couch regarding the body. The surgeon performed his preliminary work.

"Instant death — shot through the heart," the surgeon reported. "Shot fired at close range — shirt powder marked and slightly burned over wound."

The surgeon stood back and Tim Murphy surveyed the body and then glanced around the room.

"He fell awkward," Murphy said, half to himself. "Never knew what hit him, I suppose. And the gun —"

He picked up the revolver and ascertained that there had been but one cartridge exploded. The weapon was of an old pattern.

There was but one door, opening into the hall. The four windows had networks of steel bars outside. There was nothing much to see — just the dead man and the revolver. But Tim Murphy called the surgeon to his side again and whispered to him, and as the surgeon again bent over the body to make a more careful examination, Murphy beckoned the butler to a corner and bade him be seated. The fingerprint expert stood near, listening.

"Tell me about it," Murphy commanded.

"The young woman shot him, sir."

"The one we just took out of this room?"

"Yes, sir."

"And who is she?"

"I — I do not know, sir."

"My man, you are rather tangled in your statements. I followed that young woman to your door about half an hour ago, and you declared to me that she was Sellington's niece."

"I must crave your indulgence, sir, for the falsehood," Bramley said. "I was acting under orders, sir."

"Whose orders?"

"Mr. Sellington's, sir," Bramley said.

"Um! Well, tell your story, and don't miss anything."

"I have been with Mr. Sellington for years, sir," Bramley said. "So has Mrs. Albright, the housekeeper. We have rather a small household for such a large residence, but Mr. Sellington has not entertained since the death of his wife —"

"Get down to cases."

"Yes, sir. I tell you these things, sir, to show how peculiar the whole affair is. Mr. Sellington, as far as I know, has no relatives except a nephew, Mr. Gerald Sellington, a young man about town. Mr. Gerald is a proper young man, sir. He has means of his own from the estate of his mother, and never came to Mr. Sellington for funds, I am quite sure. And so we do not see much of him.

"As a usual thing, Mr. Gerald paid a duty call about twice a month, often to dine and spend the evening. Besides Mr. Gerald Sellington, scarcely anybody came to the house save Mr. Sellington's attorney and broker."

"Cut it short," Murphy commanded.

"Some time ago Mr. Sellington told me, one morning, that he expected a young woman to call. She did, and I ushered her into the study, acting according to his orders. She remained less than ten minutes, and hurried away. She has called half a dozen times since. It was — well, rather peculiar, sir, and Mr. Sellington acted in an odd manner about it. He gave me orders to say, if anybody should ask, that she was his niece, a poor relation. That is why I told you the falsehood half an hour ago, sir."

"And the young woman is the same as is now in the other room?"

"Yes, sir."

"What about today?" Murphy asked.

"You know when she came, since you followed her, sir," Bramley replied. "I told you the story Mr. Sellington had ordered me to tell if anybody questioned. I did not understand the business, and was only obeying orders, I conducted the young woman to the study immediately, as usual."

"Was Mr. Sellington alive then?"

"Oh, yes, sir. He was at the door, and closed it himself after the young woman entered. I walked on through the hall, sir, and happened to meet Mrs. Albright, the housekeeper, who was making her rounds. We held some conversation."

"What about?" Murphy demanded.

"Well, sir, Mrs. Albright is a prejudiced woman. She had observed me escorting the young woman to the study, and when she met me, she says 'So that hussy is here again, is she?' I reminded her that she was questioning the integrity of Mr. Sellington by her remark. She started to reply to me — and at that instant we heard high words, sir."

"In the study?"

"Yes, sir. We heard Mr. Sellington say something that we could not understand, and then the voice of the young woman. 'You'd better give it to me!' we heard her cry. And then there was a shot — and a groan. I rushed to the door of the study immediately, sir, with Mrs. Albright hurrying along behind me. Just as I reached the door the young woman threw it open and would have dashed past me, but I caught her. I drew her back into the study with me. Mr. Sellington was dead, just as you see him now, sir. The young woman seemed dazed. Mrs. Albright shrieked and almost went into hysterics. We were alone in the house save for the cook, who was in the rear, and as much inclined to hysterics as Mrs. Albright. I did all that I could, sir. I forced the young woman to remain in the study — locked her in — sent Mrs. Albright to her room, and telephoned for the police."

Detective Tim Murphy looked at him for a moment, and then at the body on the couch.

"That is all?" Murphy asked.

"Yes, sir."

"And you know nothing else? You heard nothing, at any time, to suggest what was occurring between Mr. Sellington and this young woman?"

"Nothing at all, sir. It was a very peculiar affair."

"How many times have they met?"

"I should judge, sir, that she has called here five or six times."

"And you have no idea why this young woman called upon him?"

"Not the slightest, sir. I thought at first that it was one of Mr. Sellington's charity cases, but not after her second visit. Save for the initial investigation, charity cases were always handled by Mr. Sellington through his attorney."

"Then this is the substance of it: This unknown woman called upon your employer; and there was some mystery about her visits; he directed you to say she was a poor niece of his if anybody asked; today she came as usual, they had words, a shot was fired, and when the door was opened Mr. Sellington was dead and the young woman was in the room."

"That is it, sir," Bramley said.

"Did you notice the revolver?"

"Yes, sir, when I thrust her back into the room. It was on the floor, still smoking."

"Careful, now. About how long was it from the time you left

the front door after your conversation with me until the shot was fired?"

"I should say not more than five minutes, sir. I walked the length of the hall and engaged the housekeeper in conversation — and then we heard the shot."

"Then when the officers arrived a few minutes ago, it could not have been more than half an hour after the shot was fired?"

"I should judge, sir, that Mr. Sellington had been dead about half an hour."

Detective Tim Murphy stepped across to the surgeon, who had completed his examination, and they exchanged whispers again. And then the detective whirled toward the butler once more.

"A nice, concise story," he said. "It is a pleasure to find a man under such circumstances who is not rattled and not unable to tell just what happened. You say the housekeeper is Mrs. Albright? May I see her?"

"Kindly come with me, sir, and we'll ascertain. She may need the services of a physician, and I have not called one."

"Here is the police doctor who will act, if necessary."

Bramley opened the door. Murphy stopped for an instant beside the fingerprint expert.

"Take charge of that revolver and examine it," he directed, "and keep the result of your examination to yourself until I see you at headquarters."

Then he followed the butler into the hall and up the stairs. Mrs. Albright, it appeared, had recovered from her hysterics. She looked as if she had been weeping. Murphy questioned her closely, Bramley standing by and not saying a word. Her story was exactly the same as Bramley's, except that she made a few remarks about the "hussy."

Detective Tim Murphy led the way down the stairs to the first floor again, a puzzled Tim Murphy; a Tim Murphy who looked at this affair from many angles and wondered whether there was something vital that he had overlooked.

He hesitated a moment before the door of the big living room, and then threw back his shoulders and entered, Bramley behind him. Kitty Crade, weeping, was crouched on a divan.

IV.

The Big Chance.

"What have you to say to me, Kitty?"

Tim Murphy had seated himself on a chair before her, and was bending forward to catch the first expression on her face as she raised it and looked at him. He spoke in a soft voice, a voice to foster confidence.

Kitty Crade sobbed again, and then lifted her head. She struggled to speak.

"Take your time," Murphy said. "And then tell me your story, Kitty. And let nobody else say a word until she has finished."

"It's — it's terrible," Kitty said, moaning. "I — I'll go insane!"

"Is this Kitty Crade speaking?" Tim Murphy demanded. "Is it for a girl like Patrick Crade's daughter to go to pieces and not be able to control herself?"

Kitty Crade fought to end her sobs, and wiped her swollen eyes. She gasped for breath, and then, head hung low, poke.

"I — I don't know where to begin," she said.

"Begin with the department store, where I saw you take the comb," Tim Murphy told her.

She hung her head again, for shame, but fought it back and began to talk.

"I — I didn't mean to steal — didn't think of it as stealing," she said. "But when I knew that you had seen me take the comb, I thought I'd get away without letting you speak to me, and declare afterward that you had made a mistake, that it was some other girl. I was afraid you'd tell mother, you see."

"Go on, Kitty."

"And you kept following, and I had to leave the trolley car. And I just ran up the steps and rang the bell, and when the butler opened the door I told him that a man was annoying and following me, and asked him to pretend that I lived here. And he did. Then he said that he'd go out and be sure that you had gone away. He told me to step into the study while he did that. He put me in there, and locked the door."

"And then what did you do, Kitty?"

"I just waited. It was almost pitch dark. And then I — I began to grow frightened because he did not come back. I imagined that I could smell blood. It got on my nerves, I guess. I started for one of the windows to raise the shade, and stumbled against the couch, and I — I got it on my hands."

She ceased speaking, shuddered, struggled to go on with the story Detective Tim Murphy wanted to hear.

"I sprang to the window and raised the shade — and I saw the dead man. Then I screamed."

Again she bowed her head and sobbed because of her shame and fright. Murphy touched her on the shoulder.

"Have you ever been in this house before, Kitty?"

"Never. I didn't know who lived here."

"The butler has told me his story, Kitty," Murphy continued. "He says that you have been here several times, and that Mr. Sellington gave orders that it was to be said you were his niece, if anybody asked. The butler says you came as usual today, and that he ushered you into the study and that Mr. Sellington met you at the door. Then he and the housekeeper heard you quarreling with Sellington, there was a shot, and they found you alone in that room with a dead man, and prevented your escape. And the housekeeper, Kitty, tells the same story."

"Why — why —"

"They say that you shot Mr. Sellington," Murphy said. "They say you murdered him. They found you alone in the room with his body and the —"

Kitty Crade sprang to her feet, screeching.

"It's a lie — a lie! I didn't know him — never was here before. He was dead when I raised the shade. Oh, say that you don't believe it."

"It looks bad for you, Kitty Crade. Murder is the worst that can be."

"Don't look at me like that. I didn't. I didn't even know him."

"But the butler and the housekeeper, Kitty — there is their story. They say you've come here several times. Why did you, Kitty?"

"I didn't," she shrieked. "I — I couldn't kill anybody. What does it mean? Why should this trouble come to me?"

"Can't you see how it looks, Kitty? Alone in a room with a murdered man — and the stories of the butler and the housekeeper and all that!"

"I didn't kill him. I didn't know him. I never was in this house before."

"But the stories of two servants stand against you, Kitty — old servants who have been with Mr. Sellington for a long time. I'm sorry for you — knowing your father as I did — knowing your mother as I do. This will almost kill your poor old mother."

"What do you mean? You — you believe it?" she cried.

"There is the evidence, Kitty," said Detective Tim Murphy.

"You're going to charge me with such a thing? You're going to arrest me?"

"I'll have to send you in, Kitty."

He turned away, but Kitty Crade hurled herself upon him, begging, imploring. Tim Murphy signed to two of the others, and they forced her back.

"Take her to headquarters," Murphy said. "She is arrested on suspicion. Don't put her name on the blotter, and don't let it out. Tell the newspaper boys that Sellington was shot by a young woman, and that we are trying to find out about her. Tell them nothing else at present."

Kitty Crade was beyond imploring now; she was sobbing again, and would have collapsed had not the two officers supported her. They led her away, out to the police automobile, and the drive to headquarters began.

Detective Tim Murphy faced the butler.

"It looks like a clear case, Bramley," he said. "We may have some difficulty discovering a motive, unless this young woman talks and we find out about her. I know her, you see, and this thing is a puzzle to me. And we'll have to make the usual examination of all concerned, of course, as a matter of form. You've nothing more to tell me?"

"Nothing, sir. I gave you all the facts — little enough, but all I know, sir."

"Thank you, Bramley. I'll notify the coroner's men, and they will take the body away. You'll telephone Mr. Sellington's attorney and tell him of the tragedy, and notify the nephew, also."

"I'll attend to it, sir."

"What other servants are there?"

"I believe I mentioned the cook, sir. Then there is the chauffeur. He went downtown on an errand for Mr. Sellington; I gave him the orders myself. He was to get some books Mr. Sellington had ordered."

"Very well. All the servants will remain at the house for the present, of course, including yourself. I may want to question some of you."

"Very good, sir," Bramley said.

"I'll leave one man on duty here for the present. But I want to investigate a bit more before I go."

Murphy went back to the study and made a careful examination, while Bramley telephoned to the attorney and left a message at Gerald Sellington's club. Tim Murphy remained until the coroner's men had come and taken the body away. And then he left the house, shaking his head as if perplexed.

Down at headquarters he told the story to the chief, first sending out an order that Joe Draylon be picked up. He was — within three blocks of the Sellington house. Draylon had seen the weeping Kitty Crade taken away in the police department automobile, and had loitered in the neighborhood to ascertain what had occurred.

"Have the girl brought in here," Murphy instructed. "Bring in Joe Draylon also. Chief, I understand that I am handling this case myself?"

"It's in your hands, Tim. Issue your own orders. But it looks like a quick case to me."

"It's nothing of the sort," Tim Murphy said. "It's a complicated case, and take it from me we are going to be surprised when we come to the end of it."

"But the girl in the room —"

"Just wait, chief — and listen. I've been on the force a good many years, and I've seen some strange things. I'm a man of fifty-five, you know. I knew this girl's father, and I know the girl, and young Draylon. Just listen, chief."

Kitty Crade was ushered into the office and told to take a chair. She was still weeping, and in her eyes was the horror she felt at her predicament. Joe Draylon was brought in a moment later.

"We've had enough tears, Kitty Crade," Murphy told her. "Hold up your head now, and listen to some words of wisdom. I've got Joe here for a reason. First of all, I suppose you know how serious this is? Almost any jury would bring in a verdict of guilty. The story of the butler is perfect, and the housekeeper backs him up. It would be a better story if it wasn't so perfect, and if the butler tried to add a few facts."

"You don't believe I did it?" Kitty cried.

"I don't!"

"Thanks — oh, thank you."

"Listen to me — and Joe, too. I've had my eyes on you, Kitty. You're starting on the wrong road. I knew your old father well — may his soul rest in peace! I know your mother, a splendid woman. And what have you been doing? You've been petted too much, you've found life too easy and too free of responsibilities. It's not a little thing to steal a bit of lace or a comb at a department store. It's a start on the wrong road.

"And you, Joe Draylon! A fine lad you are, but you're on the wrong track, too. Loaf around pool halls, you do, instead of getting an honest job and working for your money. I've been watching you, too. 'Tis on the road to love you are — you two. That is the right road, but there's a wreck ahead for you, if you don't change. Smart you are, both of you. Clever, too. But you're using your cleverness for the wrong things."

He stopped for a moment, and looked them over. They were clasping hands now, trying to give each other courage.

"I'm going to give you a chance," Detective Tim Murphy said. "I am going to try and have that cleverness of yours directed right. Use it in upholding the law instead of breaking it, and you'll win. You'd make a fine pair to work together, with love to aid you. And you're going to work together."

"What do you mean, Murphy?" Joe Draylon asked.

"You know the evidence? Very well. Then you know that the only way Kitty can be saved is for us to find the guilty one. And that'll be the job for you two. I'm going to make detectives out of you. I'm a bit puzzled by this case; it's a deep one. I know the butler lied, but we've got to prove it, and find out why he lied.

"My father was a contractor. He built that Sellington house when I was a boy. I played all around it, and I know things about it that Sellington himself didn't know. You'll go into that house, you two, tonight, and you'll solve this mystery. I'll show you how to get in and how to conceal yourselves. Nobody there but the butler, housekeeper, and cook. The chauffeur eats there, but sleeps in the garage. Maybe the nephew will be there, but that's all — you'll have it easy enough if you're clever.

"And you'll be doing honest work, and you'll get paid for it. We have an emergency appropriation, thanks to a sensible city council. Everybody must think that the woman accused of shooting Sellington is in jail, and that we're trying to find out all about her. I'll see your mother, Kitty, and I'll tell her you're doing some work for me. Your name isn't on the blotter. Do you understand? If you succeed, nobody ever will know that you were the girl accused. And you'll be on the right track then. I'm thinking you'll steal no more combs after this."

"Oh, Tim!" Kitty Crade cried.

"Save your thanks until the mystery is solved, Kitty. Use your heaven-given woman's weapons — wit and cleverness. Save yourself and atone at the same time. And you, too, lad! Win, and I'll make honest detectives out of you both. You've love to help."

"We've got to go into that house and work on the inside?" Joe Draylon asked.

"Exactly, lad. I'm thinking the regulars might have a hard time doing it. I want that butler to think that we are satisfied Kitty did the killing. I don't want him to have any suspicions at all. So you must be careful. I'll arrange some things with you — signals and the like — and we'll be watching on the outside."

"Pardon me, Murphy," the chief interrupted, "but maybe you're going too fast just because you happen to know this girl and her folks and have confidence in them. That butler told a pretty straight story. How do you know that he lied? How do you know that you are not helping this girl make a getaway, and giving her a man who's in love with her to help her do it? When you come right down to it, how do you know that she didn't kill Richard Sellington?"

"The butler lied," Detective Tim Murphy declared. "And I know that she didn't kill Sellington. I'd say as much if she was some woman I never had seen before. According to the butler, she killed Sellington soon after I left the door of the house. That means that Sellington hadn't been dead more than half an hour when the boys got there. And the surgeon told me that the man had been dead for two hours at least!"

"And that means —"

"It means Sellington was dead long before Kitty Crade went

into that house. It means she was thrust into the study and a deliberate attempt made to fasten the crime on her. The butler's story made me suspicious even before the surgeon told me the truth; it was too perfect, and the story of the housekeeper matched it entirely too well. Had they been honest stories, they would have differed here and there in unimportant details."

"You mean that the butler —" the chief began.

"I mean only that Sellington was dead before Kitty got into the house, and that the butler knew it, and that he and the housekeeper deliberately tried to hang the crime on Kitty. That's what I mean. And our little job now is to find out why these things were done, and who really did kill Richard Sellington. If we don't land the guilty person, it may go hard with Kitty Crade. You understand that, Kitty? It's up to you and Joe. Use your wits, your woman's weapons, Kitty. Every human being gets a big chance some time in life — and this is yours."

V.

On The Inside.

Late that afternoon, while Kitty Crade slept in the matron's room at the jail and prepared for the ordeal before her, and Joe Draylon loafed in a private room adjoining the office of the chief and smoked innumerable cigarettes, Detective Tim Murphy made his way toward the residence of the late Richard Sellington.

The sensation had struck the city; the newspapers had come out with extras telling how Sellington, the aged and feeble philanthropist, had been shot down in his study by a mysterious young woman who had made several visits to his house.

The butler had been interviewed, and had told the same story that he had told to Tim Murphy. The prisoner, the papers said, was being kept in seclusion in. police headquarters, and not even a description of her had been given out. It was intimated that she refused to talk, and that the police were endeavoring to learn her name and place of residence, and fix some motive for the crime.

Tim Murphy had read all that the newspapers had to say,

and with disgust. Often Tim Murphy had taken the right trail in a case because of some insignificant sentence in a newspaper article. But Bramley was still sticking to his story, it appeared, and that story had not been changed in the slightest.

"Too perfect — altogether too perfect," Tim Murphy told himself. The body had been removed, the attorney had come and gone, the morbid crowd had looked upon the house where the tragedy had occurred, and everything was quiet when Tim Murphy arrived, save that a patrolman was in front of the residence to disperse any crowd that might gather, and a detective was inside on guard.

Bramley opened the door at Murphy's ring, and bowed him inside.

"Anything new?" Murphy asked.

"Nothing at all, sir."

"No peculiar telephone calls, or anything like that?"

"No, sir."

"Nothing suspicious?"

"It has been quiet, sir."

Murphy grunted and walked slowly along the hall. Bramley was a hard nut to crack. Murphy gave him leads to enlarge upon his story and thus leave himself open for an entanglement, but Bramley refused to take advantage of these leads.

"He's a clever scoundrel," Murphy mused.

The detective went into the study again. Aside from the fact that the body had been removed and that the fingerprint expert had taken the revolver away, everything was as it had been at the time of the tragedy. Before leaving headquarters Murphy had ascertained from the fingerprint expert that he could not help. The revolver was an old one, of an ancient pattern. Its grip had taken no fingerprint impressions.

Murphy had the weapon in his pocket now, and suddenly he pulled it out and thrust it at the butler.

"Ever see that weapon before, Bramley?" he demanded. "It's the one that killed Mr. Sellington."

There was no fright or hesitancy in Bramley's manner as he took one step forward, extended his hand, and took the revolver. He turned it over, inspected it, looked at it carefully without the least sign of nervousness.

"I am quite certain, sir, that I never saw it before the

murder," Bramley said. "The first time I ever saw it was when it was on the floor of the study, after Mr. Sellington had been shot. An old sort of weapon, isn't it, sir?"

"Yes," Murphy assented.

Bramley was a puzzle to him. Bramley had been in the study at the first investigation, and had not quailed in the presence of the dead man, as a murderer popularly is supposed to do in the presence of his victim's body. And now, Bramley handled the sinister weapon as if it had been nothing more than a stick of wood.

Murphy sat down before the desk in the study and gazed around the room, while Bramley waited respectfully near the door. Finally Murphy beckoned him across the room.

"How long have you been with Mr. Sellington?"

"Almost twenty years, sir, and Mrs. Albright for the same period. We were here while Mrs. Sellington was still alive."

"A man who has been a servant in a house for twenty years should know something about his employer," Murphy said. "Know anything about Mr. Sellington's business?"

"Very little, sir," Bramley replied. "He retired from active business when his wife passed away. He was supposed to have a large fortune, sir; he always was giving money away to hospitals and such. His broker and attorney have attended to his business lately, sir — such as he had."

"I believe that you said his nephew, Gerald Sellington, was his only living relative."

"The only one of whom I have any knowledge, sir."

"Tell me what you know about the young man. I'm having him looked up, but I want to hear what you have to say."

"Mr. Gerald is a splendid young man, sir. As I told you before, he came here once or twice a month, generally to take dinner with his uncle — merely duty calls, sir."

"Didn't come to ask for money?"

"Mr. Gerald's parents, now deceased, left him a large fortune, sir. He had no reason to ask Mr. Richard Sellington for money, as far as I know."

"Ever hear them quarrel?"

"Never, sir. Mr. Gerald is not like the usual run of young men around town. He appears to be very much the gentleman, puts up at the best clubs, is welcomed in the best of polite society. I understood that he was engaged to marry some young lady."

"Perfect, is he?" Murphy asked.

"Compared to some of the young men of the day, sir," said Bramley.

"Did he ever bring anybody here with him?"

"Not that I can recall, sir."

"When was he here last?"

"Now that I come to think of it, he was here for a few minutes today."

"Today? At what time?"

"I should say about half an hour before the young woman came, sir."

"Know what he wanted?"

"Yes, sir. When he was here a couple of weeks ago he brought a rare Japanese print of some sort to show to Mr. Richard Sellington, and when he went away he forgot it. He came today to get the print, sir, saying that he wished to show it to some friends of his who were interested in artistic things."

"Did he get the print?"

"I think that he did, sir; at least he carried a package with him when he left the house."

"Tell me a little about this visit."

"He went directly to the library, where Mr. Richard Sellington was at that hour, and knocked. He entered at Mr. Sellington's call. They came out immediately, and went to the study, where the print had been left. Mr. Gerald was not there more than fifteen minutes, sir. I heard him talking. And then he came out and went away."

"Did you see Mr. Richard Sellington alive after that?"

"Oh, yes, sir. He came to the study door with Mr. Gerald. Then he turned back into the study, sir. He remained there until the young woman came. He was all right, sir, after Mr. Gerald left, if that is what you are driving at. The housekeeper happened to be in the hall, sir; she saw him alive and well after Mr. Gerald left."

Their eyes met. Detective Tim Murphy smiled grimly.

"It appears to me," he said, "that the housekeeper always is around to corroborate anything in the way of evidence. It. is very fortunate."

There had been a hint of satisfaction in Bramley's utterances. It was if he had told Tim Murphy in so many words that he could back up whatever story he saw fit to tell. He stepped back against the wall again as Murphy got up and continued his examination of the room.

"Know anything about Mr. Richard Sellington's will?" Murphy asked suddenly.

"Only what he mentioned to me at one time, sir."

"And what was that?"

"He said, sir, that Mr. Gerald did not need money, since he had a fortune already and had invested it wisely. And so, he said, he was going to give all his fortune to different charitable institutions. I think he spoke of endowing an old folks' home, sir. His attorney would know about that, of course."

"Leaving all his money to charity, eh?" Murphy said.

"He had only Mr. Gerald, sir, so he said. If this — er — young woman had any claim upon him, I do not know what it is."

"And how about his faithful servants?" Murphy asked.

He watched Bramley narrowly, but the face of the butler was inscrutable.

"He had cared for Mrs. Albright and myself, sir, so he told me. He took out two life insurance policies some six or seven years ago. One was for Mrs. Albright and the other was for me. Each was for five thousand dollars, sir. It was to be our reward for a score of years of faithful service."

"So you each get five thousand dollars by his death?" Murphy asked.

"That is what the policies call for, sir."

Murphy glanced at him narrowly. There was nothing in Bramley's manner to denote that he felt himself in a delicate situation, that he imagined for an instant that the detective could think he might have slain his master to get the five thousand dollars of life insurance.

And Tim Murphy was doing some hard thinking now. He knew, of course, that Sellington had been dead before Kitty Crade entered the house, and that the butler and housekeeper were making an attempt to fasten the crime upon her. And who was being shielded by that method?

Had Bramley told the truth concerning the relations of Gerald Sellington with his uncle? Had Gerald Sellington, a few minutes before Kitty arrived, slain his uncle, and was Bramley trying to save him? The surgeon had said that Sellington had been dead for two hours.

"Tell me again when Mr. Gerald called," Murphy commanded.

"About half an hour before the young woman came, sir."

"Sure it wasn't longer than that?"

"Quite sure, sir. The housekeeper will bear me out in the statement."

"I suppose so," Murphy sneeringly told him.

He looked at the other angle of the case. Had the butler and housekeeper slain their master to cash in on the insurance policies? It did not appear to be so, for, in such event, how had they hoped to escape detection? They could not have known, of course, that Kitty Crade was going to enter the house an hour and a half later and lend herself to a trap.

Murphy concluded his examination — and then went out into the hall again.

"How about the cook and the chauffeur?" he asked.

"I have instructed them to remain close about the house until you say otherwise, sir."

"Very good," Murphy said. "I think that is all at present."

"Pardon me, but have you discovered anything about the young woman, sir?"

So Bramley had a little curiosity, did he? Murphy turned to face him.

"Nothing much," he replied. "She declares that she never had been in this house before, and that Sellington was dead when you put her into the study."

"She persists in that preposterous story, sir?" Bramley said.

"I suppose she is fighting for her life," Murphy reminded him. "We are going into the case well, of course. We'll know all about it before we are through."

Detective Tim Murphy felt that the butler grinned after he had closed the door. The case puzzled him, and he hoped that Kitty Crade and Joe Draylon would be able to do something once they were inside the house.

Murphy went to his home and ate the evening meal, saying nothing to his wife except that he was working on the Sellington case. And then he went to Kitty Crade's home and greeted her mother.

"Worried about Kitty?" he asked.

"She went downtown this mornin' to get her a job, and she hasn't come home," said Mrs. Crade. "We're keepin' her supper hot."

"Better eat it. Kitty won't be home tonight, Mrs. Crade."

"She — she's not in trouble, Tim."

"She's working for me," Murphy answered. "I've got Kitty and Joe Draylon helping me with a case. They have a lot of cleverness between them, and they ought to make good. And I'll see that they're paid liberally for it. So don't you worry about Kitty, Mrs. Crade. I'm taking care of her. She may be home tomorrow, and maybe not for a few days — but don't you worry."

Then Detective Tim Murphy went back to police headquarters and called Kitty and Joe Draylon to the conference room.

"We'll start soon after dark," he explained. "I'm giving you pocket flashlights and automatics and handcuffs, and be mighty careful how you use them. It's wit you want to use. And don't forget for a moment, Kitty, that you are still in somewhat of a pickle. If we don't get the guilty party, we'll have to put you on trial, maybe. It is up to you and Joe."

"We'll do the work," Draylon said.

"Here's a rough sketch that I made of the house. Bend over the table, and I'll show you a few things. This is the second floor, and you can work from there. You'll have to be mighty careful. Make a break, and they'll be on guard. Understand?"

"We'll be careful," Kitty Crade said. And Tim Murphy knew from the expression on her face that she was alert, every sense attuned, a pretty female bloodhound on the trail.

Murphy had a taxicab call at the side entrance, the curtains at the windows drawn. They hurried out and got into it, and it drove away. To the public the mysterious woman accused of shooting Richard Sellington was in jail and probably undergoing the third degree; in reality she was outside working to free herself of all charges.

Three blocks from the Sellington residence they left the taxicab at a dark corner and slipped quietly down the street until they came to the mouth of the alley that led to the rear of the house.

They turned into the alley, and Murphy left Kitty Crade and

Joe Draylon crouching there in the darkness while he went ahead to reconnoiter.

He opened the gate in the alley wall, went inside the grounds, made sure that the chauffeur was in his rooms over the garage, busy reading the evening papers. Then he slipped back and got the other two, and took them safely inside the grounds and to the rear of the house.

There seemed to be no lights in the front of the residence, but lights were burning in the servants' quarters and in the kitchen. It was half past eight o'clock, and Tim Murphy supposed the servants had eaten their dinner and were in the servants' parlor talking of the tragedy.

At the side of the house was a small door that opened into a tiny hall. It was seldom used, having been constructed at first as an entrance for men putting fuel into the basement. Murphy worked at the door for a moment, and finally threw it open. They slipped inside, and stood listening.

No sound came to them. Murphy led the way along the hall until they came to another door.

"Remember those plans?" he whispered. "When you get into the other hallway, slip along it and manage to get up the front stairway. You'll have to be ready to dodge, of course. Get to the second floor and find that closet I told you about. Ready?"

"Ready," Kitty Crade whispered in reply.

"And don't forget for an instant what it means, Kitty Crade. Use your woman's weapons all the time. Joe is here to protect you if the worst comes to the worst. I'm trusting you, too, Joe."

"It'll be all right, sir," Joe Draylon said.

Detective Tim Murphy shook hands energetically with both of them.

"Good luck to you, Kitty Crade — and to you, lad," he whispered. "There are men watching outside, remember. And I'll be on the job myself, too. Good luck!"

Then he slipped quietly back along the hall and let himself out through the little fuel door. Kitty Crade and Joe Draylon, their hands clasped, stood against the door that opened into the rear hall on the first floor of the house — alert, listening, determined. They were safe inside the Sellington residence; now their work began.

VI.

Unexpected Discovery.

"**A**fraid, Kitty?" Joe Draylon whispered.

"No. We've got to do it, Joe. I'll be afraid if we don't. Oh, what I let myself in for when I tried to dodge Tim Murphy! I've been a bad girl, Joe."

"Don't worry about that now, Kitty," he told her. "You'll be a good girl from now on. I guess I haven't amounted to much either."

"It isn't that we're bad at heart," she declared. "We've just been careless. We were just playing at life, Joe."

"And now we'll take things seriously, eh, Kitty? I'll get a job and work hard. And we'll be married —"

"We can't talk of that now, Joe. Can't you see the predicament I am in? There's an awful case against me, Joe. Maybe the jury wouldn't find me guilty, but I'd have the disgrace just the same. Everybody will know that I got mixed up in it because I stole a two-dollar comb and tried to dodge Tim Murphy. It'd kill mother, Joe. We've got to make good."

"We'll make good, Kitty," Joe Draylon promised.

He gripped her hand for an instant, and brushed his lips against her cheek; and then Joe Draylon became a cool, self-possessed, determined man with an object in view.

He whispered for silence, unlocked the door with one of the keys with which Detective Tim Murphy had provided him, listened a moment, and then swung the door open half a foot or so.

The hall was dark except for a single, tiny incandescent light near the front door. There was nobody in sight, but they could hear voices coming from the servants' quarters on the second floor of the house.

"Come," Draylon whispered.

They crept out and closed the door, crept along the hall through the semi-darkness, making not the slightest sound, stopping now and then to listen, always alert and cautious.

Past the door of the study they went, Kitty Crade shivering a bit as she saw it, and toward the front of the hall. There they crouched beside the stairs for a time.

"We've got to go up, Kitty," Joe whispered. "We've got to take the chance. Everybody in the house is up there, and we can't learn anything by remaining on the lower floor."

Cautiously they started. It was deathly still in the house now. Two steps they took — and then the peal of a bell rang through the house.

They stopped, their hands clasped again, breathless, half-frightened. On the upper floor a door was slammed.

"It was the front door bell," Draylon whispered. "Somebody will be coming, Kitty — the butler, perhaps."

There was no need to say more. Already she was down the two steps and into the big living room, Joe Draylon at her heels.

"The divan," she whispered.

They reached it, got behind it, crawled beneath it and stretched there almost breathless, scarcely daring to breathe. They heard some one walking down the stairs, knew that lights had been turned on, heard the door opened, and then heard the voice of Bramley, the butler.

"It is you, Mr. Gerald? Come in, sir."

"I didn't hear of it until I got to the club this evening," they heard Gerald Sellington saying. "This is terrible, Bramley — terrible. Why, I must have seen my uncle less than an hour before it happened. Tell me, Bramley, tell me all about it."

"Step into the living room, Mr. Gerald, sir, and try to compose yourself," Bramley said. "I'll tell you all that I know, sir."

Kitty Crade and Joe Draylon heard them come into the room, and knew that the lights had been snapped on. Gerald Sellington sat down on the divan above them, and Bramley stood before him.

"Sit down, Bramley — sit down and tell me," young Sellington commanded. "You make me nervous standing there."

"If you say so, sir," Bramley replied.

He was always the perfect servant. Now he got a chair and placed it near the divan, and sat down.

"There isn't much to tell, sir," he said. "Your poor uncle is gone."

"And in such a way! The police — they were here, of course?"

"Yes, sir."

"And what questions did they ask, Bramley? What did you tell them?"

"I told them, sir, that you had seen your uncle about an hour or so prior to his death."

"Bramley! They'll be saying that I did it — that I quarreled with him, or something like that."

"Did you quarrel with him, Mr. Gerald?"

"For the first time in my life," Gerald Sellington replied. "It is a terrible thing to remember, Bramley."

"I am astonished to hear it, sir. I had thought you were on very good terms with your uncle, sir."

"I had been — always. But I — well, I don't mind telling you, Bramley. You're such an old servitor of my uncle, and so closely associated with my early boyhood, I feel I can confide in you. I wanted to get married, Bramley — and he didn't fancy the girl."

"Indeed?"

"Just because she is a shop girl, Bramley — a nobody. But she is a splendid girl, for all that."

"I am certain of it, sir."

"Uncle was furious; we had talked the matter over before. He threatened to have nothing more to do with me."

"Surely he would not say that, sir."

"But he did, Bramley. It wasn't money, you see — for he already had informed me that he would leave me nothing in his will, since I had a fortune of my own. I told him that I wouldn't touch a cent of his money if he did leave it, and then we had words. And the police may think —"

"Pardon me, sir, but the police will not bother you. They have no idea that you had anything to do with your uncle's death. They are satisfied, sir, with the story told by me, and by Mrs. Albright."

"Tell me, Bramley."

"A young woman called and was ushered into the study. She had high words with Mr. Sellington. A shot was fired, and I got to the door just as the young woman opened it. I saw Mr. Sellington dead, and detained the girl until the police came."

"But — this young woman —"

"I did not know her name until I heard one of the detectives mention it, and I believe that I have forgotten it now. You understand, sir, that this young woman has been here several times to see Mr. Sellington."

"Bramley! Did you insinuate —"

"I shielded your uncle's honor, sir. Nobody, I am sure, knowing his age and his poor health, would consider that he had been carrying on a clandestine love affair, or anything like that."

"But the explanation —"

"There is no explanation, Mr. Gerald, there is no explanation at all."

"The police will demand one."

"Then let them find it," said Bramley softly.

Gerald Sellington got up and paced the floor.

"I don't know what to do," he said. "I don't know where to begin even."

"Do nothing, Mr. Gerald. The attorney will attend to everything, and make arrangements for the funeral, consulting your wishes of course. Grieve for your uncle — grieve naturally — and let us attend to everything."

"Bramley! You speak as if I had had something to do with my uncle's death."

"Oh, nothing of the sort, sir! The idea is preposterous," Bramley said.

"I — I want to stay here tonight, Bramley."

"I'll have Mrs. Albright prepare the front room for you, sir. Is there anything else?"

"That girl —"

"Oh, they have the person in jail, sir. The case is quite complete against her, I believe. Mrs. Albright and I will be compelled to give testimony, I suppose. We are really the only witnesses for the prosecution."

"You think they'll convict her?"

"Undoubtedly, sir."

"But they'll investigate, Bramley; they'll find out all about her."

"I suppose she will make some sort of a defense, sir, but it scarcely will stand against the testimony Mrs. Albright and I can give them."

"It seems so terrible that a girl —"

"Yet, sir, if she killed your uncle —" Bramley said.

Gerald Sellington paced the floor again, then sat down on the divan once more.

"Just have my room prepared, Bramley, and then go about your business," he directed. "I'll remain here for a time, then go upstairs. You needn't come down again. I'll snap out the lights."

"Very good, sir," Bramley said.

Kitty Crade and Draylon heard him moving away, heard him go up the stairs. A door slammed.

Gerald Sellington remained sitting on the divan for a time. And then he got up, walked toward the center of the room, and turned. He spoke in a quiet voice.

"I have an automatic pistol in my hand, and I can use it. Come out from beneath that divan, whoever you are. Some sneaking detective, I suppose. Come out! The next time you try such a trick, don't wear cheap perfume that nobody in this house would use. I have very good nostrils. Come out!"

VII.

Evidence Wanted.

Kitty Crade warned Draylon by a pressure of the hand, and whispered into his ear, a whisper that was no more than a breath, yet that he could understand.

"Let me go out. He expects only one. You can come out if it is necessary."

Before Draylon could utter a protest she had started crawling backward. Free of the divan, she stood up and faced Gerald Sellington, who stood within a dozen feet of her, an automatic in his hand.

Sellington showed his surprise by recoiling a step at sight of the girlish figure.

"Who are you?" he asked. "What were you doing under there?"

"I am the girl they say killed your uncle," Kitty Crade said simply.

"You —" Gerald Sellington gasped his astonishment, and almost allowed the automatic to drop. "Is this a joke?" he demanded.

"It is no joke, Mr. Sellington," Kitty Crade declared.

"But your statement is preposterous. The girl who is said to have killed my uncle is supposed to be in jail undergoing an examination. How did you get into this house? What were you doing beneath the divan?"

Kitty Crade found it necessary to tell a little lie.

"I — I escaped from the matron's room and came here at once," she said. "This is the last place the police would look for me, isn't it? Getting into the house wasn't difficult. And I had to hide when I heard you ring, and the divan was the easiest place."

"Sit down," Gerald Sellington commanded.

Kitty sat down and looked up at him. "I am the girl they accused, but I had nothing to do with your uncle's death," she declared. "I came to this house accidentally, and the butler thrust me into the study. Your uncle was dead when he did that. It was a trick to throw the blame on me. The butler and the housekeeper made up their story and then telephoned for the police."

"I scarcely can believe that," Gerald Sellington said.

"You think I killed your uncle?"

"They tell me that the proof is conclusive."

"And I know that Mr. Sellington was dead when I was thrust into the study," she said. "You had called upon him just before that. I just heard you tell the butler that you quarreled with him. Are you sure that you didn't kill your uncle yourself?"

"You — you mean to insinuate such a thing?" he demanded.

"If you knew that I was under that divan — or that somebody was — why did you send the butler away before you called to me to come out?" she asked.

"I — I was worried. I didn't know what I was doing. This thing has made me nervous."

"Well, here I am," said Kitty Crade. "Do you want to call the police and give me up? Or do you want to talk?"

Gerald Sellington looked at her for a moment, and then sat down in the chair Bramley had vacated. He still held the automatic in such a position that he could use it quickly if called upon to do so.

"We'll talk," he said. "What did you have to do with my uncle?"

"Nothing. I never spoke to him in my life. I never saw him alive."

"You expect me to believe that?"

"I do. The butler put me into that study; he and the housekeeper made up the story. Did he do it to shield you?"

"You insinuate —"

"I know that I am innocent, and I know that I will be suspected until the guilty person is found. That is one reason I came back here — to try to find the guilty person. You quarreled with your uncle; you had the chance —"

"Don't dare say it," Gerald Sellington commanded hoarsely.

"The evidence points to you as much as it does to me. The story of the butler makes no difference to me, you see. I know that I am innocent."

"Who are you?" Gerald demanded. "Why did you come to this house today?"

"I am a working girl — a shop girl, like the one you said you wanted to marry. I stole a comb, and a detective saw me, and chased me. I came to the door of this house, and when the butler answered my ring, I said that a man had been following and annoying me, and asked him to act as if I lived here. He put me into that study; it was pitch dark. He didn't come back — and I found your uncle there, dead."

"And you expect me — or anybody else — to believe such a preposterous story?" Gerald Sellington asked. "Why should Bramley make up such a story?"

"Perhaps to shield the real murderer. Perhaps to shield you," she said.

"You dare say that again?"

"Why should I kill your uncle? What had I to gain?" she asked. "I never spoke to him in my life. I have told you the entire truth."

"In that case, who did kill my uncle?"

"That is what I want to discover," she said, "I know that I did not, and you say that you did not; then who —"

"Don't even speak of it again," he commanded.

"You were afraid, according to the way you spoke to the butler, that the police might think so."

"I'm nervous — worried — scarcely know what I am saying."

"Well what are we going to do about it?"

"Tell me the truth."

"I have."

"If it is possible that you had relations with my uncle, and he mistreated you, tell me the story."

"I have told the truth."

"Then I can do but one thing — call the police and hand you

over," Gerald Sellington said.

"And so protect yourself."

"That is not necessary. I, too, know my innocence."

"You had the chance to kill him, and you had quarreled."

"My uncle was alive when I left him last. And, looking at it in the cold light of reason, I had no reason for wishing his death. I was not his heir. I would not benefit. And I am not the sort of man to kill in a sudden passion — especially my uncle, who has been like a father to me. Scores of my friends can testify to that."

Kitty Crade looked at him closely.

"Then we are both innocent," she declared. "I did not commit the crime, and I feel sure that you did not."

"I cannot feel so sure about you. The story you tell is preposterous."

"Bramley's story sounds better, does it? Possibly. And he has the housekeeper to back it up."

"I will turn you over to the police," Gerald Sellington said, with sudden determination.

"You'd do that?" Kitty Crade got up and approached him, her arms extended, as if imploring him to change his decision. "Don't you know what it would mean for me? I am innocent, I tell you."

"Then your innocence can be proved."

"You know the story. It will be hard to disprove," she said.

"Did you know Bramley?"

"I never saw him before today."

"Then why should he attempt to fasten upon you a crime you did not commit? What would be his object, if not to shield me? And you have said that you do not believe me guilty."

"He is shielding somebody else," she replied.

"We'll let the police solve the riddle. You escaped, you said, and so you are a fugitive."

"You'll hand me over?"

"Yes."

She crept closer to him, agony in her face, begging him, imploring him. Kitty Crade would have made an excellent actress. Gerald Sellington was off guard for a moment, fighting to decide between a desire to aid a woman and another desire to do his duty. And in that moment Kitty Crade acted. She grasped him by the arm, tore the automatic from his hand, and sprang backward, menacing him with his own weapon. The expression of her face changed; she was no longer the supplicant, but one in command of a situation. And she spoke, softly.

"Joe! Come out!"

Gerald Sellington, in amazement, saw a man creep from beneath the divan, a man who held a weapon of his own.

"Not a word out of you," Joe Draylon warned.

"Two of you!" Sellington exclaimed with a gasp.

"Two of us determined to find the guilty person," Kitty Crade said. "I do not think you are the man, Mr. Sellington, but really I am not sure."

"What — what are you going to do?" Sellington asked.

"Simply keep you from bothering us while we continue our investigation," she replied, "There'll be no violence unless you force us to use it. We'll go into the study."

"The study!"

"Exactly. Into the study where your uncle was killed. They say a murderer shudders to look upon the scene of his crime. I am not afraid to go into the study. Are you?"

"I — no."

"And let me advise you not to make a noise and attract the servants. Come."

She led the way to the door. Joe Draylon walked immediately behind Gerald Sellington, who could feel the muzzle of Joe's automatic against the back of his head.

When she reached the doorway Kitty Crade snapped off the lights in the living room. No sound reached her ears, and she supposed that the butler was upstairs with the others. She led the way along the hall.

The door of the study was unlocked. They went in, the door was closed, lights were snapped on. The body had been removed, of course, and the study cleansed of gruesome reminders. Still, Gerald Sellington shuddered when he looked around the room.

"Sit down," Kitty Crade commanded. "Stay close to the door, Joe, and listen."

Sellington sat down, and Kitty Crade sat down on another chair just before him. She spoke in a low voice, and demanded that he answer in whispers.

"Granted that you did not kill your uncle, and that I did not, what person would you suspect?" she asked.

"I don't know. I didn't know that he had an enemy in the world."

"How often did you visit him?"

"Once or twice a month," Sellington replied. "I really knew very little of his personal affairs."

"Business troubles?"

"He had none, I am sure. He had retired from active business, and had only some investments. He had been rather broken since the death of my aunt. I was astounded when I heard that a girl had shot him. He always respected women."

"Any old business enemy?"

"I am quite sure not. My uncle did not make his fortune by riding roughshod over other men. His father left him considerable money, and he made more by judicious investments. There never was any trouble of any sort. My uncle wasn't the sort of man to make enemies. He was mild, satisfied with the things that life had given him."

"How about the servants?" Kitty Crade asked.

"Bramley and Mrs. Albright have been with him for years — were with him before my aunt died. The cook is an elderly woman who has been here about three years. The chauffeur has been here a year. It would be ridiculous to suspect one of the servants."

"Yet somebody killed your uncle," Kitty Crade said. "It is seldom that a man is murdered except by somebody with a motive. And there was no mistake. He was killed in his own study, which has but one door, and the windows are barred."

"If somebody called upon him —"

"Nobody but the butler would know that, and the butler, please remember, says that he let me in, and that I shot Mr. Sellington."

"The gun —"

"I heard them talking about that at police headquarters. It is an old gun of a common make; anybody might have one like it. They investigated it for fingerprints, and found none. The old handle and rusty trigger didn't take prints readily. We can get no help from the gun."

Gerald Sellington had been looking at her peculiarly.

"Can't you see," he said, "that the further you carry on this conversation the more it makes things look bad for you? Tell me the truth!"

"So you still think I am guilty?" she asked.

"What else can I think?"

"We don't seem to be getting anywhere," said Kitty Crade. "We'll have to look farther, I guess. And I can't have you bothering me, you know."

"What do you intend doing."

"Just render you helpless for a time; that is all. Don't shriek for help, and don't fight against us. You perhaps understand that I am desperate."

She nodded to Joe Draylon, and he stepped forward as Kitty Crade kept Sellington covered with the automatic. Joe had guessed her plan. He had been wondering why she did not stop talking to Sellington and bind and gag him. And now he hurried across the study and tore down the cords at one of the windows, and stepped swiftly back to the chair and began lashing Gerald Sellington's hands behind his back.

"I — I don't want to be left in here," Gerald said.

"It shouldn't trouble you if you are innocent," Kitty Crade told him. "Hurry, Joe."

Sellington did not struggle, nor did he object when Joe Draylon made a gag and affixed it. All this was beyond Gerald Sellington — the tragedy, the mystery of this girl, the advent of Joe Draylon when Sellington had thought that he was dealing only with a woman.

His natural courage seemed to leave him. He submitted tamely, not only because he feared that an automatic might be brought into use against him, but also because he did not seem to know just what to do. And before he could determine a course of action he was a prisoner, bound and gagged and helpless, lashed to a chair, placed in a corner where he would be as comfortable as possible, and the chair lashed to two window casements.

"Sorry, but it is necessary," Kitty Crade whispered to him. "You wouldn't give me a chance, and you know it. You'd telephone for the police. We'll release you as soon as possible."

VIII.

In the Closet.

It was not that Kitty Crade feared the police if Sellington tele-phoned, for she knew that Detective Tim Murphy had the sanction of the chief and would take care of her. But she was afraid that those at headquarters might send out men to make an investigation and so attract the attention of Bramley and put him on guard. And she wanted Bramley to think that everything was secure.

Draylon turned off the lights, and they left the study and slipped into the hall.

"It might be a good thing to break the telephone wires," Joe told her.

"Silly! You'd have to go outside to do it. There are probably several phones in the house. And we haven't the time to spare. We'll go upstairs now, Joe."

"You don't think that young Sellington did it?"

"No."

"What makes you so sure?"

"I don't know, Joe; just instinct, I guess, or whatever it is that they call it. He's more worried about his uncle's good name than anything else — which means his own good name, of course."

"Well, then, who did kill Sellington?"

"Joe! You're not suspicious of me, are you?" Kitty Crade whispered.

"Don't talk like a fool," Joe Draylon said. "But, since you didn't kill him, and you think that young Sellington didn't, who did? That's what I want to know."

"Ask me something easy," she said. "Bramley, the butler, is shielding somebody, of course. That is why he tried to put the crime upon me. I just happened along and walked right into a trap."

"But, if Mr. Sellington had no enemies —"

"Did it ever occur to you," Kitty Crade whispered, "that the butler might be shielding himself? Or the housekeeper, Mrs. Albright?"

"But they are old servants. Why would they want to do away with their employer?"

"Looking for a motive, are you?" Kitty Crade asked, "Well, so am I, Joe."

They went along the lower hall carefully, fearful lest Bramley put in an appearance and detect them. There was no question but that they could handle Bramley if they took him by surprise, but they did not want to clash with him. They wanted him to feel secure, wanted him to do or say something that would put them on the right track. There was no doubt in the mind of Kitty Crade that the butler held the key to the situation.

They reached the bottom of the stairs and went up cautiously, a step at a time, listening for sounds from above. Now and then they heard, as if from a distance, a muttered word. Somebody was holding a conversation in the servants' sitting room.

They came to the top of the stairs.

"That closet must be half way to the rear of the house," Joe Draylon whispered.

"And on the left-hand side," Kitty Crade added. "Got the keys ready?"

"Yes. If that butler comes out while we're trying to open the door it'll ruin everything, I suppose. We'll just have to take the chance, Kitty."

"I'm not afraid, Joe, not when I remember what it all means for me," she replied, "Let's go!"

Detective Tim Murphy, who had played around that house as a boy when his father's men were constructing it, had told them about the peculiar closet. It was in reality a good-sized room opening off the hall, a sort of storage room for odds and ends. On one side of it was the servants' sitting room, but without a connecting door; and on the other side was the butler's room, and beyond that rooms for the other servants.

Detective Tim Murphy had explained to them that the walls of that closet were as nothing. If they could get into it they might be able to overhear what was said in the servants' room, might hear something that would give them a clew.

Joe Draylon led the way along the hall. Now they could hear the voices in the servants' room easily, but could not make out what was being said. They came to a door, passed it, and came to another. Joe Draylon stooped and tried to look through the keyhole.

"Dark," he whispered to Kitty Crade. "This must be the closet, all right."

He took from his pocket the keys Tim Murphy had given him, and set to work. Kitty Crade moved a few feet away toward the door of the servants' room, ready to take command of the situation if Bramley came out unexpectedly. It seemed an age to them before Joe managed to get the door unlocked. Kitty Crade backed toward him swiftly, and went inside. Joe Draylon followed. They were not a moment too soon. As the door of the closet was closed, the door of the servants' room was opened, and Bramley stepped into the hall.

"What was it?" they could hear the housekeeper say.

"Nothing, I guess. Thought I heard somebody. Thought possibly Mr. Gerald wanted something, but I suppose he has retired."

The butler stepped back into the servants' room and closed the door, and Joe Draylon turned the key in the lock of the door to the closet. Then he followed Kitty to one of the walls, where they secreted themselves behind empty trunks and packing cases.

Detective Tim Murphy had been correct. They could hear every word that was spoken in the servants' room. The cook, it seemed, had gone away for the night, declaring she could not endure to sleep beneath the roof of the Sellington residence the first night following the murder of her employer.

"All the better," Joe whispered to Kitty Crade. "We've only the butler and the housekeeper to handle now."

"Listen," Kitty commanded.

"There is nothing to fear, Mrs. Albright," Bramley was saying. "It is no more than our right, and you want to look at it in that way. Should not old servants be protected? We have served faithfully for a score of years, and we are entitled to some reward. Do you want to be penniless in your old age?"

"No; I couldn't endure that," the housekeeper replied. "But I — I am afraid."

"Of what?"

"They may find out the truth."

"And how could anybody do that?" Bramley asked her. "I

flatter myself that I have arranged things so that the ignorant police will not discover the truth. All you have to do is to stick to the story we have told. If you grow frightened, or think that you are getting into a tight corner, you can weep and threaten to collapse or go into hysterics; say that you cannot endure it because you served Mr. Sellington for so long. They will think nothing of it. They expect a woman to be nervous and peculiar after the murder of a person she has known well."

"Still I am afraid," Mrs. Albright said.

"You must conquer your fear then!" The voice of Bramley was stern; there was the ring of command in it. "If you do not, you may ruin everything. We have gone so far, and we cannot back out now, Mrs. Albright. Think of the money, and what it means! Think, rather, of what it will mean for you if you do not get it. We are growing old, Mrs. Albright; we need money for our declining years. Are you going to let silly fear, sillier scruples, rob you of comfort in your old age?"

"I know," she replied. "I — I must have the money. But I hate it, Bramley; I hate it. If they find out —"

"How on earth are they going to find out?" the butler demanded. "Our story is perfect, and we want to be sure not to add to it. That girl has come here several times to see Mr. Sellington. We do not know her, nor her business. She came today, was ushered into the study as usual, and later we heard a shot and found her in there with Mr. Sellington murdered and a smoking revolver on the floor. Beyond that, Mrs. Albright, you know nothing, and please remember it. No matter if they ask you a million questions, you know nothing more. There is no danger. We simply stick to our story and let it go at that. It is for the police and the courts to do the rest. You simply say as little as possible, Mrs. Albright, and leave the rest to me. Tomorrow at the inquest, weep like the faithful servant over the death of a kind master, and they will be lenient with you and not ask too much."

"And — that girl —"

"What of her?" Bramley asked.

"Suppose they convict her, Bramley? Suppose they should send her to prison, or to death?"

"Bah! You have too much consideration for other people. Let the girl fight her own battle, Mrs. Albright. She was running away from the police or she never would have entered this house. It is fortunate for us that she entered just when she did. I suppose she will make a defense. She probably will declare that she never was in this place before, and the jury may believe her and may not. The fact remains that she was in the study with Mr. Sellington's body, for the police found her there. She's a pretty girl, and I suppose the jury will give her the benefit of the doubt and let her go. But we do not have to trouble about that, Mrs. Albright. We do not care whether she is convicted or not, so long as they think she did it and do not snoop around to find somebody else to put on trial."

"It — it seems a terrible thing to do."

"Do you want them to know the truth?" Bramley thundered. "Are you weakening? Well, I am not. And I want protection, remember. We'll go ahead as we planned, Mrs. Albright, and you'll kindly do your part. You'll be thanking me after you have your five thousand dollars safe in the bank and the thing is over."

"If Mr. Sellington never had taken out those insurance policies!" the housekeeper exclaimed. "Why, if he wanted to reward us, didn't he just put us in his will?"

"Every man does his business in his own way," Bramley replied. "The fact remains that the will gives everything to charity, and that the insurance policies take care of us. Five thousand dollars each, my dear Mrs. Albright, is a goodly sum. It is worth doing many things to get. Are you weakening?"

"I — I dare not weaken now."

"You are as deep in this as I am, remember," the butler told her. "It is to your interest as much as it is to mine to act correctly. Silence your silly conscience, if that is what is troubling you. Mr. Sellington is dead and cannot be returned to life, and we might as well go ahead and take our profits. What is the difference — now?"

"I'll try to do as you say."

"You must do it," Bramley repeated. "Pull yourself together. It will not be a long ordeal. Tell your story at the inquest, weep a bit, and they'll not question you too closely. Let me handle the affair. There will be the trial of that girl, of course, but you can say that you told all you knew at the inquest. It will be easy. And there is the money to be considered."

"I — I'll do it, Bramley."

"Very good. Be sure that you do not weaken. It is too late for that now. You'll be in trouble the same as I will be, if there is a mistake made. And now you'd best go to your room and retire, I think. Try to get some sleep; take some drug, if necessary. You must be calm for the inquest tomorrow."

Kitty Crade and Joe Draylon heard Bramley open the door, and heard Mrs. Albright sniffling as she walked along the hall. A door opened and closed — the second from the closet, Joe Draylon judged. Bramley went back into the servants' sitting room. They heard him scratch a match.

"A cool customer," Joe whispered to Kitty Crade. "A born killer, that man — and at his age, too. Money — he'd do anything to get money so that he can live easy during his last years."

"You think he did it?" Kitty asked.

"Don't you?"

"I'm not sure. He and Mrs. Albright know the solution of the mystery, of course. We heard them as good as admit that."

"Well, you heard what they said about the money, didn't you?" Joe Draylon asked. "They couldn't wait until he died naturally, I suppose. He was a fool to do a thing like that, if you ask me, even if they had worked for him for years. It was a mighty big temptation. And, if I size that Bramley up right, he'd kill a man without blinking an eye. And he'd put the crime on you, just because you happened to walk into the house at the right minute. I'd like to get his throat between my two hands for —"

"And spoil everything," Kitty Crade said. "It is facts we want, Joe, and we've got to get them. We've got to have evidence, not guesswork. Remember what it means to me, Joe."

"Well, what are we going to do now?" Draylon asked. "Here's where you use those women's weapons Tim Murphy spoke about."

"The woman will be the easiest to work on, Joe, because she is frightened half to death already."

"That's true, all right."

"But I think we'll wait until Bramley retires, and get him first. I have a little scheme."

"Let's hear it," Joe Draylon said.

IX.

Dealing With Bramley.

For half an hour they could hear Bramley moving about the servants' room, now and then striking a match; for half an hour Kitty Crade and Joe Draylon crouched in the closet, not making the slightest noise, fighting against the impure air in that unventilated chamber, the perspiration streaming from their faces and hands.

"Smoking, and flaming up some more stuff," Joe whispered in Kitty's ear. "I hope he doesn't keep that up all night."

"Why not?" Kitty asked. "I've been thinking, Joe. Why not walk in on him now. I suppose the door is unlocked. You go, and gel the drop on him. Then I'll come in."

"It's a good idea at that," Draylon commented. "No use wasting any more time."

"And remember what it means to me, Joe," Kitty Crade begged.

"I'll not be forgetting that for a moment, Kitty," he replied. "We'll go through with this thing, all right. Just you trust to me, Kitty."

They left the wall of the closet and crept silently to the door. Joe Draylon unlocked it. For an instant he hesitated. To their ears came the sounds of the butler's ceaseless pacing back and forth across the servants' sitting room.

"All right, Kitty," Draylon said.

He opened the door an inch at a time, fearful of creaking hinges. The hall was dark save for a little light that came from the front of the hall below. There was no sound to disprove the fact that Gerald Sellington was safely confined in the study where they had left him.

Draylon slipped out into the hall, holding his automatic ready. Kitty Crade remained in the closet doorway, watching him, glancing now and then at the door of Mrs. Albright's room.

At the door of the servants' room Joe Draylon hesitated for a moment. Again he heard the butler strike a match, and then the pacing back and forth across the room began once more. Draylon grasped the knob of the door with his left hand, held the automatic ready in his right, and suddenly wrenched the door open.

"Hands up!" Draylon commanded.

Bramley whirled at the sound, saw the menacing weapon, and slowly put up his hands. Draylon noticed, in that instant, that the man did not seem the least frightened or disconcerted. There was a cold, calculating gleam in his eyes.

"Who are you? What do you want here?" Bramley demanded in a low, tense voice.

"You keep those hands of yours up. It'd be a pleasure to plug you, and I'd do it first chance," Joe Draylon told him. "I've got you, my man. Don't look for any help, because I've attended to the young man who was downstairs. And I'm not afraid of the housekeeper, and that is all of you."

"Are you a burglar?"

"Is it any of your business?" Draylon demanded. "Sit down on this side of that table. Put your hands before you, spread out. And don't make a move unless you want to get what Sellington got earlier in the day. Understand?"

Without taking his eyes off those of Joe Draylon, Bramley walked slowly around the end of the table and sat down as he had been directed. He spread out his hands on the table before him.

"If you have come to rob, I cannot prevent you. You are armed, and I am an old man," Bramley said. "And this is the house of death tonight. But you know that, since you spoke of Mr. Sellington."

"Don't talk except to answer questions," Joe Draylon warned. "And never mind about that old-man stuff. You're able to take care of yourself, all right."

"What do you want with me?"

"We'll come to that after a bit," Draylon said.

He stepped back toward the door and hissed peculiarly. Kitty Crade came into the room.

Bramley's eyes flickered for an instant when he saw her, and his face went white for a moment, but he quickly regained his composure. Kitty Crade closed and locked the door, and stepped to Joe Draylon's side.

"What do you want?" Bramley asked again.

"You know this girl, don't you?" Draylon asked.

"She is the young woman who killed Mr. Sellington."

"Enough of that. That's a lie, and you know it," said Joe.

"What are you doing here, young woman?" the butler asked. "I thought the authorities had you in charge."

"They did," said Kitty Crade. "But there is such a thing as escape, you know, when a police matron is careless. I suppose you know why we are here."

"I do not."

"We are here," said Kitty, "to hear you say why you tried to fasten that murder on me."

"I — I don't understand."

"Yes, you do understand. Why did you lie to the police about me?" she demanded.

"I told the truth," Bramley answered.

"So you still say that I killed Mr. Sellington?"

"I do."

"And that I have made several visits to him here in this house?"

"That is the truth."

"It is a lie," Kitty Crade declared "And it will do you no good to keep it up. Why did you lie? Why did you put me into that study and then call for the police? You know that Mr. Sellington was in there dead when you locked me in. Hanging it on me and shielding somebody else, are you? It may interest you to know that we were under the divan downstairs while you were talking to Gerald Sellington. We heard all that you said. Is it Gerald Sellington you are shielding?"

She was giving him the chance to change his story now. She was giving him the opportunity to intimate that perhaps it was, to escape by swinging the blame from her to Gerald Sellington, by saying that he did it to save the family name and honor. It was a trap to weaken his story. But Bramley refused to walk into it.

"This is preposterous," he declared. "Mr. Gerald had nothing to do with his uncle's death. You came here, young woman, and I ushered you into that study, and a few minutes later Mr. Sellington was dead. You know the story I told, and I still tell it."

"Going to stick to it, are you?" Draylon sneeringly asked. "And you think that you can get away with it? We want the truth out of you, Bramley, and we want it right now. You'll get what Sellington got if you —"

"Killing me would not change my story," the butler said. "I fail to see how it would help you, young woman. It would simply be two murders instead of one."

Bramley almost smiled. As long as he maintained his story he would hold this man and woman at a disadvantage, and he knew it. He was not to be frightened; Joe Draylon was instantly aware of that fact, as was Kitty Crade.

"It was a good story you told," said Kitty Crade. "It was almost a perfect lie. But, you see, we happen to know that it was a lie! And now you are going to listen to the truth."

"I am interested," the butler returned with a sneer.

"Mr. Sellington took out life insurance policies for you and the housekeeper, to reward you for faithful service. You couldn't wait until he died. You plotted with the housekeeper. You killed your employer, Bramley, to get that money."

"Preposterous! As for the policies, I told the police about them — told them freely. I scarcely think they believe I committed the murder."

"Perhaps you think there is no evidence that you did?"

"I know that there is no such evidence," the butler replied. "On the other hand, both the housekeeper and I are willing to swear that you came to this house several times on some mysterious mission, that you called today, were closeted with Mr. Sellington, quarreled with him, shot him. That is perfect evidence, you see. You may declare you never were in this house before; but you cannot deny the fact that the police found you here early today, in the room with the dead Mr. Sellington."

"Going to see it through, are you?" Draylon said. "Well, Bramley, you're going to the electric chair, and the housekeeper is going, too!"

"I have told my story. I have nothing more to say," Bramley declared. "And what are you going to do about it?"

"There are ways of making you talk."

"My dear young man, you could torture me, and I'd not open my mouth; you can kill me, but you can't make me change my story. Think that over."

"Tough bird, are you?" Draylon said.

"And this young woman's escape merely makes the case

against her more complete. Any atrocity you commit in this house tonight will make it the harder for her."

Kitty Crade looked at him closely. She knew that the butler could not be cowed. He held the advantage, and he knew it.

"You — killed — Richard — Sellington," Joe Draylon intoned, walking nearer him.

"I scarcely think you can make anybody believe that," Bramley retorted.

"And you are trying to hang the crime on this girl. That's enough to give me an excuse for killing you."

"Killing me will not help her," the butler replied.

There did not seem to be a nerve in his body. His voice was calm, his manner self-possessed. It was as if he had absolutely no fear, no dread, no apprehension at all. He almost smiled as he looked first at one and then at the other of them.

"Your little visit to me is netting you nothing," Bramley said. "If you want to steal, I suppose I cannot prevent you. You are threatening me with a weapon, there are two of you, and I am an old man."

"An old scoundrel. A murderer of the worst type. A man who would shoot down his employer of years for a few thousands of dollars, and then try to fix the crime on an innocent woman," Joe Draylon declared.

"If she is innocent, no doubt she can prove it. The fact remains that the police found her in the room with the dead man."

"She is innocent, and she will prove it," Draylon declared.

"She'll have to tell a better story than she has, then," the butler said. "No jury in the world —"

"We've had enough of your talk," Draylon said angrily. "Now we'll get down to business. We'll see whether —"

"I have nothing more to say," Bramley asserted.

Joe Draylon approached him, menacingly, and Kitty Crade, knowing that this was the crucial moment, stepped rapidly forward.

"Cover him, Kitty," Joe said.

Kitty obeyed. Joe Draylon whipped the covering from the table and rapidly tore it into strips. Then he approached Bramley once more.

"I'm going to bind your wrists and legs and lash you to that chair," Joe Draylon said. "And then I'm going to have the truth out of you, if I have to kill you to get it."

"I am an old man. I cannot resist."

"Resist, if you feel like it; small good it will do you," Draylon said.

He bent forward, strips of cloth held ready, and grasped one of the butler's wrists. And then Bramley acted. His manner changed in an instant. He heaved forward, hurled Joe Draylon to one side, whirled him back and before him, so that Kitty Crade dared not shoot. In an instant they were struggling, fighting like maniacs. Bramley had age on his shoulders, but he also had muscle in his arms. Joe Draylon found that he had his hands full.

Now one was on top, now the other. There was a sudden shriek in the hall, a sudden pounding on the door. The housekeeper had heard the commotion.

"Hurry, Joe," Kitty cried.

Draylon had his hands around the butler's throat now, and was trying to choke him into submission. But the butler had fight left in him. Once more he whirled Joe Draylon aside, and Kitty Crade ran in. The automatic rose, and fell. It thudded against Bramley's head.

The butler weakened for an instant, and in that instant Joe Draylon conquered. Bramley's head fell to one side, and he breathed like an unconscious man.

"Hurry, Joe."

The housekeeper was still in the hall, screeching, pounding on the door, crying for Bramley to open it and tell her the trouble. Joe Draylon worked like a maniac. He bound the unconscious butler's wrists and legs, put him into the chair and lashed him there, gagged him effectually with one of the strips of cloth. And then he sprang back, toward the door.

"Get her into her own room — and leave the rest to me," Kitty Crade whispered.

Joe Draylon unlocked the door quickly and threw it open. Mrs. Albright had a quick vision of Bramley, bound and gagged in the chair, his head hanging to one side. And then she felt her arms seized, had a shriek stifled in her throat, felt herself whirled away from the door and down the hall toward her own room.

X.

Mrs. Albright Talks.

The door of Mrs, Albright's room was open, the lights were burning. Instantly Joe Draylon had her in her own apartment; she crouched on the side of the bed, badly frightened, her eyes bulging

"Who — what?" she asked, gasping.

And then her eyes bulged again. For, through the door came Kitty Crade, a stern expression on her face, her fists clenched at her sides. She walked to within six feet of the housekeeper and stood before her, her fists resting against her hips now.

"You — you —"

"So you know me?" Kitty asked.

"I — that is —"

"You should know me well," Kitty Crade said. "According to the story Bramley told the police — and according to your own — I paid several visits to Richard Sellington in this house."

"You — you're the girl —"

"Suppose you get over your hysterics, Mrs. Albright. I'm the girl you and Bramley accused of murdering Richard Sellington, and you know that I did not. I am the girl you would have sent to prison for life, or seen executed, that you might protect yourself. Well, I am free now, thanks to a careless police matron. And I have come here to have a settlement with you."

Mrs, Albright, thoroughly frightened, stared at her, incapable of making a reply.

"I'm trying to decide what to do with you," Kitty Crade said. "I thought at first that I'd simply shoot you down."

"No — no! I —"

"Keep quiet. I knew that I was innocent, you see, and I wondered why you and the butler blamed me. I judged that you were shielding somebody. I thought at first, this evening, that it was Gerald Sellington. Then we got hold of Bramley, and made him talk."

"He — talked?" the housekeeper asked.

"He did. It was a clever trick, but it didn't work," Kitty told her.

"And what did Bramley say?"

"The truth, I suppose. You'll soon know how it feels to be in jail, accused of murder, life sentence or death staring you in the face."

"What do you mean?" Mrs. Albright screeched.

"You know very well what I mean." The housekeeper stared at her. Then she gave another shriek, and gave way to hysterics. She writhed and twisted on the bed, beat at her face with her fists, jabbered meaningless phrases.

"We're on the right track, Joe," Kitty Crade whispered. "Find a bathroom and bring water. We must get her out of this."

Draylon hurried into the hall, opening door after door, searching for the nearest bath. He found one, finally, seized a small pail that he found in a corner, and filled it with water. He felt as Kitty Crade had said, that they were on the right track now.

Carrying the small pail filled with water, Joe hurried from the bathroom and started along the hall. He turned into the main hall — and looked into the muzzle of a revolver.

"Drop that pail and put up your hands!" commanded the voice of Gerald Sellington.

Joe Draylon could do nothing but comply. His own weapon was in a pocket of his coat, and he could not reach it. And by the way Gerald Sellington's eyes gleamed in that fitful light, Draylon did not care to take a chance with him. Sellington had every right to shoot. Joe Draylon, as far as Sellington knew, was an intruder. Joe put up his hands. "Step into this room," Sellington commanded.

He opened a door, and Joe went in, still holding his hands above his head. He had no chance to get the automatic out of his pocket before Gerald snapped on the lights.

"Well, the tables are turned," Sellington said. "You got Bramley, did you? I didn't have time to release him, but I got you. And I'll get that girl as soon as you're secure, and then send for the police. Your little game is at an end."

Joe Draylon sank into a chair and put his palms upon his knees.

"Just a minute," he said.

"Well?"

"I suppose you are a gentleman; that's the general idea

around town. And I don't think for a minute that you had anything to do with your uncle's death. And I know that Kitty Crade
did not have —"

"The authorities can decide that," Gerald Sellington interrupted.

"Your uncle was killed before Kitty came to the house, and
the police know it. The surgeon says your uncle had been dead
an hour or more before Kitty came here. You want your uncle's
murderer to pay the penalty, don't you?"

"Naturally."

"Well, we're on the right track now. I'll let you in on a secret.
Kitty didn't escape. She was released, and Detective Tim Murphy, whose father built this house, brought us here and got us
inside. We came to solve this puzzle. Murphy wanted the butler
to believe that the police were satisfied that Kitty had done it;
that's why the police aren't handling it themselves."

"A likely story!"

"It is the truth," Joe Draylon declared. "We got the butler,
but he sticks to his story. But we heard the butler and the
housekeeper talking, and it was peculiar talk. They spoke of the
money each is to get because of your uncle's death. The butler
stood firm, but the housekeeper has broken down."

"You mean to insinuate that Bramley or Mrs. Albright killed
my uncle?"

"Something like that. At any rate, they know all about it,
and they can clear Kitty Crade."

"I think we're wasting time."

"Don't you understand, man?" Joe cried. "This is our only
chance, Kitty's only chance. Possibly we can get the truth out of
the housekeeper now. She is in hysterics. Give us a chance."

"What do you want me to do?"

"Just play fair with us — give us our chance," Draylon
begged. "I have an automatic in one of my pockets. Take that;
search me for other weapons. Let me go back into that room with
some water, and you stay just outside the door and listen. Leave
the door open a crack and watch. I'll be unarmed. Kitty has a
weapon, but you'll have the advantage. And we can't escape, if
we are in that room. Are you afraid to give us a chance?"

Gerald Sellington looked at him closely. Joe Draylon's voice
had the ring of sincerity in it.

"I'll give you the chance," Sellington said. "But if you try a trick I'll shoot first and ask questions afterward. You're an intruder here, and so I have the right to shoot. And that girl, as far as I know, is a fugitive. Get up and turn around."

"Thanks — thanks," Joe Draylon said.

He got up and turned around, holding his hands above his head. Gerald Sellington took away his automatic and searched him well.

"Remember," he said, "don't try any tricks. I may be a fool to act like this, but no man can ever say that I didn't give him a chance. I'll stand outside the door, and watch and listen. Go get the water. And you're not to intimate to the girl that I'm in the hall, remember."

Joe Draylon picked up the pail and hurried along the hall, and got the water, Gerald Sellington at his heels. Joe did not hesitate. He went into the room, leaving the door open half a foot, in order that Sellington could see.

"Thought I'd never find a bathroom," Joe told Kitty Crade, handing her the pail.

Mrs. Albright was still in hysterics. She beat at her head with her fists, kicked at the foot of the bed, writhed and twisted like a crazy woman. Kitty Crade dashed water into her face. She gasped, tried to turn away. But Kitty twisted her back, and threw more water into her mouth and nostrils.

"Stop your nonsense," Kitty cried. "Sit up and listen to me. I'll hurt you if you don't."

She grasped the woman by the shoulders and shook her. Mrs. Albright was as old as Kitty's mother, but Kitty Crade was remembering what she faced unless she could ascertain the truth. And suddenly the hysterics ceased, and the tears came.

"Stop crying and listen to me," Kitty commanded. "You'll have to listen some time, and it might as well be now. Bramley has talked, I told you. Want to hear what he said? It was a pretty plot, but it didn't work, Mrs. Albright. And there's punishment coming to you for what you did, and for trying to put the blame on me."

"Bramley — Bramley — I can't —"

The woman seemed unable to talk.

"He told us all about it. It took a little persuasion, but he finally told. Murder your old master, would you, for a few filthy dollars!"

"I — He didn't —"

"Oh, he told us! And now you are going to jail, and probably to prison for life — if they don't send you to the chair."

"What do you mean?" the woman shrieked.

"You know very well. Bramley told us, I said."

"But I don't understand. What did he say?"

"The truth, I suppose. He told us about the life insurance policies. He told how you hated to wait for the money, and that he didn't want to wait, either. And so you plotted Mr. Sellington's death. You got the old revolver, and oiled it, and filled it with cartridges. But Bramley couldn't bring himself to do it at the last moment. But you, with the thought of that money in your mind — you went into that study, faced your old master, and fired the shot that killed him."

Mrs. Albright sprang from the bed, her arms flung out, shrieking at Kitty Crade at the top of her voice.

"It's a lie — a lie. I never touched him. Don't believe it. Bramley is lying. He's trying to shield himself. I didn't do it — didn't —"

"Bramley has told the story. You did it, all right," Kitty Crade declared.

"I didn't. I'm innocent. There was a plot — yes! — but that wasn't it. I've been — been afraid ever since. I didn't want to do it in the first place, but Bramley made me."

"So you killed him?"

"No — no, I didn't mean that," she shrieked. "You must believe me. Bramley has been telling lies."

"Did Bramley do it, then?" Kitty asked. "Are you two accusing each other? Is that the game? Well, we'll just let the police decide between you. They'll have the truth out of you when you get to headquarters."

"You'll not call them?"

"In about a minute. I've got to protect myself, haven't I? You were ready and willing to see me sent to prison for life. And now you're going there. Either you killed Richard Sellington, or Bramley did. In either case, you knew about it. You'll both be sentenced — one for life, the other to the chair. Maybe it'll be the chair for both."

Mrs. Albright threw herself upon the bed again, shrieking

once more, tearing at her hair.

"I didn't kill him," she cried. "I didn't want to have anything to do with it. Bramley made me. It was Bramley. I couldn't go against his wishes; I didn't seen to have the strength. Bramley always has made me do as he wished."

"So Bramley killed Mr. Sellington, did he — and you were to keep quiet and help put the blame on me — and get your money? Joe, telephone for the police."

"No — no," Mrs. Albright cried. "Wait. Please wait. I'll tell — I'll tell it all!"

Gerald Sellington, standing just outside the door, heard an interesting recital.

XI.

The Truth.

And when the recital was at an end Gerald Sellington walked into the room, to stand before the housekeeper and look down at her accusingly.

"Oh, Mr. Gerald," she cried. "You heard?"

"I heard."

"Don't let them be too hard on me, Mr. Gerald, sir. It was Bramley. I always did whatever Bramley said from the first day I came into this house."

"I know that Bramley always dominated you," Gerald Sellington replied. "But do you realize what you tried to do? You backed up Bramley's story. You subjected this young lady to arrest and humiliation. But for her courage and the help she has received she might have had to stand trial for murder. Though she had been acquitted she always would have a stained name. And you, a woman, did that to her, another woman. Deliver me if that's what the charity of women means."

"Mr. Gerald —"

"Now things must be put right immediately. The innocent must be cleared and the guilty suffer."

Kitty Crade stepped up to him; Joe had told her what Sellington had done, how he had given them a chance.

"I want to thank you, Mr. Sellington," she said. "But our work is not done, you see. We have Mrs. Albright's story. but there is Bramley. We must force him to admit the truth. Will you let me handle the affair?"

"Gladly. If I can be of service —"

"You can. Please go to the front door with Mr. Draylon. Joe, you call for Tim Murphy, please."

She sat down near the weeping Mrs. Albright, on guard, and Draylon and Gerald Sellington hurried down the stairs and to the front door, turning on the lights in the hall.

Murphy had said that he would be outside, or that some of his men would be there if he was called away. Draylon took a whistle from his pocket and blew a signal. A moment later Detective Tim Murphy was at his side.

"Well?" Murphy asked.

"We've done it, Mr. Murphy — Kitty did the most of it," Joe said. "This is Mr. Gerald Sellington. We had to handle him rough at first, but he helped us before we got through."

"Well, what's the answer?" Murphy queried.

"We've got to handle the butler yet, sir. Kitty has some plan for that. She told me to call you. She's upstairs watching the housekeeper. Please come up, Mr. Murphy."

Murphy went up the stairs at his side, and Joe Draylon talked rapidly, telling of the housekeeper's confession.

"You see; we've got to deal with Bramley. It will be easier if we can get Bramley to confess, too."

"That'll be the hard job."

"I think that Kitty has some plan, sir. We want actual proof, of course."

"We have to have it," said Detective Tim Murphy.

They entered the room. Mrs. Albright was weeping, now, stretched full-length across the bed. Kitty Crade, a smile on her lips, went across the room to Tim Murphy and outlined her plan. And Detective Tim Murphy said that it was good.

And then Kitty Crade led the way along the hall and to the door of the servants' room, Gerald Sellington leading Mrs. Albright. They had arranged the scene, but they were uncertain as to its success.

Bramley was conscious by now, struggling with his bonds, but he ceased when Kitty and Joe Draylon stepped into the room, and glared at them.

Without speaking a word Joe Draylon took off Bramley's

gag, and then loosened some of his bonds.

"Gave it up, did you?" Bramley asked, with a sneer.

"We did not," Joe answered. "We had a little talk with the housekeeper after I put you to sleep. And she talked."

"She talked, did she? Well, she didn't say anything that will bother me."

"Didn't she? I think she did," Kitty Crade said. "You played a fine game, Bramley, but you didn't reckon on a woman breaking down and confessing."

That was the cue for the entrance of Gerald Sellington with Mrs. Albright. Bramley's eyes bulged when they stepped through the door.

"Mr. Gerald, these persons have assaulted me," Bramley said. "Can you not come to my assistance?"

"Would a man assist the murderer of his uncle?" Gerald Sellington asked. "I suppose I should thank you for not telling the police that I did it."

"What do you mean, sir?" Bramley cried.

He glanced from Sellington to the housekeeper. Mrs. Albright burst into tears again.

"They — they made me tell, Bramley," she said. "I couldn't help myself. They threatened me with prison and the —"

"It's all off, Bramley," Joe said. "She's told the whole truth, all right. She told how you arranged to kill Mr. Sellington, so you could get the life insurance money. And you had a chance when he was in his study. You, the servant he trusted, walked into that study, faced him, and shot him down in cold blood as if he had been a mad dog instead of a kind, old man —"

"It's a lie," Bramley screeched. He showed some fright now. "Oh, Mrs. Albright tells an excellent story, Bramley. Her testimony will be enough to send you to the chair. Mr. Murphy!"

Detective Tim Murphy stalked into the room. Draylon motioned toward Bramley.

"There's your man, officer," he said. "You can take him in on the murder charge, and I guess that clears Kitty Crade."

"I didn't kill him. That hag is trying to save herself," Bramley cried. "Are you saying that she did it?"

"No. Neither of us did it. Mr. Sellington killed himself."

There was silence for a moment, and Kitty Crade exchanged meaning glances with Tim Murphy.

"Fishy," Murphy said. "It's too late to spring that story on me, my man. You might have got by with it if you had told it at first. But we can't take in that suicide rot now. If Sellington committed suicide, why did you not say so at first? Why did you try to fasten the crime on this young woman? I guess you're done, Bramley."

"I'll tell the truth; I —"

"Mrs. Albright already has told what we wanted to know."

"I didn't kill him. She lies if she says that I did. Mr. Sellington killed himself, I tell you."

"Then why didn't you say so at first, Bramley? Why did you try to make it look like a murder, and try to make us believe this girl killed him?"

"Wait. I'll tell. He killed himself. He has been in poor health, and he never got over grieving after the death of his wife. He told me a score of times he was going to do it, and I always talked him out of it. He had that old revolver for years. I hid it once, but he found it again, and put it away somewhere.

"And Mr. Gerald came, and they had a little tilt because Mr. Gerald wanted to marry some girl of whom his uncle didn't approve. Mr. Gerald went away, and then I heard a shot in the study, I rushed in there — and Mr. Sellington was dead, stretched on the floor."

"On the floor!" Murphy exclaimed.

"Yes, sir. I was shocked, of course. And then I did some quick thinking, sir. I had been with Mr. Sellington a score of years, and so had Mrs. Albright. And I knew that he had left us nothing in his will. He had given us each a life insurance policy for five thousand dollars. And even that was gone, I feared."

"How do you mean?" Murphy asked.

"The suicide clause, sir. The policies are void if the insured takes his own life. Can't you understand, sir? I saw myself penniless in my old age, and Mrs. Albright, too. It would be difficult for either of us to get a good place again.

"And then the young woman came to the door, escaping from the detective. It came to me like a flash, sir, I would put her in the study and send for the police. I made up the simple, direct story, told it to Mrs. Albright, demanded that she stick to it. I forced her to do it, sir, telling her how easy it would be for us to get the money if it was thought that Mr. Sellington had been murdered.

"And you know the rest, sir. I was just trying to protect myself in my old age. I didn't stop to think of the young woman. I supposed she was a criminal, sir — thought she probably would be acquitted and the case always remain a mystery. Mr. Sellington killed himself. It is all over now, sir."

"You cur," Tim Murphy cried. "You'd make an innocent girl stand trial for murder, face imprisonment or death, just to get a few dollars. It's a pretty tale, Bramley, but it doesn't go. Your suicide story is too late. We'll keep Mrs. Albright away from your influence, and I guess her testimony will fix you. You killed Sellington, and you know it."

"No — no. It's as I told you."

"And what proof have we?" Tim Murphy demanded.

"Unfasten my hands. I'll show you."

Murphy nodded. Joe Draylon took off the strips of cloth that bound the butler's wrists and arms. Bramley reached into the inside pocket of his coat and pulled out a sheet of paper.

"Mr. Sellington left a letter," he said. "I found it on the table in his study after he killed himself. I took it, so the police would not find it. I left the revolver on the floor, but I lifted Mr. Sellington's body and sprawled it across the couch, as if he had fallen there when shot, as if he had been standing before it talking to the person who shot him. Here is the letter, sir. I have told the truth. Mr. Gerald will know the handwriting."

Murphy took the letter, and Gerald Sellington stepped to his side.

"It is my uncle's writing, sir," he said.

Murphy read it quickly, the last epistle of an old, lonely, brokenhearted man whose fortune had not been enough to pay him for dragging out existence:

> I am going to take my own life. My dear wife is gone, and I have nothing for which to live. I have been told that spirits meet in the new land, and I am going to her. There is nothing left for me on earth.

"Just what we wanted," Tim Murphy said. "You've won, Kitty Crade. Bramley can't change his story in court now. There'll be no necessity for you being mixed up in this further.

Nobody need ever know the part you played. It's just a plain case of suicide, without a bit of doubt. With this letter before the coroner, the testimony of Bramley and Mrs. Albright will be enough.

"As for you, Bramley, I could make you suffer for this, but not without bringing this girl into the public gaze, and I don't care to do that."

"I understand, sir. I'll tell a straight, short story at the inquest."

"Be sure that you do," Murphy said. "You may remain here for the present, but one of my men will be in the house, and you'll be watched until you have given your testimony at the inquest. Mrs. Albright, you'd better retire to your own room."

Tim Murphy went back into the hall, and the others followed. A few minutes later Gerald Sellington conducted Murphy and Joe and Kitty Crade to the front door.

"I'm glad that the puzzle is solved," he said. "I forgive you two freely for handling me the way you did. I can appreciate what a terrible ordeal it must have been for the young woman."

Down at the corner where Murphy had a taxicab waiting the detective turned to clasp Joe and Kitty Crade by the hand.

"Let this be a lesson to you, Kitty, girl," he said. "No more foolishness after this."

"You may be sure of that, Tim."

"And you, lad — you've got a treasure here. Why not start working for her? It's well along the road of love you are; why not travel it hand in hand?"

"You can depend upon me, Mr. Murphy."

"Go along home, now. Kitty, tell your mother that you're done working for me for the present. I'll see that both you and Joe get some pay out of our emergency fund. And I may need you again one of these days. There are lots of times when a couple of outsiders can learn the truth of things quicker than the police. Go along home in this taxi. And if you exchange a kiss or two on the road, it will be no crime."

Detective Tim Murphy raised his hat and turned away, chuckling softly to himself; there was something reminiscent in his chuckle. Kitty Crade and Joe Draylon got into the taxicab, gave the chauffeur their address, and were driven swiftly down the avenue.

"Kitty, you know what Murphy said," Joe whispered. "It

would be no crime."

"Well," said Kitty, "so long as it is not a crime —"

www.ingramcontent.com/pod-product-compliance
Lightning Source LLC
Chambersburg PA
CBHW030446250626
47154CB00003BA/1155